Bewitched, Bothered, and Beheaded

The Alvarez Family Murder Mysteries
Book 10

by
Heather Haven

Wives of Bath Press, The
5512 Cribari Bend
San Jose, Ca 95135

http:// www.heatherhavenstories.com

ISBN: 979-8-9880502-1-6

Praise For The Series

♥ "Heather Haven makes a stellar debut in *Murder is a Family Business*. With an engaging protagonist and a colorful cast, Haven provides a fresh voice in a crowded genre. We will be hearing more from this talented newcomer. Highly recommended." **Sheldon Siegel,** *New York Times* **Best-Selling Author of** *Perfect Alibi*

♥ *A Wedding to Die For* "Wonderfully fresh and funny!" **Meg Waite Clayton, Author of** *The Race For Paris*

♥ "I Just finished *Death Runs in the Family* and I loved it! This has turned out to be one of my favorite series and I sure hope there will be another installment in the near future!" **Becky Carbone, Global Ebook Awards**

♥ *DEAD...If Only* "A must-read 5-star series!" **Cindy Sample, National Best-Selling Author**

♥ *The CEO Came DOA* "This is a strong work in the genre of the mystery/thriller!" **San Francisco Book Review**

♥ *The Culinary Art of Murder* "This latest installment of Haven's murder mystery series offers a twisty whodunit laced with a healthy dose of suspense. A solidly entertaining mystery" **Kirkus Reviews**

♥ *Casting Call for a Corpse* "There was never a dull moment in this entertaining cozy mystery, which includes plenty of action, a well-balanced range of twists and turns, and even a few laugh out loud moments." **Cassidy's Bookshelves**

♥ *Love Can be Murder* (ebook only) "If I could give this series ten stars I would!" **Amazon Reader**

♥ *The Drop-Dead Temple of Doom* "Even Indy Jones would be puzzled, but leave it to Lee Alvarez to not only discover the crimes beneath the crimes but who in the party had the motive to kill. Read the whole series. You'll be glad you did." **Cellophane Queen**

♥ *Bewitched, Bothered, and Beheaded* "As a huge fan of cozy mysteries, Bewitched, Bothered, and Beheaded hit all the right notes for me. The victim is portrayed as someone who wasn't well-liked, and many characters had valid reasons to off the victim, other than just for the inheritance. The whacky mannerisms of the Alvarez family, the blend of humor and sarcasm in the dialogues, and the eccentric traits of their pets added to the comedic element of the story. I could imagine being part of the audience watching this narrative being played out as an interested bystander, all while cheering for the Alvarez family and especially Lee to get to the bottom of the mystery. Heather Haven has developed each of the characters well with their unique speech patterns and mannerisms, and although previous cases were mentioned in the narrative, I could easily follow along as a first-time reader of the series. This author has successfully added me to her fanbase." **Pryia Matthews, Readers' Favorite Book Reviews**

Acknowledgements

I want to thank Mat Franco, magician extraordinaire, for his help with understanding the mind of a magician. When he uttered the words, "think of magicians like musicians. Their approach is much the same," I understood completely. Being married to a musician for forty-two years does drive certain things home. I also want to thank Mat for introducing me to the Animal Foundation of Las Vegas. Even though I live in California, I try to support this organization in their very worthy cause of rescuing and saving animals. Wherever in the world there is an animal in need, we should try to help.

I also want to thank my beta readers, Linda Osborne, Kathy Weatherford, and Mary Wollesen. Where would I be with these three amazing women? They really help keep me on course.

And last but not least, special thanks to editors Paula and Terry Grundy. It was a lucky day when I found them.

Dedication

This book is dedicated to families everywhere. And not just the mother and father with two-point-one kids, an SUV complete with dog, and a thirty-year mortgage. This book is mainly dedicated to people who are a family because they love each another, share their lives, hopes, and dreams, and stick together no matter what. That's what family is all about.

This book is also dedicated to my beloved mother, Mary Lee, passed but much alive in my thoughts and prayers. Lastly, to my wonderful husband, Norm Meister, who gives me endless love and support, which is not always as easy as it sounds.

Table of Contents

Bewitched, Bothered, and Beheaded

Chapter One
Sunday

"I always knew I'd see you behind bars one day, Lee."

Frank Thompson's black eyes were razor-sharp as they glared at me. I blinked back at my deceased father's best friend, my godfather, and the Palo Alto chief of police. I could tell Frank's role at that moment was outraged godfather. His dark skin was mottled by a redness that probably started at his toes and ended at his hairline. Blood pressure up, tolerance level down.

As shocked as I was to see him at one o'clock in the morning at the San Franciso hoosegow in a rage, I was even more shocked by his appearance. Debonair is a word that often goes hand in hand with Frank Thompson. He usually looks like he stepped off the cover of *Gentlemen's Quarterly*. Now he looked like a reject from *Hee Haw Magazine*. Uncombed hair going every which way, stubble on his face, collar of his wrinkled shirt half in and half out of his jacket, and a black pair of slacks with—yikes—brown shoes. The Frank Thompson I knew wouldn't be caught dead in a ditch wearing that outfit.

"Frank. What are you doing here?" I asked. Too late, the reason occurred to me. He was here because of the spot of trouble I was in. Actually, murder is more than a spot. It's sort of *101 Dalmatians* wearing pink polka dots, riding in a ticker-tape parade. Only not as endearing.

I swallowed hard. I wasn't sure what was worse, being detained on murder charges or being confronted by Frank's wrath. He ground his teeth together as he spoke, but somehow managed to enunciate each word perfectly.

"What am I doing here? I am here because I was awakened by a phone call in the middle of the night from Bill Fenner. He was awakened himself by his second-in-command with the news that you were in jail on a possible homicide charge."

"It's not what it looks like, Frank."

"You remember Inspector Bill Fenner?" he said, as if I hadn't spoken.

"Of course I do."

Once again, he acted as if I hadn't said a word. "Deputy chief of investigations of the San Francisco Police? He's a buddy of mine. And your father's, who must be spinning in his grave. You may have met Fenner a couple of times throughout the years during another one of your many escapades."

"Now, Frank."

"In case you don't know, Inspector Fenner doesn't take kindly to being awakened in the middle of the night, any more than I do!"

His voice steadily rose on each succeeding word until it reached a crescendo. Maybe he forgot he was only talking to one person and not giving the Sermon on the Mount. But I didn't feel that was something I could mention at the moment.

"This wasn't my fault."

"It never is."

The volume of his voice had lowered but he still ground his teeth together. My dentist has told me to never do that, but I didn't feel it was the time to mention that, either.

"Honest, Frank!" For emphasis, I grabbed at the bars with scratched and dirt-covered hands, ending with decimated fingernails. Needless to say, although I will say it, the condition of my nails would probably seal my fate with my manicurist, who is never happy with the ten I present her, at the best of times.

Frank continued again as if I hadn't spoken. "Resisting arrest—"

"I wasn't resisting arrest. I was trying to catch a suspect."

"Fleeing the scene of a crime—"

"I wasn't fleeing. I was trying to catch—"

"And finally, murder."

"I didn't murder anybody. How come nobody thinks of it as an unspeakably horrid accident?"

"Because, according to forensics, the safety lever on the guillotine wasn't in the position it should have been in. Someone tampered with it."

"Well, it wasn't me. Do I look like the kind of person who would behead someone?"

"And yet it has a unique touch for which you are famous." His voice held a sense of irony but was cold enough to chill a martini, something I could have used just then.

"I don't know anything about the trick. I don't know what happened," I protested. "Come on, Frank. I was just filling in, doing a job—"

"What job?"

"A magician's assistant for this charity thing I got roped into, although it seemed like a good idea at the time. You know, the Sons and Daughters of Fallen American Heroes."

"Is that why you look like a Las Vegas showgirl who did battle with a bulldozer and lost?"

My eyes traveled first to the wristwatch that didn't make it, smashed crystal and all. Then on to the formerly glamorous, sparkly costume that once could be described as part bathing suit and part mirrored disco ball. Now ripped, dirt-stained, with missing or wounded sequins, it shed broken strings of silver beads like a Labradoodle sheds hair. My eyes ended at shoeless feet in torn fishnet stockings. Dang. I loved those silver stilettos, so easy to slide into, so easy to be left somewhere in a cave-in.

I snapped my head back up to face Frank. The quick movement caused the red ostrich plume, which had bobbed above my head when I started the magic show, to flap to the side of my face. Now kaput and ladened with mud, wisps of feathers got in my eyes and mouth. I tried to blow the maimed plume away from my face, but it waved about listlessly only to land right back where it started. Determined little bugger.

"Oh, this!" I decided maybe the cool approach was the way to go. "This happened when the tunnel caved in. I had to dig my way out. Come on, I was undercover, pretending to be the magician's assistant. The real assistant disappeared a few days ago. You have to understand—"

"I don't have to understand anything," he interrupted. "And don't be blinking those baby blues at me, all innocent. You are in the women's holding tank, waiting to appear before Judge Plenca on charges of first-degree murder by decapitation."

"Not me." I shook my head for emphasis.

"Yes, you! Never mind. Where's Lila?" He looked behind me, taking in the holding cell.

"She's over there talking to Misty Waters, in for soliciting."

I pointed to a dark corner where my cool blonde mother sat. She was wearing a floor-length black-and-white strapless evening gown, similar to the one worn by Rita Hayworth in the film *Pal Joey* when she sang the song, "Zip." Playing the same role of Vera Prentice-Simpson for our local community acting group, the Palo Alto Players, I was glad Mom hadn't changed into the blue peignoir set for the second number, "Bewitched, Bothered, and Bewildered." It might have been embarrassing running after me in a nightgown, even a French one.

My mother seemed so deep in conversation with Misty Waters that she hadn't heard us. Or possibly Mom was using selective hearing. That seems to go around a lot. Her companion, Misty, was a fiery redhead who'll never drown, if you get my meaning. Her costume was purple shorts and a revealing emerald-green, latex tank top. Not nearly as classy as Mom's, but made a certain statement.

Frank turned to me. "How you managed to involve your mother in all of this—"

"She followed me when I took off after the suspect."

"And Richard gave chase, too?"

"He followed Mom. And before you ask, Tío's home recuperating from the flu and Gurn's in DC."

"Ah! That explains why they're not part of this madness."

"Where is Richard, anyway? Do you know?"

"Your brother's in the men's holding tank facing possible accessory charges, same as Lila."

"Yikes. I'll bet he's not happy."

"You think? The three of you should be locked up."

"We *are* locked up."

"Not anymore," Detective Inspector Bill Fenner said, stepping out of the shadows. How long he had been standing there, I didn't know. At five foot nine, or ten, and about fifteen pounds overweight, he didn't look to be in as good a physical condition as Frank, but he had a sharpness in his eyes akin to Frank's. He focused those eyes on me now, and I felt a little uncomfortable under the intensity of them. He was as unshaven as the first time I'd met him when he was still coming up in the ranks. That time he'd been working around the clock, filling in for officers out on sick leave. This time it was because he'd been awakened in the middle of the night by the mess I was in. He didn't look any happier than Frank.

"You're being released under Chief Thompson's recognizance." He went on. "The paperwork is being done now. Instead of going home and back to bed, I have to return to the theater and deal with the fallout of this beheading. Two ushers quit. Several people fainted. One man had a mild heart attack. He's going to be all right, but his wife is talking about suing the theater. And the press is having a field day. It led the eleven o'clock news on six channels."

"Oh, wow," I said lamely.

"Oh, wow? Oh, wow? That's what you have to say?"

"How about, *soy inocente*?"

"You're innocent? So, you say. But for now," he thundered, "you will return to your home in Palo Alto, and then in three days' time, you will drive back to San Francisco, where Chief Thompson will present you to the judge in chambers for an eleven a.m. hearing. And for the record, I had to call in every favor owed me to get the charges against Lila and Richard dropped. For Bobby's sake."

"Thank you, Fenner," I said, trying to be friendly. "This is really nothing more than a horrifying—"

"That's *Inspector* Fenner, deputy chief of investigations, to you," he interrupted with a snarl. So much for being friendly. I have discovered the longer someone's title is, and the more they throw it in your face, the madder they are. I would say on the one-to-ten scale, Inspector Fenner, deputy chief of investigations, was a twelve. So, I said nothing. "Don't poke the bear" — that's my motto.

"Come Wednesday, you will explain yourself to Judge Plenca, and if you're lucky, she will let you post bail, pending further investigation. If not, you'll be right back where you are now, facing murder charges. First-degree murder charges. Well, I think that's it for now." He turned to leave, paused, and wheeled around to face me again. "I trust I will not be seeing any more of you tonight. I have enough to deal with. Go home!"

I watched him stride away in the scant lighting of the jail's hallway. Then I turned to my godfather. "Frank, he acts like he thinks I did it. I didn't kill the man. You know I didn't."

"Of course, I know that. That's why I'm sticking my neck out for you," he stated. He gestured to an older, seasoned officer standing a few feet away, who was probably counting the minutes until retirement.

The old duffer stepped forward, holding a set of keys and looked at me with disdain. I surveyed the disaster that was me and tried to give him a winning smile. Shafts of feathers found their way into my mouth and down my throat again. I started to cough. A look of fear came to his face. He raised the N95 mask from around his neck, covering his nose and mouth with it.

"Step back," he ordered.

"Listen," I said, still hacking, "it's just the plume. I don't have—"

"Step back!" he said again, louder and with more authority. He rested his free hand on the billy club at his side.

"Better do as he says, Lee," Frank said evenly.

"Stepping back," I said, raising my hands to a surrender position.

My godfather and I have a complicated relationship. He thinks of me almost as his youngest daughter, meaning I should do as he says without asking questions. Medicine was the first profession Frank tried to push me into. Then he wanted me to pursue my childhood dream, that of becoming a ballerina. He didn't care, as long as it wasn't anything like what he or my dad did. Even when Dad opened the family-owned detective business, Discretionary Investigations Inc., Frank thought I was meant for other things.

But the fates conspired against him. My Latin sucked, so medicine was out. And even though I lived for ballet, I wasn't a good enough dancer to be anything more than in the chorus of a second-rate dance company. But what I seemed to excel at was finding evidence and piecing things together, long after the fact. So, I wound up following in Dad's footsteps, much to Frank's never-ending disappointment.

While waiting for the cell door to be opened, I yanked the offending plume off my head, taking bobby pins and a clump of brunette hair with it. My eyes watered from the pain, but I looked at Frank with hope. "So, you're really getting us out of here?"

"I will probably rue the day, but yes." He paused. "I also managed to borrow a coat from lost and found for you to wear, given how you're dressed." He reached behind him for a tan coat two sizes too big and not my color at all, but beggars can't be choosers. "Put it on, grab Lila, and let's get out of here, Lee."

"Thank you, Frank!"

Relief flooded through me. Spending the night in jail, especially with a mother who was the queen of I-told-you-so's, was not something I was looking forward to. I've said it before, and I'll say it again: being a private investigator is not all it's cracked up to be.

Chapter Two

By the time the paperwork was done, and Mom, Richard, and I had piled into Frank's car—Mom's Jaguar having been impounded—we arrived in Palo Alto around 3:00 a.m. Not much was said on the drive home that I can remember, but I fell asleep shortly after sliding into the back seat of the car.

Once home, the three of us stumbled out of Frank's car. As he pulled away, he said, "I'll be back tomorrow around eleven. We can talk then."

For an instant I watched the red of his taillights disappearing into the night, then turned to look at the house. Tío was waiting at the front door with Vicki, Richard's wife.

Even at this hour, Tío looked elegant in his black-and-white-striped pajamas and matching robe. With silver hair and aquiline features on his trim six-foot frame, he could have joined Frank as one of the more mature models on the cover of *GQ*. In actuality, he's made the cover of many a foodie mag but as the executive chef of Las Mañanitas, a well-known gourmet Mexican restaurant in San Jose.

Since he retired, and wasn't cooking for his family, or meals for a women's shelter, he made special dietary food for rescue animals. He was the busiest man I knew. When he wasn't down with the flu.

"I have made the chamomile tea," Tío said as we trouped into the kitchen. He handed Richard and me a full mug of steaming tea. I undid the belt on the coat and took a sip of chamomile.

"Thank you, Tío," Richard said. "I could use some after tonight." My brother crossed to the kitchen table, dropped into a chair, and swallowed huge gulps of tea. Vicki sat down beside him, and the two of them began to nuzzle and whisper to one another.

"The tea is spiked with something, I hope, Tío," I said, drinking half the cup down. "It sure tastes like it."

"*Como no*," he said with a wink. "I make with the golden rum."

I studied his face, a face I loved with my heart and soul. His eyes were clear, and he no longer looked feverish.

"You're feeling better, Tío. I can see. But please don't do things too fast. We don't want a relapse."

"I only do what I am capable of doing. It is for you that I worry." He turned to Mom. "Lila, I have the chamomile tea without the rum, as well."

"*Thank* you, but I'll *pass* on *tea*, Mateo," Mom said, using his given name and stressing several words in the sentence as usual. "What I *need* is a good *soak,* then *off* to bed. Good night, *everyone.*" But instead of leaving, she turned to me. "*Liana,* you look *dead* on your feet."

Mom reached out, and without saying anything, drew me into a quick mother-daughter hug. She pushed me away immediately, though, once she got a whiff of my dirt-caked body. Looking down at the bodice of her gown, she brushed off a few specks of schmutz.

"And *you* need to shower *immediately*. And just *look* at the *condition* of your nails. *Disreputable*. I'll call Anita and make an *appointment* for you to have them done. The coat Francis *borrowed* for you to wear needs to be dry-cleaned *before* it's returned. But *I'll* take care of that, too. But *first*, you need some *sleep*. *Then* you need to *concentrate* on what happened tonight and how it *impacts* you."

I was trying to keep up with the orders, but said, "I would say it impacts me a lot, Mom."

"We'll have a meeting *tomorrow* morning to discuss it, as *Francis* says. Be here *precisely* at eleven."

"Sounds good. And Mom," I confessed, "I'm sorry about all this. I mean, ruining the fundraiser and everything."

"Liana, please be *mindful* that *you* did not *deliberately* set *out* to *ruin* the fundraiser. In fact, if you had *anything* to do with what *happened*, I would be *very* much *surprised*."

Relieved and pleased, I said, "Thank you, Mom. I—"

"And as for *fundraisers*," she went on over my words, "the *dates* of them can be *altered*. *True*, the event becomes more *work*, but we can *do* it."

"Thank you, Mom. I—"

"However, we will *continue* this conversation at a *later* time. At the moment, *all* five of my senses are *suggesting* that *you* recently *returned* from *wallowing* in a *sewer*."

"Image-worthy. Got it. Shower."

"And *Liana*—"

"Yes, ma'am?"

"I *am* sorry you've had to *experience* something so… *unsettling*."

"Thank you, Mom. But I think Tío's spiked tea is going to help." I drank down the last of my tea.

With a nod to everyone in the room, Mom turned on her Jimmy Chu's and was gone.

I watched her depart, wondering—and not for the first time—how anyone could say so many of the right words and yet leave the recipient of those words feeling as if their slip were still showing.

"Your mamá," Tío said, coming up from behind, "is suffering, also. She expresses herself sometimes in a different way, but her *corazón* always beats for you."

"Gracias, Tío," I said, as he refilled my mug with more steaming tea. "You always know what to say to make me feel better. And I'm so glad you're feeling better."

"Si, the worst is passed," he said. "I would have come up to San Francisco to get you, but Victoria and I wait here as Frank instructed. You have had a bad night, *sobrina*." His eyes were sympathetic as they looked into mine.

"Well, it's not every day your niece sees someone's head chopped off." I tried to smile, then bit my lower lip. "Forgive me. That sounded glib. I'm feeling anything but glib." I guzzled the tea down, then went to the table and poured myself another mugful.

"I saw it from the wings, Lee," my brother said. "It's something I'll never forget." He involuntarily shivered. Vicki wrapped her arms around him but said nothing.

Tío gave me another one of his bear hugs. "We will talk about all of this tomorrow," he said. "Now you must finish your tea and go to bed."

Vicki stared at me. "You look exhausted, Lee." Then she turned to Richard. "You, too. Let's go home. I should have gotten a babysitter for Steffi. I should have been with you."

Richard leaned toward her and kissed her forehead. "Given all that's happened, I'm glad you weren't. Where is our little angel?" Richard asked, taking her hand.

Trying to lighten the tension in the room, Vicki put on a bright smile. "You wouldn't be calling her that if you'd seen the tantrum she threw earlier tonight about having to go to bed. The terrible-twos have descended. Right now, she's asleep in the family room. I'll go get her."

A minute or two later, Vicki rolled the stroller out containing my sleeping niece, the most gorgeous two-year-old in the world, not that I'm prejudiced or anything. Then Vicki shuttled Richard and Steffi into their car and drove him home.

After kissing Tío good night and pouring myself yet another cup of rum-laden tea, I left the kitchen, exiting into and through the back garden. Once at the garage, I climbed the stairs to my husband's and my apartment, my body screaming with each step I took. Then it occurred to me. I'd have to feed the cats before I did anything else, even took a shower. They hadn't had their dinner yet, and it was nearly morning.

I opened the door expecting to see two half-crazed, hungry cats who had been alone for nearly eight straight hours. Instead, Tugger and Baba were asleep on the sofa curled up together in a yin-yang position.

"Of course," I said aloud after looking into the kitchen and noticing their half-full cereal bowls. "Tío was here and took care of them." I took a sniff of the air. "And he brought me chicken soup."

Without disturbing the cats, I went into the bathroom and stripped, throwing the borrowed coat on the laundry hamper and what was left of the torn and ripped costume into the wastebasket in the corner, filling it to the brim.

I felt bad about the destruction of the costume. Billie Evans, the theater's wardrobe supervisor, had scrounged it up for me out of stock at the last minute, fitted it to me, and then spent much of the day making alterations. I hadn't even gotten it until five minutes before I went onstage. The silver-spangled and beaded costume had grabbed at me here and there but was a credit to Billie's sewing skills. I'd have to buy her a bouquet of flowers the next time I saw her. I looked in the wastebasket. Maybe a flower shop.

I rinsed most of the gunk off in the shower, then filled the bathtub with hot water laced with scented bath oil and stepped into the warmth. Submerging myself for a few seconds, I came up for air. I fought back tears of exhaustion and sadness as I assessed the scratches covering most of my body. Superficial. Time and Neosporin would take care of them. But nothing could change the fact that a man was dead. True, he was a nasty man—by all accounts, a despicable man—but he was now a headless man. And someone used me to kill him. Anger bubbled up from my gut, overtaking the sadness.

I took a deep breath, forced myself to relax, and rested my head against the tub while I reached out for my cell phone in its usual spot by the tub. It wasn't there. I sat up so abruptly, water sloshed over the top of the tub and splashed onto the travertine flooring.

Realization hit me. My phone was still in the dressing room, along with my clothes, purse, and keys. After the ghastly climax to the act, running after the person I believed to be the culprit, and being arrested, I never went back to the dressing room to retrieve my things. Clawing your way out of a collapsed tunnel tends to make you forget the small stuff.

Wait a minute, I thought, trying to focus my frazzled brain. My car! Where was my car? Oh, that's right. Downstairs in the garage. It was lucky Richard and I had driven up with Mom in her Jag. Otherwise, it would have been my car that had been impounded. How did I get in? Oh, yes. The door was unlocked. Tío must have done that. That's right. He did mention he'd left the door open for me.

"I'm sure you're in shock, Liana," he'd whispered in his thick Spanish accent. "Seeing a man die like that is very shocking. I left your door unlocked and soup on the stove. Have some, *mi sobrina*, before you go to bed."

And I will as soon as I soak away some of the stiffness, I thought. I settled back and tried to relax. Again. After soaking until the water had turned lukewarm, I took a shower and washed my hair. Wrapped in a terrycloth robe, long hair bound up in a towel, I felt near human as I headed for the kitchen. Not hungry, I put the chicken soup in the fridge and microwaved the remainder of the tea. The kitchen clock said 4:30 a.m. That meant it was 7:30 back East. I should call Gurn. I didn't want him to hear this from the news or somebody else. Fenner's words about the press having a field day with this bounced around inside my head. I picked up the landline and called his cell. He answered on the first ring.

"Hi, darling," I said, trying to keep the tremble out of my voice.

"Sweetheart! Something's wrong. What is it?" he asked. "It's four thirty in the morning there."

"I'm all right. I want you to know that up front. I'm all right."

"When you start out with that, something bad has happened. Is your mother okay? Rich? Vicki and the baby?"

"Sorry, darling, everybody's fine. Physically. Well, not everybody. There's a magician, Marvin the Magnificent, who's not all right. He's dead. In fact, he was beheaded."

"Did I hear you right? Someone was beheaded?"

"You could say I was the instrument of his demise."

"What? Are you all right? What happened?"

"I'm shaken, to be honest, but I'm all right. As to what happened, I'm not really sure. One minute Marvin was barking orders at me to—"

"Why was he barking orders at you?"

"That's right. You don't know any of this. Day before yesterday I became his assistant. All undercover for this job I was doing. And then after the head of cabbage had been cut in half, he… then it happened to him, too." I rushed on before Gurn could say anything. "Even though the lever was to the right and pushed in, just like he told me it should be, and he checked it before I hit my pose, too. And then after I lowered the pillory over his neck—"

"Slow down. What's a pillory?"

"It's a wooden framework with a hole for the head. It's in two pieces, top and bottom."

"Okay, so you lowered the pillory over his neck," Gurn prompted.

"After locking it in place, I dropped the guillotine, and turned to face the audience. There was this sound behind me, like a thump, and then…"

My voice strangled in my throat. I stopped speaking and without warning, drew in a half sob, half breath. I paused and tried to pull it together.

"Honey, I should come home. You don't sound like you should be alone."

"No, I guess I shouldn't. I've never seen anything like it in my life. The audience started screaming even before I came out of my pose, so I turned around and looked at where his head should be, and it wasn't. It was in the basket on the floor. And there was blood everywhere. They think I killed him on purpose."

"I'll be on the next plane home," Gurn said. "We'll sort this out. Even from what little you've told me, it sounds like an accident, nothing deliberate. There's an aircraft cargo plane leaving for San Francisco in forty minutes. If I hurry, I can be on it."

"What about your Sunday afternoon meeting? That's why you're there, to talk about your team's experiences in Afghanistan to the top brass. Learn by the Past, that's your lecture." The spiked tea hit me like a sledgehammer. "People are counting on you," I managed to say.

Gurn is a lieutenant commander in the Navy Reserve and a former SEAL. Navy SEALs are named after the environment in which they operate, the sea, air, and land, and are the foundation of Naval Special Warfare combat forces. His experiences on the ground and in the air during the last days of the US Central Command of warfare in Afghanistan made him invaluable to the Pentagon. Hands-on experience wins the day.

"I'll think of something," he said, as I felt myself drifting off. "Try to get some sleep. I should be home by the time you wake up."

I rallied. "Absolutely not, Gurn. They called this special meeting on a Sunday because that's the only time all of them could be there to hear you. You told me with the current crisis, time is of the essence. You have to stay. One more day won't make that much of a difference for me."

I lied. I had three days to clear myself, or it was off to the clink for me. Every minute counted.

"Besides, I've got Frank and the whole family to help me sort this out."

"You're sure?"

"Yes."

"All right, then. I'll stay. I'll catch the red-eye and be back Monday morning."

"Thank you, darling." I let out a hiccup. "Excuse me. Tío made me chamomile tea with a shot of rum in it. I'm feeling a little woozy right now."

"How many cups have you had?"

"Three. Maybe four."

"Good. Go snuggle up with the cats. Get some sleep. Things will look better in the morning."

"It is the morning. And things don't look so good."

"Then later this morning."

"Mom and Richard shouldn't have followed me down to the basement," I said, my words becoming slow and slurred. "Thank God they didn't follow me into the tunnel. It collapsed when I was in there, but I got out."

"A tunnel collapsed on you?" I could feel his anxiety through the phone.

"Rats. I didn't mean to mention that yet. We can talk about that when you get home. Jeesh, we'd still be in jail, but Frank pulled a few strings as did Bill Fenner. You remember him? He, Dad, and Frank went to the police academy together. Anyway, between the two of them, they got the charges against Mom and Richard dropped, and I've been released into Frank's recon... reconna... recarceration, or something like that."

"Recognizance."

"Yeah." I felt myself nodding off but got with it enough to add, "You know, darling, I don't understand. The lever was right where it was supposed to be, and yet forensics said it had been tampered with. And I am the only likely candidate. I don't understand."

"Go to sleep, honey. I'll talk to you when you wake up. And I'll see you Monday morning. I love you."

"Even if I go to prison?"

"Even if you go to prison."

Chapter Three

I woke up hours later with a start, not really remembering where I was or what was going on. I lay in bed with Tugger sleeping on one side of me, Baba on the other, both warm and familiar. I looked at the clock on the side table. Ten thirty-five a.m. Then it all came back to me. I reached out and clutched at each sleeping cat, realizing that orange, while it may be the new black, was simply not my color.

The landline rang. It was Mom.

"Are you *awake*, Liana?"

"Heart hammering nicely, thank you."

"Then get *dressed* and come down. We are *awaiting* you. In the *family* room."

Putting aside that my mother tends to stress certain words within sentences, which drives me mad, she also doesn't use abbreviations, nicknames, or colloquialisms. In short, my mother tends to sound like a reading of a Charles Dickens' novel. And often with Mr. Dickens' ability to find the darkest moment of every hour. Watch *Saturday Night Live* or Bugs Bunny? Not happening.

"I cannot *impress* upon you the *importance* of this meeting," she went on. "It is *dire*."

"Who's there?" I asked, throwing back the covers and getting up, much to the annoyance of the cats.

"In *attendance* are Richard, Mateo, Frank, *and* I. Victoria and Stephanie remain at *home*."

"I wish little Steffi was there. I could use a friendly face. I'll need a strong cup of coffee before I meet the 'grand inquisitors.'"

She sniffed. "There are *no* grand inquisitors. We have a common *purpose* for this meeting. *Your* freedom. *Humor* is *not* appreciated at this juncture, *Liana*."

"No, ma'am."

"Coffee is *waiting* for you. *As* are *we*," she added. "*Ten* minutes."

"Yes, ma'am."

But while the spirit was willing, the flesh was not. Every part of me ached from the evening's wild chase ending with the cave-in I had to dig my way out of. I decided to take a shower to help with the stiffness but wondered if once I got in, would I just stand there and let the hot water run over me until it was gone? We had a large water heater. There was no telling how long it would take to run out of hot water. I forced myself to hurry, but it took a good fifteen minutes of running water to relieve tense muscles.

Already late, I threw on my favorite purple sweats, old and faded but clean, and ran down the stairs to the outside of the garage. It wasn't until I got to the bottom of the staircase did I realize I'd forgotten to change out of my fake leopard-skin slippers and into actual shoes. Oh well. Mom already hated it when I wore sweats no matter how clean they were. May as well send her over the edge with fuzzy house slippers.

Out of breath from running across the backyard, I entered the family room and huffed a "good morning," with a big smile planted on my face. No one returned it. Richard looked deep in thought, Tío concerned, Mom annoyed—especially after she got a load of my feet—and Frank worried. I liked it better when he looked angry.

"Sorry I'm late. I took a quick shower."

Silence fell on the room. Then all of a sudden everyone started talking at once. I couldn't understand any one person, but I did hear a lot of who, how, what, and when questions. Finally, Frank's voice bellowed above all the rest. He gives good bellow.

"Quiet, everyone! Quiet!" The room fell silent again. "That's better." He turned to me. "I want every detail of what you did, who you saw, and what you said from the moment you entered the theater several days ago. No, start at the beginning of this assistant-magician fiasco. Oh, and there are your car keys, phone, and purse." He gestured to a pile of my things on the coffee table. "I took them from the dressing room this morning. Fortunately, it wasn't designated as part of the crime scene."

"Thank you, Frank! You drove all the way up to San Francisco. That was so thoughtful." I smiled at the man who was back to looking well-groomed and stylish, sporting a mustard-colored cashmere V-neck sweater worn over caramel-colored slacks.

The same brown loafers as last night, but of course, they worked better with this outfit.

"You're welcome. Now start talking."

"It's a long story, and first I need some coffee." I crossed the family room to the small kitchen area hidden behind a marble counter, with its small fridge, stove, and sink. The room, done in two of Mom's favorite colors, beige and white, had at least been given some life with the golden oak floors and wall shelving.

Speaking of beige, mom was wearing her favorite beige tweed pantsuit with a high-necked, soft-blue blouse. The slacks had narrow cuffs on wide-legged pants with razor-sharp pleats. A matching jacket was draped over the back of her chair for when she left the house. Naturally, Mom's feet were encased in Manolo Blahnik stilettos, exactly the same color as the pantsuit. The queen of understated elegance, stud pearl earrings and a gold wedding band were her only jewelry.

I looked down at my faded purple sweatsuit, then wiggled my toes in the fake leopard-skin scuffies. Sometimes the fruit falls far from the tree. Sometimes it falls in the next county.

Sighing, I headed to the counter with its carafe of hot coffee, cups, milk, and sugar. Then I noticed a plate of Tío's incredible *roles de canela* or cinnamon sticky buns and cheered up considerably. I grabbed the largest bun I could find because I am a pig.

"Give me just a minute to inhale some caffeine and get my heart started."

"You can see I make for you some breakfast before I go," Tío said.

I turned and threw Tío a grateful smile. Ah! The friendly face I'd been looking for. A white linen Nehru shirt with trim black slacks outfitted him, and he never looked better. Or healthier. He crossed to the closet and took out a black jacket and threw it over one arm.

"You look *ready* to resume your *life*, Mateo," Mom said. "And no *doubt* the women's shelter has *missed* your cooking for the past few days."

"Is that where you're going?" I asked. "Please don't overdo, Tío."

"I will be good, little mama," he said to me with a wink. "But it is time for me to go to the shelter to make *almuerzo*, the lunch, and to give some of the residents words on how to cook the tortilla soup."

"Do you mean tips on how to cook tortilla soup?" I asked. Now and then I help Tío out with the English language, and it has become an enjoyable habit for both of us.

"Si, si. Tips, not words," he said with a laugh. "English is not always so easy." Then his face took on a serious look. "But if you have need of me, sobrina, I will stay."

"Tío, I always have need of you, but in this case, I think between Mom, Richard, and Frank, we've got this."

"Mateo," Mom interjected, "please *go* and do your *work* at the shelter."

"They need you, too," Richard put in, looking up from his laptop.

Tío looked at me. "Of this, you are sure?"

"I am sure. We are sure."

And with that he nodded his head in acceptance, waved goodbye, and exited the house.

I watched him leave, then picked up a napkin and bit into the still warm, sticky bun. I poured myself some coffee, added the 1 percent milk being offered—Mom's homage to healthy living—and stirred in a teaspoon of sugar. After several slurps of coffee and two bites of the sticky bun filled with cinnamon, brown sugar, and chopped pecans, I crossed back to my waiting audience and plopped down in one of the white leather overstuffed chairs.

"Okay, I think I can go on." I wiped the sugar off my mouth with the napkin and took another slug of coffee. "I do want to go on record as saying it was my stupid idea to do this, thinking of it as a great opportunity. Mom just went along with me."

"I did *not* 'just go *along* with you,' Liana," Mom said in rebuttal.

"I'm the one who insisted I take over the magician's assistant duties when the assistant disappeared."

"Liana I do not see *why* you are trying to take the *entire* blame for this," Lila countered. "I am *just* as *responsible* as you. After all, I *am* the CEO."

Aha, I thought. We're in work mode.

"Oh, pa-leeeze, Lila," I said, glad I remembered to call Mom by her given name. "You may be the CEO of Discretionary Investigations, but I am the in-house investigator. Tell her, Richard," I said, turning to my brother.

As usual, Richard retreated inside the neck of his blue T-shirt, pulling it up over his nose. He stretched out an already stretched-out ribbed neckline. Combined with the saying on the front of the shirt, "Half A Brain Is Better Than Wallowing," the shirt and its owner looked pretty weird. I had no idea what the motto meant, but my motto was "Keep your trap shut." Asking only led to a theoretical conversation about computer stuff which was incomprehensible to me.

"I really need to concentrate on this," Richard finally said through the fabric, then leaned back in his chair and stared at the ever-present laptop in his lap.

Frank intervened. "Ladies, you can get into the mother-daughter who's-the-most-guilty act when we have more time. Right now, let's concentrate on the business at hand. In three days, Lee, you appear before a judge who might hold you on premeditated murder charges. Whoever manually switched that lock from Safe to Danger is going down for premeditated murder. Let's try to figure out who it can be." He paused. "Besides you."

I swallowed hard. I was supposed to be flying to Bali with Gurn in less than a month on a second honeymoon. Being indicted for murder could interfere with the trip big-time. Actually, being indicted for murder could interfere with life, big-time. I took a deep breath and started talking. Babbling might be a better description.

"A few days ago, right after Gurn left for DC, Lila called me into her office. Apparently, Richard had made some headway on finding the real address of the cyberterrorist who's been hacking into Heart's Desire's site and screwing with their clients. You know, sending them wrong information, or having them meet at two separate places, or fixing them up with the family dog. At first, Richard followed the IP address to Bombay, but that was just a ruse. They were in Silicon Valley all along."

"Wait a minute. What's this Heart's Desire?" Frank said.

"That's what brought me to the theater in the first place. A job DI was doing for a client."

Even though Lila was in the room, I accidentally used the initials of Discretionary Inquiries, the family-run Silicon Valley-based detective agency, instead of saying the full name. I saw her flinch out of the corner of my eye, but she kept silent. Frank continued.

"Sounds like a lonely-hearts website."

"They *are*," Lila said, while I took another bite of sticky bun. "*And* they are in every *major* city *throughout* the country. It is a *multi*million-dollar company. And our *latest* client."

"Multimillion-dollar company?" Frank looked shocked. "I thought it was an online club for people trying to find a date. Or a little action."

"An *apt* description," Lila said. "But when Richard tracked *down* the name of the hacker, it was the *husband* of Marvin Del Vecchio's *daughter*. Professionally, Marvin *Del Vecchio* is known as Marvin the *Magnificent*."

Frank looked surprised and said to Lila, "You're kidding."

"*That* would never *occur* to me," Lila said, after thinking over his comment. "The *alleged* hacker we sought is the son-in-law of the *dead* magician."

"So, let me get this straight. Marvin the Magnificent's daughter's husband is the hacker you've been looking for? What's his name?"

" Steven Kutner. And he's a real cracker," Richard put in.

"And you don't mean a Florida cracker, do you," Frank said, with a wink.

"No. He's a cybercriminal. He's good at what he does," Richard said. High praise from my baby brother, a computer prodigy, who can hack with the best and is better than most. He's also head of Discretionary Information's IT department. Richard continued, with his rare admission: "He had me running in every direction but the right one for nearly a week."

"But you found him?" Frank asked.

"I found his location," Richard corrected.

"*Unfortunately*, not the *man* himself," Lila said. "*He* seems to have *disappeared*. But he *is* employed by True Love Forever, a *competing* online dating service."

"But we did find out he was related by marriage to Marvin the Magnificent," I said when I could finally get a word in edgewise. "And that M the M was doing his act for the same charity show as Mom's amateur theater group. That made it too good a chance to pass up."

"So you were there on a related case," Frank mused. "You'd better give me the cast of characters." Frank looked at me.

"Okay." Internally I shivered, thinking about the man who was decapitated. He may have looked as if he'd never had a happy day in his life, but nobody wants to lose their head over that.

Aloud, I said, "Magician Marvin Del Vecchio, fifty-eight years old. A dark-haired man with coarse features. Frown lines deeply etched into his face. He seemed pretty bitter about the fact he wasn't thought of well in magic circles. From what I understand, his act was a flop with audiences most of the time. He didn't get many bookings. Not that he needed to."

"He was just playing at being a magician?" Frank asked.

"No, he took it seriously. Very seriously. What I mean is, he was independently wealthy due to inheriting a chain of chicken-fat-processing plants, a mansion in Sea Cliff, and a portfolio of stocks and bonds from his father who was something of a financial genius," I said.

"That's interesting," Frank said. "Go on."

"Marvin Del Vecchio had a son and daughter by his second wife of three marriages. David, age twenty-six, an up-and-coming magician. It seems to run in the blood. But the son is reported to be good, unlike his father. David won some sort of big-deal television contest recently, which is supposed to have helped launch his career. He's out on the road perfecting his act. I don't know what he looks like, as he's never been around the theater or, at least, not when I've been there."

"So, the son is everything the father wanted to be," Frank remarked, mainly to himself.

"Then there's Donna, Donna Del Vecchio Kutner, the youngest. She's twenty-four, but looks and acts even younger. She's about five four, slender, pretty, with long, dark hair down to her waist, although she wears it up for the performances."

"She's the one with the dog and married to our hacker," Frank said.

"Yes. Then there's Del Vecchio's current wife of four years. The former Madison Cartwright, thirty-three and holding. Visualize a Barbie doll and you've got her. Although, Madison likes to wear blue polish on her fingernails and toes, which is very un-Barbie. Third marriage for her, too."

"They're all players?" Frank asked.

"Until we know better," I said.

"Marvin, Madison, David, Donna," Frank repeated.

"And Steven, don't forget," I said. "The man who started it all."

"Marvin, Madison, David, Donna, Steven. Steven's the hacker. Got it. Sounds like a bad soap opera. So why didn't you just tell Lonely Hearts who did what?"

He looked at Lila questioningly, but Richard spoke up first.

"When I finally got through the security system and into his online files, they were encrypted to self-destruct without another password being entered within five seconds. Which they did. I should have anticipated that. Because of my blunder, we have nothing."

"You're being too *hard* on yourself, Richard," Lila said, more motherly than not.

"No, I'm not," Richard refuted. "He's a black hat—malicious, unscrupulous, and knows every trick. I should have known he'd program his files to self-destruct without a second password. But he has to have a backup someplace. Probably carries it on him."

"We can't anticipate *everything*." Lila turned back to Frank. "But *because* of that, we have no real *evidence*, merely *speculation*. And I *promised* to have proof for Lonely Hearts by the *end* of the month, *eight* days' time."

"That might be our undoing, Lila," I said. "But we've all got things to answer for in this case. Mine would be being in the wrong place at the wrong time when somebody gets murdered. Lucky me."

Frank turned to me. "Never mind the self-pity. How did you come to be Marvin's assistant? What happened to his own assistant?"

"That would be Donna," I said, chewing on the last of the sticky bun.

"*Don't* talk with your *mouth* full," Lila said, less motherly than not.

"Sorry." I swallowed quickly. "She disappeared two days after her husband, Steven, along with her dog."

"Her dog?" Frank looked at me.

"Yes, a little honey-colored Pomeranian, aptly named Honey Boy. Very cute but a yapper. When she's onstage, she leaves him in the dressing room. When she's not onstage, he's always in her arms."

"I don't have to remember the dog's name, do I?" asked Frank.

"*Liana*," Lila said, "You've *allowed* yourself to be *sidetracked*."

"Sorry," I said. "No, you don't, Frank. Anyway, Marvin needed an assistant tout de suite. And as I said, it seemed like a golden opportunity."

"So, who of these people would be viable suspects for killing Marvin Del Vecchio?" Frank asked. "We have to get you off the hook, Lee," he said, turning to me.

Before I could reply, Richard jumped in. "I've been looking into that. I've dug up some interesting facts that could influence a number of people to do the deed, including a member of the household staff."

"When did you do that, Richard?" I asked.

"Around six this morning."

"After everything that happened last night?" I was aghast.

"I'm used to sleeping in spurts." He looked down at the small but powerful computer in his lap, one he'd put together to his own specifications. "Anyway, I got some info on the value of the assets, plus the chicken-fat-processing plants. The processing plants alone gross fifteen to sixteen million annually."

Frank let out a whistle. "That's a lot of chicken fat."

"Of course, I can't get into his actual will, but the processing plants are only part of an estate left in trust to Del Vecchio by his father, Lionel Del Vecchio, when he died fifteen years ago. That's public record. Besides the plants, there are stocks and bonds and real estate, including the mansion in

Sea Cliff currently lived in by the family, and valued at over twenty mil. The entire estate is worth roughly around one hundred and sixty million dollars. Marvin Del Vecchio had an annual income plus access to the interest of the estate but could not touch the principle. Upon Marvin's death, the assets are passed on to each of the children, David and Donna, and also—"

"So," Frank interrupted, "David and Donna inherit half of nearly one hundred and sixty million dollars once their father dies. That seems like a lot of motive to me."

"That's not quite—" Richard said.

I jumped right in, overriding my brother. "Maybe it was Donna I saw in the wings right after the guillotine fell. He or she was dressed in black and had a black hoodie over the face and hair, so I don't know for sure. But whoever I was chasing wasn't big, and ran like a woman."

"I didn't know *women* ran differently than *men*," Lila said.

"Trained athletes, no. But some women have more hip action. This one did."

"Listen, I—" Richard tried again.

"You think Donna might have sabotaged the guillotine?" Frank asked, looking at me. "Maybe she and her husband were in it together."

"Killing her own father?" I was aghast. "And in such a ghastly way?"

Frank looked at me knowingly. "It wouldn't be unheard of. And from what you've told me, he didn't seem like such a nice man."

"*Possibly,*" Lila said. "But I don't *know.* She *strikes* me as a naïve and *simple* young woman. As *Liana* said, *young* for her age. And she *certainly* was kept under her father's *influence.*"

"I have to admit," I said, "while being front and center gave me a lot of latitude, he was the nastiest, most sexist man I ever met in my life. It wasn't until I told him I would break his hand if he grabbed my rear end one more time, did he stop. And then he started throwing his swords *at* me instead of *to* me. If I had the job for real, I would have quit in an instant. The two days I worked with him were an eternity. I don't know how Donna took it."

"Helloooo," Richard put in rather loudly.

"She probably didn't *know* any better, Liana," Lila said. "*Sad* child."

"Excuse me," Richard said, raising his voice theatrically, "but I would like to continue with the rest of the information I found."

The three of us turned and looked at my brother.

"Sorry," I said.

"*Dear* boy, *apologies,*" Lila said.

"Well, spit it out, son," Frank said.

"There's more to this trust." He cleared his throat dramatically. "It's not half to each child, it's a third. The remaining third is split between two nephews and all the wives, whether they are still married to the blood heir or not, and—"

"*Surely* you can't mean *ex-wives*?" Lila asked in shock. "*Nephews* I can understand, but *former* wives?"

I could see annoyance on my brother's face at being interrupted again, but he recovered. "Yes, the trust includes Marvin Del Vecchio's two ex-wives, as well as the current one. When Lionel Del Vecchio's wife, Marvin's mother, passed away, he never remarried. He referred to her in the trust as the 'love of his life.' But before he met her, she had been divorced by her first husband, who left her destitute. Del Vecchio the Elder never forgot that and tried to be honor bound to any woman who married into the family, widowed or divorced, as long as she never remarried."

"This is the *oddest* thing I've ever *heard*," Lila remarked.

"I haven't gotten to the odd part yet," Richard said. "But first I want to mention the butler, Mr. Wong Chen. He's been at the job for nearly thirty years and is also in the trust. Now that Marvin is dead, Wong receives two percent of the entire estate off the top. That's around two and a half million dollars."

He paused dramatically while the three of us tried to take it in. Richard leaned forward.

"And drumroll, please, because *here* comes the odd part: Del Vecchio the Elder set up the trust almost as a tontine, in that when Del Vecchio Junior died, the properties were to be liquidated, the monies combined and kept in another trust. The heirs receive a share of the interest of the sum annually, not the principle. All except for Wong. He receives his two percent immediately, and then is out of the picture."

"Where's the tontine part?" I asked.

"I'm getting to it. When and if any of the heirs die, and that includes one or both of Marvin's children, that person's share is distributed in like percentages among the remaining survivors."

"Is that *legal*?" Lila asked.

"Oh yes," Richard said, "but it needs a battery of lawyers making sure everything is copacetic at all times. Only larger estates can afford to do it."

"Let me get this straight," Frank said. "When one of the heirs dies, their piece of the pie is split among the remaining living heirs?"

"Do the heirs know about this strange will?" I asked, following Frank's query.

"According to the terms of the trust," Richard said, "the heirs are supposed to be notified immediately of Marvin's death and have six months from the date of the reading of the trust to accept the terms and claim their inheritance."

"And if they don't accept the terms?" I asked.

"Then they are stricken from the trust. As I said earlier, during that six-month period, the properties are to be sold and compiled into one lump sum and kept in a savings account. After that time, depending on each heir's place in the trust, percentages of the interest are to be distributed to them on a yearly basis, changing only if and when one or more of them dies. Then in true tontine fashion, the last one alive inherits everything. No more percentages. They get the whole kit and caboodle, chicken fat and all."

"That *means* they could *all* wait *years* to inherit the real *value* of the estate," Lila said.

"Unless one of them decides to start bumping the others off to speed things up," I said. "My, my, my, my, my. And that, my friends, is called motive."

Chapter Four

"Let's *return* to the *nephews* in Marin. Who are *they*?" Lila asked.

Richard looked at his computer screen. "Wyman and Winston Del Vecchio, twin brothers living in Mill Valley."

"*Twins!*" Lila exclaimed. "How *fascinating.*"

"Sons of Lionel Del Vecchio's older brother, Mario, also deceased, and the only other living relatives. Wyman and Winston are forty-one and single. They own a pastry shop called Perfected Pastries by W. and W., in Mill Valley. In true Marin style, the pastries are organic and made with nondairy products. Online chitchat says they want to expand but have no money. The Marin side of the family has been estranged from the Sea Cliff side for decades, but that doesn't seem to have made any difference to Del Vecchio Senior. If they're related by blood, they're in the trust."

"Let's leave this Marin side of the family for the moment," Frank said. "I want to know about the two ex-wives of Marvin Del Vecchio." Frank looked at Richard. "Got any of their names?"

Richard turned to the screen of his computer. "Elizabeth Hofsted was wife number one. They married young; she was eighteen, he was twenty. That was thirty-seven years ago. They were married ten years. No trace of her that I can find yet, not even an online photo—which is strange—but all of this was before the internet got to be what it is today. If the estate lawyers don't have anything either, I'll put Andy on it. He'll do the search the old-fashioned way, i.e., make phone calls, to find either a birth or marriage certificate. Hopefully, both."

Andy is Richard's second-in-command and an even bigger geek. He lives on Diet Pepsi, yogurt, and pizza, and at five foot six, tips the scale at a hundred pounds. He shares his home with a sulcata tortoise named Buster, who weighs more than he does.

But I digress. Richard went on.

"As I said, Elizabeth Hofsted was married to Marvin Del Vecchio for ten years. From what I can glean, she was a bit of a mouse. Didn't even drive a car, so no driver's license. No online ID at all that I can find. No kids. Del Vecchio dumped her for Claudia Gracioso, a Miss Italy, who gave him David and Donna in the six years they were married. Claudia left him for Paul Rinken, owner of a chain of health clubs in the Bay Area. Never married him, though. Del Vecchio got custody of the kids."

Richard tapped on a key or two, then said, "Wife number three, Madison Cartwright. They married four years ago. She's an on-the-fringe socialite who makes a specialty of marrying older men. She signed a prenup, which meant if she divorced Del Vecchio or he left her, she wouldn't get anything. But if she survived him, which she did, she splits a third of the estate with his two ex-wives and nephews, roughly ten and a quarter mil each. And as for Donna," Richard added, waggling his eyebrows. "She doesn't look as dumb to me as she acts."

I digested this. Putting waggling eyebrows aside, Richard has a vast knowledge of all things technical and digital, but his people skills are wanting. They were practically nonexistent until Vicki came on the scene. His wife more or less socialized him, something his family could never accomplish. But he still eats liverwurst and onion sandwiches right before client meetings and often forgets to put his shoes on, so I can't give him any marks for socialization higher than a C minus.

"Good Lord," Frank said. "I need a chalkboard and a pointer. Just how many people are in this trust, Richard?"

"Let me think. Eight. Two kids, two nephews, three wives of various standings, and a butler."

"I wonder why Marvin got custody of the kids," I said. "Isn't that a little unusual?"

"Not so much now, but back then, for sure. No idea why. I'm looking into that. I think a judge is involved, but I'll let you know."

"Can you send me whatever you have on file for these people?" I asked of Richard, waving my phone at him. "Include the butler. Is he the only member of staff that is in the trust?"

"Yes," he said. "The rest of the staff are paid well but tend to come and go. Mr. Wong was hired by Lionel Del Vecchio, and according to what I found out, could not be fired by Marvin Del

Vecchio or anyone else, unless there is clear proof he is..." Here Richard paused and read from his computer. "'Unless there is clear proof he is stealing from the estate or household funds.' Needless to say, Wong's monthly household accounting is scrupulous."

"Wow," I said. "In some ways, I feel sorry for Marvin the Magnificent. Talk about controlling things from the grave. He didn't even have the power to fire a member of staff."

"When did you say the old man died?" Frank asked.

"Fifteen years ago," Richard answered. "Pneumonia. I've got more, but those are the highlights."

"A job *well* done, Richard. Well *done*," Lila said.

"Yeah, but from my point of view," I said, "it's all a little daunting." I closed my eyes and rubbed them with my hands.

"*Liana*," Lila said, becoming Mom again. I opened my eyes and looked at her. "*Don't* rub your *eyes* like that. It *causes* wrinkles."

"Anything else going on? Where does the case against Steven Kutner stand now?" Frank asked loud and fast. I don't think he wanted to hear about Lila's beauty dos and don'ts. It worked. Lila became distracted and turned her attention back to him. And I stopped rubbing my eyes.

"*Yesterday*," Lila said, "Richard came across some *emails* from Steven to Donna. They were sent from *North* Lake Tahoe. Apparently, the Del Vecchios have a *rustic* log cabin there."

"Not only do I want to find Steven, now I want to find Donna," I said. "She's become my main suspect in her father's demise. I could almost swear it was her I saw in the wings, but I may be talking myself into that. Before all this happened, my plan was to fly there this afternoon, look around, and take the last flight back. I'm going to still do that."

"You're not supposed to leave the Bay Area, Lee," Frank said. "A condition of your release into my custody."

"I've only got three days to prove my innocence. I have to go," I protested.

"Then I'll go with you," he said mildly. "It's Sunday. All Abby and I are committed to is a party at a friend's who makes the driest grilled chicken on record. Abby won't mind going by herself." He rose. "But first, I'm going home to change into something wilderness appropriate. I'll meet you at the airport in an hour. So, shake a leg. And get two round-trip tickets on the Tahoe Express. Your treat," he added with a smile.

* * *

I settled into the seat on the aisle and looked over at Frank in the window seat. He'd changed into a long-sleeve, black turtleneck shirt and black jeans. Thrown over his lap was a black utility jacket. I looked down at my faded sweats. I was in such a rush to get our tickets and hightail it to the airport, I hadn't even thought about changing anything but my scuffies for sneakers.

The plane was about to take off, and Frank's head was already leaning against the window, eyes closed. It was only an hour and ten-minute flight to Reno, but a snooze was a snooze. And when you're a policeman, you learn to catch your z's whenever you can. From Reno we'd do the forty-five-minute drive to North Lake Tahoe in a rental car. It would be shortly after three when we arrived at the Del Vecchio cabin, last known address for Steven Kutner. Sunset was scheduled for 8:12. Plenty of daylight to do a search of the area.

Before I put my phone in airplane mode, I downloaded the JPGs of Del Vecchio's last two wives, Claudia and Madison; his two kids, Donna and David; the twin brothers, Wyman and Winston; Mr. Wong, the butler; and Donna's husband, Steven. Last, I downloaded the copious notes my brother sent on all eight.

I reviewed the wives' photos first. The second and third of Marvin's wives were real lookers, photographed in glamorous poses. I paused, wishing there was a photo of his first wife, Elizabeth Hofsted, glamorous or not. Even a passport photo would do. And we all know what those look like.

David and Donna were both super attractive. Looks-wise, they took after their mother, Claudia, and not their father. Good luck all around. Unfortunately, Wyman and Winston took after Marvin's side of the family. The twins photographed as disdainful, belligerent, and ill-natured. Facing either one of them down first thing in the morning for a glazed doughnut or a cruller would probably have it curdle in my mouth.

From his picture, Mr. Wong was an elegant Chinese American, a year or two younger than Marvin the Magnificent. He may have spent the majority of his life as a butler, but there was nothing subservient in those eyes. What I saw was self-assuredness and intelligence. I had a feeling I would only get out of him what he wanted to tell me.

I'd saved Steven Kutner for last so I could spend time on him. Before I read Richard's findings, I studied the candid shot of Mr. Black Hat taken at an outdoor event, pine trees in the background. Looking straight at the camera, he was a dark-haired young man with even features, exuding a warm, engaging smile. Con men always exude a warm, engaging smile. That's the devil of them. Steven looked to be no more than nineteen or twenty in the photo.

But according to Richard's report, by that time he'd already led a pretty dissident life. Born in the States as Sergey Kuznetsov to Russian ex-pat parents, his father was a tenured professor of music at UC Berkeley and mother a psychiatrist of some note. They seemed to live quiet, stellar lives. Not so with Steven.

At thirteen years old he'd managed to hack into the school system and change his grades from C's and D's to A's and B's. He was caught, but due to his tender age, put on probation, as long as he promised to never go near a computer again. He promised, but eighteen months later was convicted of breaking into the security system of a chain of pharmacies and having controlled substances sent to an empty house in Oakland. He served six months in a juvenile correction facility. Once released, his parents shuffled him off to Moscow to stay with his maternal grandmother. In the six years he was there, even Richard couldn't discover what he did, but suspects it was something along the lines of perfecting his computer espionage skills.

Shortly after Steven's return to the States from Russia, he was accused of being one of five criminals who hacked into bank accounts and stole millions of dollars. He'd turned state's evidence, the money was returned, his pals went to prison, while Steven got a slap on the wrist and bought a handgun. He even had a license to carry a concealed weapon.

That was when his parents disowned him, and he changed his name from Sergey Kuznetsov to Steven Kutner. He also managed to expunge his true identity and background on the internet. But leave it to Richard. It took him the better part of a week, but eventually, he found it. My brother has his ways.

Richard also sent me Steven's present online bio, most of which was dog doody. The newly created Steven Kutner was born in Ohio and known as a systems analyst from Detroit. Several now-defunct businesses were listed as having hired him to do some pretty impressive things. Except, according to Richard, they hadn't, and he didn't. But somehow Steven managed to snow True Love

Forever and currently worked for them. Three years ago, he married the former Donna Del Vecchio and lived in San Francisco, California.

By the time I'd finished reading up on everyone, we landed at the Reno, Nevada airport.

"You didn't tell me you put your gun in the belly of the plane," Frank said, as we waited for the luggage to be brought in from the twin-engine plane to the waiting room of the small terminal. "We might be here forever."

"Or ten minutes. All *you* have to do, Officer Smarty-Pants, is show your badge and you can carry it on board. I have to do a lot more cartwheels." I became more serious. "Steven Kutner has a license to carry a concealed weapon. Did you know that?"

"On the way home, I phoned my secretary to gather his particulars. I don't know much else about him, but I do know he carries. That's always one of the first things we find out."

He stopped talking and looked toward the double doors that noisily opened from the tarmac. Two men rolled in a luggage trolley containing boxes of fruit and goods, and several pieces of luggage. I saw my red overnight bag and made a grab for it. Frank reached down and picked up the gray duffel bag he'd carried on the plane.

"People like Kutner make me a little nervous," I admitted. "You never know."

"True enough. The man is possibly a murderer. He may also be the reason his wife has disappeared," Frank said. "I'm glad I came along with you."

"Me, too," I said.

I smiled and so did he. We'd reached a truce. Glory hallelujah.

It was a sunny afternoon, not too warm, with nary a cloud in the sky. The drive to North Tahoe was easy and uneventful. Frank took yet another snooze in the passenger seat and I listened to ABBA's *Arrival* album, humming along with "Dancing Queen" and "Money, Money, Money." I tried to enjoy the whole experience and not think about the possible prison sentence for murder hanging over my head. Like they say, "Live for the moment." That isn't my motto, but sometimes I try to pretend it is.

I followed the GPS through a public park that led to a privately owned, winding dirt road that went up into the hills. Pine trees lined both sides. At the end of the road was the — ha-ha — two-story log cabin. It was about as rustic as a Hollywood movie star's home in Pacific Palisades. The sprawling house had a dark, split-log façade that was sanded, primed, and oiled. Bright blue window boxes sat beneath a multitude of picture windows, each box crammed with vibrant red and yellow flowers. In the driveway, a shiny, late-model black Mercedes Benz sat.

I pulled onto the dirt slope on the side of the road about a hundred yards away from the house. I stopped the car and turned off the motor. The lack of movement woke Frank up.

"Are we there?"

"We are. And welcome to your average Tahoe weekend retreat. Ten thousand square feet of rustic luxury," I said. "I think that's Steven's car in the driveway. I can't see the license plates from here, but he has one like that. Wait a minute. That's strange. The front door is wide open."

For several moments, we sat ramrod still in the car, taking in our surroundings. We listened to the high-pitched chirps of the birds, the rustling of branches in the soft breeze, and the oh-so-apparent absence of human life.

"I don't like this, Frank," I finally said.

"I don't, either."

"I'm a city girl, and even I know leaving a door open invites wildlife to wander in, from a skunk to a bear."

Frank pulled his gun from his underarm holster. He opened the car door and looked at me. "Okay, change of plans. I'm going in commando. And I don't mean not wearing any underwear. We don't know what's going on in there. Whether he's in there or not, if anyone's with him or not, or if he or anybody else is armed. We know nothing."

"That just about covers it."

"Stay here," he ordered, then put his leg down on the ground, preparing to exit the car.

"Like that's happening." I opened the driver's door and got out.

"Okay," he countered, looking at me from over the roof of the car. "In that case, stay behind me." He darted to the far side of a tree and out of the house's sight line.

"Sure thing, Frank," I said in a stage whisper, crouching down and sprinting to a pine tree about five feet away. I studied the house, still as the woods surrounding it. "Meanwhile, I think we should go in from the side rather than the front or back." I pulled the nine-millimeter Glock from my pocket and gestured with it toward the house. "These trees end only a few feet from the side door. Good cover."

"Yes," he agreed. "But keep low. All those picture windows could make us easy targets. That gun you're waving around have the safety on?"

"Yes, but thanks for reminding me. I need to load it."

"It's not loaded?" His voice held an incredulity I didn't want to think about.

"I forgot." I reached into my sweats pocket for the magazine and loaded the Glock.

Watching me, Frank said, "And then you wonder why I worry about you."

"I would have remembered before we got there." I didn't add the word *maybe*.

That's the drawback of hardly ever using these things. As the in-house investigator for DI, 99 percent of the time, I sit on my derrière at my desk in a designer suit and heels, sifting through emails, memos, and other correspondence. My job is to find clues about who did what to whom. A lot of truth can be revealed by going through a company's emails and paperwork, if you're good at ferreting things out. I'm a good ferret.

Legwork on most jobs consists of walking daily to a nice restaurant for a lovely, long lunch, and then back to work. So, while I have a black belt in karate and go to the practice range to shoot regularly, most of the time I have no use at all for a weapon and keep my firearms locked away. But being the prime suspect in a murder changed that, as it has in the past when I get up from my desk only to stumble over a dead body or two.

Shaking his head, Frank squatted behind some shrubs. I did the same. Together we scuttled through brush to a tree nearest the property, maybe fifteen feet away. From there on, it was open space.

Resigned, Frank dropped down to his belly on the ground with a grunt. "I'm getting too old for this stuff," he remarked.

Glad I was still wearing my grungy sweatsuit, I dropped down as well. No grunt, but I felt one in the offing. The smell of pine needles and soil assaulted my nose. I'm not an outdoor kinda gal. I fought off a sneeze and crawled on my elbows and belly next to Frank toward the house. The oh-so-glamorous side of detective work.

"No sign of life, Frank," I whispered, as we neared the deck off the side door.

"Doesn't mean anything." He hopped onto the deck and flattened himself against the outside wall. I followed.

With caution, Frank looked inside the picture window with a view of the kitchen area. At the same time, I looked through the glass in the top of the outside door and entrance to the kitchen.

"Clear," he said.

"Nobody," I said.

I reached for the doorknob, turned it, and pushed. It opened on silent hinges. We entered the green and white kitchen noiselessly. The only sound to be heard was a ticking clock. I followed the sound and focused on the clock over a doorway leading to another room.

It was one of those Felix clocks, i.e., a black and white tuxedo cat, popular in the late thirties and early forties. Eyes and hanging tail moved in unison from side to side with each tick. It seemed like such a frivolous and lighthearted addition to a house, it caused me to consider the actual people who lived there. Thinking of suspects as people can be very unsettling.

Frank tapped me on the shoulder, and gestured he was going to check out a closed door off the kitchen. I followed as his backup. It was a laundry room. A basket filled with rumpled clothes sat on top of the washing machine.

Then we checked out the entranceway and open door. Leaves and small branches littered the plank flooring, indicating the door had probably been left open for a while.

"Don't close that door, Lee," Frank whispered in my ear.

"Wouldn't dream of it," I whispered back. But I made a note to keep my eye out for any meandering critters, small and large.

As silently as possible, we went through the living room, dining room, family room, and closets. Nada. A quick view of a small cellar basement revealed nothing but mud walls, a sump pump, and spiders. Yuck.

We crept up the stairs to the second floor. Not saying a word, we went through each of the five bedrooms, bathrooms, and closets. While one bedroom and bathroom had signs of an occupant, there was no one to be found.

More relaxed, we came back down the stairs. We sheathed our guns, and I moved to the floor-to-ceiling glass-enclosed living room, with an incredible view of the mountains beyond the outdoor patio and pool.

I opened the door to the pool area and stepped out on the patio, looking around. Frank came up behind me and whispered in my ear, "Maybe he's out hiking somewhere."

"I don't think so," I said, my voice revealing the shock I felt. I pointed to the deep end of the pool. Hidden from inside the house, a man dressed in black, floated facedown, arms extended up and outward.

"Good God," Frank said.

Almost as one, we ran to the edge of the rectangular pool and dropped to our knees on the rim. Frank reached into the water for one arm, me for the other. Together we pulled the limp body toward us and hauled the man out of the water. Turning him over, I saw it was Steven Kutner. No longer wearing an engaging smile, he stared back at me with unseeing eyes.

Chapter Five

"The ME says he's been dead for at least eight hours, probably more, so you're free to go. Just be sure to sign your statement on the way out."

Police Chief Dabuda Lel Ti looked at me and didn't exactly smile, but seemed more relaxed than our initial interview. Not much older than me, she was on the young side for being the North Tahoe chief of police. Her high cheekbones, coppery complexion, and straight jet-black hair, pulled back in a tight ponytail at the nape of her neck, told of her Native American heritage as much as the one turquoise necklace half hidden by the collar of her shirt. Understated but proud.

I was sitting on one of the lounge chairs near the pool, wrapped in a beach towel found nearby. Four hours had passed since we reported the death to the local authorities. The night had turned chilly, and I was cold. Or maybe a little shaken at finding Steven's body. The only good news was my text from Gurn. He was taking the red-eye and would be home in the morning. I hadn't updated him on the man floating in the pool yet. Time enough for that.

Frank strolled over and gestured to the woman in charge. "Chief Lel Ti here probably told you we're free to go."

"That's right," Chief Lel Ti said. "We checked with Tahoe Express. You were on it. You don't need to come down to the station, Chief Thompson. As I said to Ms. Alvarez, you can sign your statement with the sergeant before you leave."

"May I ask how the man died, Chief Lel Ti?" I asked.

"Can't say for sure," she replied with a cautious edge. "He could have slipped, hit his head on the side of the pool, and drowned. But there are several scrapes and bruises on his hands and a suspicious contusion on the side of his head. We won't know for certain until the autopsy."

"So, it's looking suspicious," Frank said.

The North Tahoe police chief turned to Frank. There seemed to be a mutual respect between the two. With the exception of the woman being in her thirties and the man in his fifties, they appeared to look at one another as total equals. Chief Lel Ti thought for a moment and seemed to come to a decision.

"Highly suspicious. Take his wallet. We found it in the bushes over there. While the credit cards were still in it, there was no cash. Not even a dollar."

"So, you're thinking that whoever killed him," Frank asked, "the motive might have been robbery?"

"It's too early to think anything, Chief Thompson. But whatever we do find, we are more than willing to share with the San Francisco and Palo Alto Police Departments. Can we count on the same? You never know what's going to cross-connect."

"Cooperation is key in these cases. All around." Frank reached out a hand to shake. "Thank you, Chief Lel Ti."

The chief took Frank's hand and shook it. "You're welcome. Call me Dabuda or Da. Whichever."

"I'm Frank, Dabuda," Frank said with a smile. "Good luck, but I'm sure you'll get to the bottom of this. I'll be in touch."

With a nod to me, the younger chief of police strode away, back to the business of dealing with death. Frank looked down at me still sitting on the lounge chair.

"Let's go find that sergeant, sign the statements, and get out of here. You okay?" he asked, searching my face.

"I'm all right," I said, removing the towel from around my shoulders and throwing it down beside me.

"Because, let's face it," he said as if I hadn't spoken, "when it comes to things like this, you're about as hard-boiled as a two-minute egg."

"I'm just envisioning someone having to tell his parents or even Donna, should they be able to locate her."

"Well, not our worry. We missed the last flight home. Right now, we've got to find a place to stay."

"And some food. I'm starving." I stood and stretched. "So, you didn't know this Chief Dabuda Lel Ti before now? I thought you knew everybody."

"Only by reputation. It was an internal promotion, nine years coming. She's had an exemplary career. It's good they recognized that. Her people, the Washoe, have been in the region for over four thousand years. She knows and respects this land."

Frank is a big believer in giving minorities and women a leg up. As a youth in East Palo Alto, he was given a chance after high school to go to Stanford University. He had the grades and ambition, but not the money. Then a scholarship came through for him as it did for my father, with a similar story. That's how they met. Both young minorities—Frank an African American and Dad a documented Mexican immigrant—proved they could make something of themselves if only given the chance.

Frank continued on about the new North Tahoe chief of police. "You'd never know this is the first homicide investigation where Lel Ti's in charge."

"She seems to know what she's doing. Does she know about me? I hope my being here doesn't get you into any trouble."

"She does and it doesn't. You're still in my recognizance. If you'd come up here by yourself and discovered the body, it would have been another story. Let's sign those statements and go. We can catch the seven a.m. tomorrow morning. I don't think we should attempt to drive home tonight. There's supposed to be an all-night diner nearby that's pretty good. And a motel, too, if I remember right."

"I thought you were asleep on the drive," I said.

"Not all the time," he said with a laugh.

Silence fell as we walked back to the car, both thinking our own thoughts. The wind had picked up, and the temperature was probably down in the low fifties. I was glad I carried a warm jacket in my overnight bag, as well as a change of clothes, and toiletries. "Be prepared" is my motto. I stole that from the Boy Scouts.

"I'll drive," he said, extending his hand for the keys.

"Sure." I reached inside my pocket and tossed them to him.

"Don't let this get you down, Lee," Frank said, as we opened the car doors on either side. The interior lights came on, and I saw the anxiousness on his face. "Your only lead petering out like this. There'll be something else. We have till Wednesday."

"I'm only a little down," I said, as I slid into the passenger seat. "I found this." I extended my hand, palm up, and showed him a silver flash drive.

Anxiety turned to surprise. "Where did you find that?"

"On the body. When we turned him over. Richard said he probably carried the backup files on him. He did."

"You took evidence from a crime scene?" His voice had that loud, accusatory tone that just makes me crazy.

"Frank, calm down. I was going to try to take it from him when he was alive. That was always the plan."

"Not my plan. I ought to march you right back and turn you in for tampering with evidence."

"Whoever killed him left the flash drive in his pants pocket. So, that's not what they were after, Frank. He died for some other reason."

He thought for a moment. I watched his inner turmoil. "Well, I guess you're not such a two-minute egg, after all."

"More like a three."

"That flash drive was in chlorinated water for eight hours. You think it's still good?"

I turned the drive around in my hand, inspecting it, as I had done five or six times when no one was looking. "It looks airtight to me, but even if water did get in, Richard says it can't hurt the data. All that might be necessary is for us to wait for it to dry out. But I wouldn't try anything myself. It could be encrypted to self-destruct, and we've already been through that song and dance. Richard says not to worry. Now that he knows, he'll deal with it. I've got faith."

"You've already talked to him?"

"You sound surprised."

"I am surprised. When did you manage that?"

"When I went to the bathroom, I gave him a quick call."

"You've gotten pretty sneaky in your old age. You're lucky you're my goddaughter or I'd arrest you myself."

I didn't say anything. He changed the subject.

"I called Fenner. Told him what's going on. Told him this death might be connected to Del

Vecchio's. He's going to talk to the widow, tell her the bad news, and see if she knows anything."

"Jeesh, a beheaded husband, a missing stepdaughter, and a dead son-in-law. I wouldn't want to be in Madison's shoes."

"She could be behind it all. The majority of times it's the spouse."

"Spoken like a true policeman."

"She's become a rich woman, and she has the potential to become even richer, if the heirs start dropping like you say they might."

"Her doing in her husband I can almost understand because he was such a hammerhead, but would she hurt his daughter? She seemed close to Donna."

"Could be an act."

"Now, that's depressing."

Frank aimed the car for the bottom of the hill before turning to me. "I think that diner is about fifteen minutes away. Why don't you give me a few more details about being Marvin Del Vecchio's assistant?"

"Okay. I'd been hanging around the theater for the last several days ever since Richard made the connection that Steven was Marvin's son-in-law. The Palo Alto Playhouse was doing a few numbers from *Pal Joey* for the benefit with Mom singing two songs, "Zip" and "Bewitched, Bothered, and Bewildered." I became lost in pride. "Have you seen Mom play the role of Vera Simpson? She's terrific. And her voice is terrific, too. When she sings—"

"Leave the reviews to the *Chronicle*," Frank interrupted. "Just tell me about your assistant's job."

"Sidetracked again. Sorry. We were hoping I could pick some clues up as to where Steven was. That was three days ago. Donna was at the morning's rehearsal but failed to show up for the afternoon's. It was supposed to be the first lighting run-through for all the acts. But she didn't answer her phone, and no one had seen her."

"What was everybody's reaction to her not being there?"

"Zack, the stage manager, was frantic. Marvin was livid, not worried, but angry. Madison kept making excuses for his missing daughter. She said things like Donna probably had car trouble or forgot. I think Madison knows more than she was saying. Donna had been Marvin's assistant for over two years after the last one quit. She got paid fifteen hundred dollars a week, when they worked. Why would she suddenly forget?"

"I must admit, it was odd Madison thought she might have."

"The next morning Donna didn't show up for rehearsal again. And hadn't been home the entire night. Everybody had the same reaction as the day before only more so, except for Madison, who kept saying Donna would show up soon. They waited a half hour, and then Marvin became a raving maniac, reaming out the stage manager as if it was his fault. I stepped in and told Marvin I was a quick study, blah blah, woof woof, and would do it for free. I think the free is what sealed the deal."

"I'm surprised you did that."

"Frank, I had to. I needed to be on scene to find out what happened to Donna and if she was with Steven. I knew from the beginning it wasn't going to be pleasant. But I went undercover, anyway."

"You're in a lot of trouble, Lee, you know that?"

"I do know that." My anger bubbled up again, overtaking me. "But I had no reason to kill him. What's my motive? I don't have one." As soon as the flash of anger flared up, it went away in a poof. Deflated, I leaned against the passenger door. "I'm sorry, Frank. I didn't mean to sound off like that. I'm a little stressed."

"Really?" he said with humor. "Imagine that."

I looked over at him. He took his eyes off the road for a split second and smiled at me. I let out a chuckle that came across as more of a grunt. But the tension I felt dropped several notches.

"The way I see it, at the very least I could be charged with negligent homicide."

"We'll make sure it doesn't come to that," Frank said. "Tell me about the guillotine trick. Fenner's looking into the collapsed tunnel. We'll know more about that, probably tomorrow."

"He might find the collapse was a deliberate act."

"I hope he does. It will work in your favor. You could have been killed. So, you think the person in the wings was Donna come out of hiding?"

"She's the most likely candidate. I was hoping we'd find her here with Steven. But not dead, of course."

"A lot of things haven't panned out the way you've hoped."

"I've been a prize schnook. Somebody set me up but good. Among other things, when we get back to the Bay Area I need to have a conversation with whoever checked out the guillotine. It can't have been regular forensics, can it?"

"No, they contacted the magic specialist that built the thing."

"Ah! Henry Swan."

"I think that was the name. How did you know?"

"His name has been bandied about as the man who makes magic tricks happen. The magician comes up with an idea, and Henry Swan creates it. Some kind of genius. But listen to this, Marvin called him the day before he died."

"Did he? Know what about?"

"I overheard Marvin say he wasn't going to pay him more than the trick was worth, and he wanted a partial refund. It got a little nasty, at least on Marvin's end. Then Marvin hung up and was in a sour mood. He told me to clean out the trunk he used in rehearsal for his disappearing act. Apparently, he'd spilled coffee in it when he was trying to get out the side. Then he sent me for more coffee, maybe so he could spill more in the trunk at the next rehearsal."

"Nice guy. But back to the guillotine."

I sat up and shook off my depression. "Marvin never showed me how the trick itself worked, just my part in it. I wasn't allowed to touch anything on the guillotine or be near it, either, unless we were performing."

"You're saying he was the only one who touched the safety lever?"

"Yes. First it's set on 'danger,' written in red letters. Then a head of cabbage is cut in half and drops into the basket at the base of the guillotine in front of the audience to show the blade is real. Then he would reset the lever to 'safe,' which is written in green letters, and indicates the blade stops at a higher, safe point. The audience can't see any of this, of course. You have to be less than a foot away."

"This 'danger' to 'safe' lever, how does that work, mechanically?"

"No idea. A closely guarded secret. But meanwhile as a distraction, the assistant's job — that would be me — was to prance around the stage like a circus pony, ostrich plume and all. You know, the one thing I did learn is, magic and illusion are mostly a case of misdirection."

"Give me the step-by-step of your part in the trick last night."

I closed my eyes so I could remember everything exactly. "My every move was choreographed and timed precisely. Tighter than any dance routine I've ever done. After he put the lever to 'safe,' he gave me a signal to move directly to the left of the guillotine where I stood and struck another pose. I looked over at the lever to double-check it still read 'safe.' It did. He, meanwhile, lay down on his back on the platform, looking up, his neck ready to be locked in the pillory, directly under the raised blade of the guillotine."

"What's a pillory?"

"It's a wooden board cut in two pieces. Some call it a stock. The top and bottom halves have a half circle cut out of the wood, making a full circle when put together. That's the hole for the neck to rest in."

"Go on."

"He adjusted his neck in the bottom half of the pillory and waved to the audience. Then I strutted to the top of the platform, picked up the top half of the pillory, showed it to the audience, and set it down over his neck and locked it in place. This kept him from being able to move his head. The orchestra did a drumroll ending with a crash of cymbals, and I released the rope to drop the blade, all the time posing and smiling at the audience."

"Once you made sure the lever read 'safe.'"

I shook my head. "No, Frank. I did that *before* when I was to the left of the guillotine. That happens when I stand near his waist as he lies on the platform. As I said, it's all very precise. That particular spot gives me a clear view of the lever. I looked at the lever to make sure it read safe — once again, written in green letters — because he couldn't see it from where he was. After I made sure it read safe, I moved up to his head at the end of the platform, lowered the top half of the pillory over his neck, and locked it into place. We must have rehearsed that part fifty times."

"So how did the lever move from safe to danger without a human hand touching it?"

"I don't know. It's all so frustrating. It changed, Frank, but I don't know how. I'm telling you it read safe before I crossed to the back of the platform, or I would have stopped the act then and there."

Pausing, I closed my eyes, seeing everything I'd done less than twenty-four hours before. I took a deep breath.

"Frank, I'm not bragging; I'm just giving you the facts. I'm a trained professional. I go through hundreds of documents looking for a word or a phrase that's going to make a difference to my clients. I'm good at what I do. There was no way that lever didn't read 'safe.' I'd bet my life on it. Actually, I am betting my life on it."

Frank thought for a minute. "That's that, then. It had to have been done another way."

Chapter Six

Praise be, the mom-and-pop all-night diner had a bar and was right next door to the motel. After I ordered a hamburger from Mom, I taught Pop, the bartender, how to make a classic martini. Come to think of it, the extent of his job was taking the tops off beer bottles and dispensing rye whiskey in shot glasses. He thought a martini was made by pouring Martini and Rossi's dry vermouth into a martini glass and calling it a day. Holy Chamole.

Now the teacher, I mixed a half ounce of dry vermouth with an ounce and a half of gin in a shaker, threw in some ice, shook the concoction within an inch of its life, poured it into a martini glass, added a green olive, and Bob's your uncle. I don't know exactly what Bob has to do with any of this, and he's certainly not my uncle, but I heard Double-O Seven say that in a movie once and it stuck with me.

After dinner Frank and I went to our respective rooms, clean but very basic. I took a hot shower, put on pajamas from my overnight case—clean but very basic—and read my messages. Gurn texted me he was soon boarding the red-eye in DC and would land around 8:00 a.m. in the morning. I texted him back some loving chitchat, but nothing about finding Steven Kutner's body. I did text we were taking the 7:00 a.m. express back to the Bay Area. We'd meet at SFO and Uber home together. Just the thought of being with him cheered me up enormously. The martini didn't hurt, either.

I made a quick call to say good night to Mom. She can be a helicopter mom when least expected. Tío got on the line, because he's always a *helicóptero* uncle, especially when people seem to be dying close at hand. Quick reassurances on both ends of the line, me about my health, Tío about the cats, and we hung up. I fell asleep before my head hit the pillow.

Chapter Seven
Monday

At 4:15 a.m., I woke up thinking about Madison Del Vecchio. The more I reflected on it, the more I wondered just what she was doing backstage nearly every minute of the last three days. I would have to look into that.

But first I needed to do a barre. Barres are used extensively in ballet training and warm-up exercises. I love my ballet barre. Not only does it keep me in shape, but it centers me. I try to follow up with a few quick karate exercises, just to keep those muscles limber, but the ballet barre is something I do every day for forty-five minutes, no matter what's going on or where I am. I find something nearby that can be used as the handrail. That day it was the top of a wingback chair. Not ideal, but doable.

I changed into my leotard and tights, tied my hair up in a bun on top of my head, pulled on my ballet slippers, put in my EarPods, and began my barre, listening to several piano pieces composed expressly for this purpose. I was no longer Lee Alvarez, private detective. In that moment, I was Anna Pavlova, arguably the greatest ballerina of them all.

Every ballet dancer in the world has Catherine de' Medici to thank for this formalized dance with its origins in the Italian Renaissance courts of the fifteenth and sixteenth centuries. Under her influence, Catherine de' Medici took the dance form from Italy to France and helped develop it even further. She was hugely responsible for presenting the first court ballet integrating poetry, dance, music, and set design to convey a unified dramatic storyline, the same as is used today. Go, Catherine!

After a quick shower, I dressed in the no-frills, teal-colored pantsuit I keep packed in my overnight case. It's made of a space-age material that doesn't wrinkle, stain, breathe, or wear out. I will probably leave it to the Smithsonian in my will. Under the double-breasted jacket, I wore a silk aqua turtleneck knit sweater. Large, filigree silver hoop earrings from Tasco, Mexico, were my only jewelry. A swipe or two of mascara, a dab of lipstick and I was done. Black socks and sneakers more or less completed the ensemble, although not really. But if people are looking down at my feet, they deserve what they get.

Once ready to face the world, I met Frank in the restaurant at five thirty for a quick breakfast and sludge masquerading as coffee. You can always tell the quality of an eatery by their paper napkins and coffee. The napkins were thin enough to read a newspaper through, yet abrasive. The coffee was thick, yet tasteless. I should have known that any place that has no idea how to make a decent martini could never make a decent cup of coffee. And thus, I groused my way through breakfast.

The only good news was our firearms were returned to us just as we were about to leave the motel. Chief Lel Ti must have had her team working through the night to get them cleared. Good lady.

"And what's on your list of things to do when we get back to the Bay Area?" Frank asked after several silent minutes in the car heading back to Reno's airport. I was making notes, reading, and sending texts on my phone while Frank drove at a fair speed.

I read from my notes. "The first thing I'm going to do is talk to Henry Swan. I've already asked Richard to look further into the background of Mr. Wong."

"You're thinking the butler did it?"

"Two and a half million dollars is a lot of inducement."

"My vote is for Madison Del Vecchio. It's usually the spouse," Frank said again, his tone sage and knowing.

"I agree, and she has been behaving suspiciously. I've only seen her with Donna for a few days before the kid disappeared. During that time, they chatted and giggled together like schoolgirls. And she certainly is closer in age to Donna than she was to Marvin. Not to sound judgmental—but I will—if Madison doesn't qualify as a trophy wife, I don't know who does."

"Makes sense. She's beautiful, expensive-looking, and twenty-five years younger than her husband."

"But here's the odd thing. After Donna's disappearance, Madison hovered around Marvin continually, seeing to his every need. Just like a doting wife. But trophy wives usually don't dote, they get doted upon. According to what I downloaded from Richard, at thirty-three, she's looking at three older husbands in her rearview mirror. The first died of old age and left her fairly well-off. The second, she divorced, but he's still paying for her house in Tiburon."

"And we know what happened to the third."

"Let's not go there, Frank. Let's just say, trophy wives require a lot of maintenance. Maybe for her, no amount of money was enough."

"So, you're thinking she might have been waiting for her time to kill him, especially with Donna out of the way?"

"Possibly. Something feels off about that whole setup. I need to talk to her."

"She may not want to talk to you. You're the one facing charges of decapitating her husband."

"True. I'll get Gurn to do it. Women like to talk to him. I'm also thinking of driving over to Milpitas. I understand David Del Vecchio is doing his magic act at one of the clubs there, Bo's Ale House."

"He didn't cancel when his father died?"

"David is performing for the next two weeks at the place. Richard says he and his family haven't talked for several years. Not even he and his sister."

"That's interesting. And where was he at the time of his father's death?"

"Backstage at the ale house in Milpitas, waiting to go on."

"Hmmm," Frank said as he ruminated. "I need to do a catch-up call with Fenner, find out about new developments, if any."

"I hope your helping me doesn't put you in a bad position."

"No. Whatever I can ask him, I'll ask him. Whatever he can tell me, he'll tell me. We both know the lines. This is his case. I'm just a bystander."

"A pretty powerful bystander," I remarked.

"He knows I'm trying to help you, and between us chickens, he doesn't think you did it. But first and foremost, he'll do his job. If the evidence leads to you, you're going down, make no mistake."

Frank sounded so matter of fact, my mouth went dry. I took a slug of my bottled water. It hurt when I swallowed. Frank went on, almost cheerfully. Sometimes he makes me crazy.

"Now, where are we meeting Gurn? SFO?"

"Yes, he flies in twenty minutes ahead of us. He said he'd meet us at the terminal."

"The way I see it, you've got a full day of talking to all these suspects. If I can fit it into my schedule, I can take his second wife, Claudia Gracioso. Of course, I'll have to run it by Fenner first. He may have already spoken with her. But I wouldn't mind meeting a Miss Italy."

"Claudia Gracioso Del Vecchio was Miss Italy twenty-seven years ago."

"Just my speed," Frank said with a laugh.

"Why, Frank," I chided. "Now, what would Abby say?"

"My wife knows it would be strictly business," he said with a wink. "Actually, I'm only kidding. I won't have time. I have a mountain of paperwork waiting for me on my desk. I'd put her on the number two list, anyway. Fenner says she's been in Marin looking after her parents for the past two weeks."

"Then why did you bring it up?"

"I just like to yank your chain. You can be so gullible."

Yup. He makes me crazy.

Chapter Eight

Gurn strode toward us as we exited the deplaning gate. Tall and muscular, with his lopsided grin and sun-streaked hair, the sight of him made my heart do a flip-flop. We may no longer be thought of as newlyweds, but I will always feel like his bride.

He set down his carry-on bag and enveloped me in his arms. I hugged him back, closed my eyes, and rested my head on his shoulder. We stood there for nearly a minute, frozen in time. Then we kissed lightly.

"You know, you two should get a room," Frank said.

Gurn and I pulled away and burst out laughing.

"Sorry, Frank," Gurn said, reaching out a hand to shake.

Frank took Gurn's hand, shook it, and laughed as well. "Listen, Gurn, wish we could have a cup of coffee and bring each other up to speed, but I've got a car waiting to take me to the precinct. Duty calls." He looked at me. "I promise to keep you posted on any developments either from Tahoe or San Francisco."

"Thanks, Frank," I said, giving him a quick hug. "For everything you did," I added.

"Try to stay out of trouble, Lee," he said, looking at me. He turned to Gurn. "Don't let her drag you too far down the rabbit hole, sport."

"I'm more likely to jump in headfirst," Gurn said with a grin.

"Two of a kind." Frank shook his head, smiled, and marched off.

Arm in arm, Gurn and I walked toward the baggage claim office, and I got my overnight bag complete with gun. Then we headed for the Uber waiting area and stood in line for a ride. Meanwhile, he updated me on DC, and I updated him on Tahoe and finding Steven's body. After assuring him I was all right—Gawd, everybody thinks I'm such a wuss—he moved on.

"So, everybody is waiting for us back at the old homestead?" he asked.

Each member of the family has a different name for the large, two-story white house which is the family home. Richard calls it The Big House. I used to call it The Mausoleum. Mom called it lonely after Dad died. But that was before Tío moved in several years ago, taking over the first floor, kitchen and all. Mom moved to the second floor with its spa and library. Good friends, they come together for meals and chitchats.

To the outside world, the house is noted for the two-story-tall marble columns that stand on either side of the entranceway. Dad brought the columns back from Mexico as a gift to Mom for their fifteenth wedding anniversary. As a teenager, I'd never seen anything like them in my life. Still haven't. The house is an homage to the Mexican American success story, Palo Alto style.

"Honey?" he asked, interrupting my thoughts. "Want to tell me where we're going?"

"Oh, sorry," I said. "Yes, home. And the entire family will be waiting for us. Darling, I've been thinking. We should scoot around to the back, jump in our respective cars, and head out right away."

"What are you talking about, Lee? I'm sure they've got some new things to tell us, especially Rich. And maybe Tío has a snack or two laid out," he added.

"Didn't you have breakfast on the plane?"

"Yes, but that was hours ago. I've been on East Coast time, remember?"

On the ride back to Palo Alto, I made two calls. One to Mr. Wong Chen, Wong being his last name. In the Chinese culture, when addressing someone, the family name comes first, and the given name last. Unless invited, I would never use a person's first name, as that denotes either intimacy or familiarity. I learned this as a teenager playing Mahjong in the park once a week with Mrs. Zhang Li-Mei, who at 103 was as sharp as a tack and then some. Mrs. Zhang taught me more than Mahjong — of which, incidentally, I never won a single game — and gave me an appreciation of one of the oldest cultures in the world.

The Del Vecchio phone rang ten times, and I was about to give up when a strong but smooth male voice answered, saying, "The Del Vecchio residence. Mr. Wong speaking." His voice was clear of any accent and sounded as if he were a television announcer.

"Mr. Wong, this is Lee Alvarez. I believe you know who I am. I am calling you regarding the recent demise of your employer, Marvin Del Vecchio."

"Yes?"

"I was wondering if it was possible for me to drop by for a little chat with you." The silence on the other end of the line dragged on for so long, I finally said, "Hello? Are you there, Mr. Wong?"

"Yes, I am, Miss Alvarez. I'm afraid that would not be possible."

"I don't understand. Why not? Aren't you interested in helping to solve the murder of Mr. Del Vecchio?"

"I have been instructed by the lady of the house not to speak to anyone about this... uh... tragedy."

"Well, the lady of the house can instruct something like that, but that might not be in the cards. And it also might not be in your own best interests. Have the police spoken with you yet?"

"I gave them a full statement Sunday evening. And I have nothing to say to you or anyone else. Goodbye, miss."

"But wait a minute," I began but was speaking to dead air. I thought for a moment and hit redial.

"The Del Vecchio—"

"Mr. Wong, don't hang up. Because you are as much a suspect in his murder as I am." My interruption was fast, rude, but succinct. "And just because the police aren't saying as much doesn't mean you aren't. Two and a half million dollars can be a lot of incentive to commit murder. Or possibly, enticed into being a coconspirator. I may have been there when the axe fell, but I had no reason to wish the man dead." I paused, then added, "Unlike you."

"In that case, I should probably retain the services of an attorney before I speak to anyone."

"You could do that. Or you could just talk to me. If you didn't have anything to do with his death, it might be to your benefit to work with me. I don't know if you're aware of this, but I am a private investigator—"

"So, the police have said," he interjected. "But I am not obliged by law to speak with you or to help you in any way." He went quiet.

"But why not? What have you got to lose? Or hide?"

"You are persuasive, Miss Alvarez. Let me think about it."

"I don't have a lot of time, Mr. Wong."

"It has been said, 'It does not matter how slowly you go as long as you do not stop.'"

"Meaning, what?"

Mr. Wong ignored my question but said, "I will arrive at a decision, Miss Alvarez, and when I do, I will let you know."

He hung up again. This time I didn't hit redial.

"'It does not matter how slowly you go as long as you do not stop,'" I repeated.

"What?" Gurn stared at me.

"Something Mr. Wong said to me. Just now."

"I thought Confucius said that."

"Did he? Good for him. I think Mr. Wong was telling me something by quoting him." I shook the reverie from my brain. "In any event, he won't meet with me right now. He wants to think about it."

"That means there's something to think about," Gurn mused.

"Apparently so. Meanwhile, are you going to call Madison Del Vecchio, use your most sultry voice, and make an appointment to meet with her? Hopefully, sometime today?"

"I called already when you were talking to the butler. She wasn't there and I left a voice mail message. I tried to use my most sultry voice, but as I have no idea what that is, I can only say I did my best."

"Your best usually does the trick, darling."

"Thank you, sweetheart."

I picked myself up out of the doldrums and dialed the number Richard gave me for Henry Swan. He was reluctant to meet at first, me having chopped off his client's head and all. Fortunately, sometimes people give me my way just to get me off the phone. It didn't work with Wong, but it did with Henry Swan. He said I could drop by his studio any time that day. Swan's studio was in South San Francisco, maybe twenty-five minutes north of Palo Alto on a good day, an hour on a bad. All depending on traffic.

Fifteen minutes later, we arrived home. Instead of going to our own garage apartment, we headed for the family house. The door swung open before I even completed knocking. Mom and Tío were standing there, each studying my face. Then they turned and smiled at Gurn.

After greetings and hugs with Mom and Tío, I looked around. "Richard and the ladies not here yet?" That's how I refer to Vicki and little Steffi.

"They're on their *way*, Liana," Mom said.

Tío shook his head. "I do not like all these bodies you are finding, sobrina," He looked Gurn in the eyes. "It makes for her the *angustiosa*," he added.

Gurn looked at Tío and then at me, having no idea what *angustiosa* meant. When Tío's upset, he tends to rattle things off in Spanish. Fortunately, I was raised in a bilingual household. Otherwise, I would have to struggle to understand what he was saying at times like these.

"It is distressing, Tío," I said, translating the word, "but Frank and I found Steven long after he was dead. It wasn't like what happened the night before." I gulped before I could go on, "With, you know, the… head… incident."

"You see? The distress!" Tío said, looking at the three of us. "*Basta!* We speak no more of this. Ricardo, Victoria, and Estefanía will be here any minute."

"Yes, it is *enough*, Mateo," Mom agreed. She kissed me lightly on the cheek and fussed with my hair, trying to push it off my face. "You should take a *brush* to your *hair*, dear, and you look *tired*."

"I did brush my hair. Do I look tired? I don't feel tired. I feel pretty good," I said, shaking my head after she was done pushing my hair around. I felt the curls rearrange themselves back to where they wanted to be, which is where they'd been. Mom sighed. People with straight hair don't get it.

"What you need is *alimento*," Tío said.

"Ah!" Gurn exclaimed, glad he knew the word. "Food!"

Tío pushed me toward the kitchen. "I cook for all of us quesadillas with the queso Chihuahua I make myself."

"Wow!" My turn to exclaim. "Thanks, Tío. I didn't know the cheese was ready." Most of his cheeses take months to mature, if not years.

I started toward the kitchen, followed by Gurn. We heard the front door open, and my brother walked in carrying little Steffi in one arm and his laptop under the other, of course. I think he sleeps with that laptop next to him every night. He was followed by Vicki, pushing their daughter's stroller.

"Hey, you three," I said, delighted to see them. "You're just in time for Tío's quesadillas with his homemade queso Chihuahua. And I've got Steven's memory stick for you," I said directly to my brother.

"Great to both," Richard said. "I'll take it to the lab right after we eat. I'm starving." He looked at Gurn and gave him a smart salute. "Welcome back, Lieutenant Commander." They both laughed and shook hands. When Richard was a student at UC Berkeley, Gurn was his NROTC instructor. They became friends, and that was how I met the former Navy SEAL and love of my life.

"Hi, Gurn," Vicki said with a huge smile, blowing him a quick kiss. "Steffi had her cereal and banana, but I'll never pass up one of Tío's quesadillas." She took Steffi from her husband's arms and rushed over to me.

No bigger than a minute with coppery-red hair, green eyes, and a complexion to die for, she stood on tiptoe, stretching up. I bent down for one of her award-winning hugs. Almost immediately, little Steffi giggled, grabbed me around the neck with both pudgy arms, and slobbered all over my face. Wet, but I loved it.

"Are you okay, Lee?" Vicki asked, handing me a baby wipe for my face. "Rich told me everything that happened to you. I couldn't believe it. I think you should leave detecting and come into business with me and design hats. I'll teach you everything I know," she added, singing at me.

Vicki is the owner and manager of The Obsessive Chapeau, a wildly successful hat shop that features her one-of-a-kind designs. As Vicki likes to say, this is specifically for the woman who expresses her heart through her hat and has no problem writing out a check in the three- or four-figure range. To my mind that's a lot of expressing, but Vicki can't keep up with the orders.

Atop her head, Vicki was wearing one of her creations, a powder-pink bowler hat with rhinestone numbers from one to a hundred randomly sewn hither and thither. This glittering chapeau was tied under the chin with a pink tulle bow jauntily tied to the side. I understand it comes in blue, too. Yikes.

The most recent lid she gave me was for Christmas. It's a felt cloche laden with seashells, seed pearls, and dozens of small, multicolored butterflies. Each butterfly rests on its own spring, so they flutter in different directions whenever you move. I've seen Beyonce shows with less action. The first time I put it on, the cats hid in the closet.

But that said, Vicki is the most wonderful thing that's happened to our family outside of Gurn. She is smart, loving, funny, sweet-natured, and, in short, perfect. So, I will wear that hat until a lepidopterist throws a net over my head.

We gathered around the family kitchen table, enjoying Tío's quesadillas and his fresh-brewed Guatemalan coffee. The large thirties'-style kitchen with its open-floor plan, roomy countertops, butter-yellow walls, and white state-of-the-art appliances serves as a backdrop for Tío's masterpieces, this morning being his quesadillas. Aside from the homemade cheese, each quesadilla was filled with sautéed mushrooms, olives, tomatoes, and onions, all lovingly prepared by Tío. Delish, delish.

"SowhatI'vegot—" Richard mumbled, having shoved the last of his third quesadilla in his mouth.

"Don't *talk* with your *mouth* full, Richard," Mom reproached him.

He chewed for a moment and swallowed. "Sorry, Mom. I wasn't thinking."

"I know the feeling," I muttered.

"So, what I've got," Richard said, after wiping his mouth and chin, "is basically an apology to you, Lee."

"Pardon?" I asked. *An apology? To me? Who was this man and what had he done with my brother?*

"If only I'd checked further," he said, contrition written all over his face, "I would have caught the fact that Steven Kutner had a cabin under his own name in North Tahoe. You and Frank might have been able to go there, but I didn't find it until early this morning."

"You were *already* on the plane, Liana, when Richard *came* upon it," Mom said.

"I didn't 'come upon it,'" Richard corrected. "I was double-checking—"

"Never mind, Richard," I interrupted. "It's all good."

Mom cleared her throat. "In *any* event, I sent *Carlson* to North Tahoe to investigate *further*. He decided to *drive* and left about *two* hours ago. He should *be* there in another *hour* or so." Before I could reply, she rushed on. "I *know* how you *feel* about another investigator *interfering* with your inquiries, but with the *time* crunch, it seemed to *me*—"

"It was a good decision," I interrupted in agreement. "With only two more days to clear me, we need as many people helping out as possible. Just ask Carl to keep me in the loop, okay?" I turned to Richard. "Here's the flash drive, and good luck with it."

My brother took it from my hand and, without looking at it, shoved it in his pocket. He wiped his mouth again and stood. "Okay, I'm walking to the office to see what we've got with this."

"Are you sure you don't want me to drive you?" Vicki asked, rising. "I've got to bring Steffi to daycare, anyway, and then get to work."

"Thanks, sweetheart, but no. It's not more than half a mile, and I could use the exercise." He thought for a moment and then said to no one in particular, "If Steven was anything like me, he made sure the stick was waterproof, but I'll know in about an hour." He turned to our uncle. "Thanks for brunch, Tío."

More manners! Surprise, surprise, surprise! Thanks to Vicki, Richard had finally been civilized. Then he burped, long and loud. Well, almost civilized.

Chapter Nine

Mom, Gurn, and I "took" a meeting in the family room while Tío cleaned up the kitchen. When it comes to his kitchen, Tío is fussy and rarely accepts any help. He likes things done a certain way, so we left him in peace.

"Liana, I do *want* to *mention*," Mom said, "Mateo is *driving* me to San Francisco as soon as the three of us *accomplish* what we need to *accomplish* in this meeting. I need to *reclaim* my car from the *impound* facility. It takes a *certain* amount of paperwork and time, so let us move *quickly*, please."

"Absolutely." I leaned forward in the overstuffed chair toward my mother, heretofore called Lila during this meeting. "You know, Lila, I forgot to ask Richard if he found out more information on the rest of the heirs. Did he mention anything to you?"

Always prepared, Lila picked up her silver fountain pen and notepad from the coffee table. She rarely uses a computer and likes to write things down on the small notepad she carries with her constantly. "Let me *see*," she said, turning several pages. "*Ah*, yes. On the *butler*, Mr. Wong. He's a *widower* whose *only* daughter lives in Portland, Oregon, with her husband. The daughter gave birth *recently* to a baby girl who has a *hole* in her heart."

"Good Lord Almighty," Gurn said, his Southern accent coming to the fore.

"How awful," I said.

"Yes," Lila agreed. "The child *can* be saved, but it requires *many* expensive operations. Even *with* insurance, the medical bills have been piling up, all which *Mr. Wong* has been paying. According to Richard, his *savings* are *nearly* depleted. Last week, he borrowed *fifty thousand dollars* from his credit union to *fly* in a heart specialist from New York to do a *lifesaving* operation. An *expensive* lifesaving operation."

"So, Mr. Wong could use this inheritance big-time," I said. "And for a very just cause."

"*Just* cause or *no*, Richard found that *several* times Mr. Del Vecchio tried to *remove* Mr. Wong from his position, and even went to court *five* years ago to *do* so. The *judge* ruled in Mr. *Wong's* favor, but I think it would be safe to *say* there was bad blood *between* them."

"Imagine working for someone who went that far to fire you," I said.

"He must make some yearly salary," Gurn remarked.

"He *does*," Lila said. "And the past few *years*, he's used *much* of it to keep his *son-in-law* from *losing* his business *during* the pandemic."

"So, he's tapped out," I said. "I hate to ask this, but how involved was Wong in Del Vecchio's act? Did he have access to the guillotine? If he did, would he know how to sabotage it?"

Lila thought for a moment before saying, "To answer all *three* questions: somewhat, yes—and possibly. Mr. Del Vecchio would *often* call Mr. Wong from *whatever* performance place he was *at* and ask him to bring missing *props, food, beverages,* or *even* a change of clothes, all tasks within the *boundaries* of Mr. Wong's job, which was written out *quite* specifically."

"Nonetheless," Gurn said, "I'll bet Del Vecchio pushed the envelope sometimes."

"It *didn't* happen at the charity show *because* Mr. Del Vecchio's *wife* was coming and going with *great* frequency. That's why we never *saw* Mr. Wong at the *theater*."

"Well, I hate to say this, but I will," I said. "Mr. Wong had means, motive, and opportunity. He might even top the list."

"Possibly," Lila said. "But why don't *you* let *me* continue with *Richard's* report before we *discuss* the suspects?" She cleared her throat. "As we have *already* stated, the *current* wife —"

"Madison," I interjected.

"Yes, *Madison.* I was *going* to say her name. *Please* don't interrupt."

"Sorry. Too much caffeine. Sorry." I leaned back in the chair. Gurn suppressed a smile.

"The *current* wife, Madison, was *backstage* of the theater for at least *eight* hours a day for the past *three* days. She could have, at *any time,* altered the safety lever."

"Yes, but how?" I blurted out. "And if she had, why wouldn't Del Vecchio have noticed it? The last thing he did was to check that lever before he lay down under the guillotine."

Lila rolled her eyes and let out a sigh loud enough to be heard across the street. "*Liana…*"

"Yes, ma'am?"

"*Caffeine* or *no*, you are to *stop* interrupting me or I will *never* get through this list. And I would *like* to pick up my Jaguar, *today*."

"Yes, ma'am. Sorry."

"May I *continue*?"

I nodded. Gurn let out a cough to hide his laughter. I tried to kick him under the table but missed.

"The *second* wife, Claudia Gracioso, was *not* in Marin with her parents, as *previously* thought. But, *rather*, she brought them to her *home* in Redwood City." I opened my mouth to speak but caught Lila's glare and merely smiled. She went on: "Which *means* that *she*, while not given the same *opportunities* as Madison Del Vecchio, is still a *viable* suspect. Now, we can *assume* that even though the guillotine is a fairly *new* illusion, each wife was at least *familiar* with his processes, and *might* have found a way to *circumvent* his safety procedures. Each *one* is a suspect, *until* we learn differently. That is *something* you and Gurn can *focus* on, I do believe. *After* I finish this report," she added pointedly.

I bit my lower lip to keep from speaking and merely nodded. Chinese water torture was nothing compared to this. The next time I "took" a meeting with Lila, I would make sure I took a Valium first.

"Now, the *first* wife, Elizabeth Hofsted, we have *not* been able to locate as of *yet*."

"Excuse me?" I burst out. Maybe I'd need two Valium. "Look, Lila, I know you said not to interrupt, but this is a biggie. Richard can find a tick on the backside of a wild burro in the deserts of the Grand Canyon in less than an hour. This has been nearly forty-eight hours. Why hasn't he located Elizabeth Hofsted yet? Don't you think that's strange?"

Gurn jumped in, "Sweetheart, you heard Rich say something like that earlier. And he didn't find Steven's cabin the first time out. Sometimes things get buried on the internet. She could have remarried, moved out of the country, be dead for all we know. How old was she, anyway?"

"Fifty-six, from the *marriage* certificate. *My* age," Lila sniffed.

"Just a kid then," I said with a smile. "So, while she could have passed on to her great reward, chances are she's alive and kicking."

"Rich will find her either way," Gurn said.

"Of *course*," Lila agreed. "It's *only* a matter of time."

"Something I don't have much of," I said.

"Liana, you must *stop* being so *dramatic*. It isn't *healthy*. You *didn't* kill the man, and we will *find* out who *did,* even if you *are* arrested."

"Wow! Something to look forward to."

"You *know* what I *mean,* Liana. Don't be *difficult*."

"I'm sorry, Mom," I said, taking in a deep breath and forgetting we were in a business meeting. "It's unbelievable. Someone managed to take a magician's trick that's been successfully done for decades if not centuries—"

"*Not* centuries, Liana. I remember *reading* that the illusion itself was created *sometime* in the 1930s."

"Whatever. Still, instead of being an illusion of cutting off a man's head, it became the real deal."

"And in *front* of an audience," she said, nodding vigorously.

"If you're trying to make me feel better, it isn't working."

"Liana, you're being too *sensitive*. *Nobody* thinks it's your fault. You were just a *witless* pawn."

"Witless?"

"Okay, ladies," Gurn said, standing. "I've got a phone call come in. It looks like Madison Del Vecchio, and I'm going to take it out on the patio. Why don't we all take five and relax a little? Or," he added, going back into the neutral zone, "continue with what you're doing. Your call. I'll be back in a few." He hurried for the sliding glass doors while answering his phone.

"And now for the *son*, David," Mom said without missing a beat. "According to *Donna*, she and her brother *aren't* speaking, but that was yet *another* illusion created by one or *both* of them. Point in *fact*, once Richard got into her *email* account, he discovered—"

"Oh, bad boy," I said. "He shouldn't do that. I'm going to tell on him."

"If that is *supposed* to be humorous, Liana, it falls *far* from the mark."

"Not just a little funny?"

"No."

"Sometimes I just can't help myself."

"Try."

"Right. Sorry. Go on, please."

"In *actuality*, Richard found *dozens* of emails from brother and sister on a *regular* basis in another email account. I read a *few* missives, and they *seem* to be quite close and share a *mutual* dislike of their father, albeit a *sad* one."

"Hmmm. I wonder why the pretense?"

"When you *find* her, you must *ask* her."

Chapter Ten

I pulled out of the driveway at around 11:00 a.m. in my 1957 Bel Air Chevy, the last gift from my father before he died. Dad bought the restored, classic turquoise convertible from a private owner, complete with power steering, brakes, and windows. The air-conditioning and seat belts were added later. They say the top speed is ninety miles an hour on an open road, but I wouldn't know. Try finding an open road in the Bay Area.

All in all, I consider the car a third pet after Tugger and Baba and would never part with it even though it tends to be hot in the summer and cold in the winter. And after several miles on the highway with the top down, nobody can get the tangles out of my hair except my hairdresser using an entire bottle of cream rinse. So, when Gurn and I make any road trips, we use his Jeep Grand Cherokee. It has all the bells and whistles, everything but a liquor cabinet. If things continued the way they were going, I would be adding one soon.

Speaking of Gurn and his Jeep, they were off to Sea Cliff to visit the young widow and see what he could find out. I was off to the magician's guru, Henry Swan. We would reconnoiter around 1:00 p.m.

According to the GPS, Henry Swan's store, Mechanical Magic, was mixed in with local auto repair and auto parts businesses. Sure enough, I found it in a long row of one-story stucco buildings with various cars, tires, or mufflers on display in between pools of drying motor oil. There were no fronts to the buildings, but rather, sliding corrugated tin doors, open for business. Above the open doors were names such as ABC Auto, Auto Repair, Inc., and Cheap Car Parts. Not imaginative names, but when you drove in you knew what you saw was what you were going to get.

Mechanical Magic, however, was an anomaly. No sliding tin doors. The stucco front had a centered thick door painted a fading black and two smallish windows on either side, each displaying an animated head. One was a white-and-red clown whose ears flapped, and eyes opened and closed. In the other, a shiny, black Darth Vader mask radiating green-and-red laser beams from the eyeholes. All in all, not a place I would ordinarily stop at in a million years.

I parked in front, noting a mechanic from across the road eyeing my car like he hadn't eaten in days and it was a pastrami on rye. I waved, and he gave me a big smile and a thumbs-up. I returned it and we both laughed. I should be admired as often as my '57 Chevy.

I knocked on the door and a voice came at me from an overhead speaker. "Yes? What do you want?"

"I'd like to speak to Mr. Swan, please."

"Who are you?" The question was suspicious and not at all friendly. "Are you a reporter?"

"No, I'm not. I spoke with you earlier. You told me to drop by anytime today, remember? My name is Lee Alvarez, and I'm a private investigator. It's about the guillotine that Marvin Del Vecchio used in his act."

There was a moment's silence and the door buzzed. I pushed it open and entered a large room littered with doll- to life-size string marionettes, new and ancient pinball machines, ticking clocks of various shapes and sizes, magicians' trunks — open, broken, or incomplete — and one old arcade bowling machine, circa 1950. I knew the date of it because my brother stuffs his basement with mid-century arcade machines and games. And Vicki lets him. What a wife.

Lounging in the middle of the single lane of the arcade bowling machine was one of the biggest and most gorgeous cats I'd ever seen. Eyes half closed, it was a black-and-tan Maine Coon with white paws, chest, and belly. A shaft of sunlight from a high window hit the cat like a spotlight, causing its white fur to gleam almost iridescently.

I ripped my gaze from the cat and looked around me. At the back, a waist-high glass counter ran the width of the room. Under the glass, parts of medieval armor were on display. Whether real or fake, I couldn't tell. A faded red-velvet floor-to-ceiling curtain hung behind it. Apparently, faded and fading were de rigueur around this place, pardon my French.

A large, heavyset man of indeterminable age stood behind the counter staring at me. Also staring at me were the large green eyes of the cat. I nodded to the man but was drawn to the twenty-five pounds or so of lounging cat. I'm going to choose a cat over a person nine times out of ten, especially if they have humor in their eyes. This one did. I reached out a tenuous hand.

"That's Sailor." The man's bass voice boomed out from behind the counter. "He comes with me to work. He's as gentle as a lamb, as long as you don't try to take him to the vet."

Sailor reached forward with the side of his face and rubbed my hand, purring softly.

The man was suddenly by my side. "He likes you. Sailor's very particular. He doesn't purr for most people, finds them too iffy. He can tell about a person right away."

"You trust his judgment." It was a statement of fact. I looked up at the enormous man, my hand now scratching the cat under the chin.

"Damn straight."

"You Henry Swan?"

"I am."

"I'm Lee Alvarez."

Being at least six foot four, or five, Swan towered over my five foot eight, especially as I was wearing sneakers. The top of his mouth was framed by a series of small lines, the kind that come from decades of pulling on a cigarette. My take was he was a committed smoker. But funny, no smell of smoke inside. His eyes were an unusual shade of pale gray, the kind that hold you in their grip. Those eyes narrowed on me.

"You're the one in the papers, the gal they say chopped off Marvin Del Vecchio's head."

"Except I didn't."

Sailor stood up and came over to me, purring his head off. I hefted him up and held him close, losing my hands in the abundance of his fur. I hugged him as much for comfort as anything else.

"That's why I'm here," I continued. "I'm hoping you can help me figure out what happened. After all, you built the guillotine. You must know how it can be rigged."

Sailor pulled out of my hug and jumped back down to the bowling lane. He walked over to Henry Swan and butted the man's stomach affectionately with his head.

"He's always telling me to lose weight," Swan said with a laugh.

Swishing his tail, Sailor turned away from both of us, stretched, and lay back down again in the sunny spot on the bowling lane. A few strands of fur floated around in the unmoving air, highlighted by the sun streaming in through the high window.

"I need to brush him. Hasn't been brushed today." Then Swan looked at me, adding in a casual tone, "Can't be rigged. No way to rig it." He smiled, nicotine-stained teeth emphasizing his grin. "It's either safe or it's danger. No in-between. You should know that. You were his assistant. He must have showed you how it worked."

He eyed me suspiciously. I shook my head.

"I was his assistant for only two days, and that was just for this charity fundraiser. He told me next to nothing. And he kept me as far away from the guillotine as possible except for three times: one, when I had to make sure the lever read 'safe,' two, to put the top half of the pillory in place over his neck, and three, remove the pillory after the trick was over. Any time I was near the guillotine, he always had me face away from it and toward the audience, smiling. I didn't even see… it… happen."

"He probably didn't want you to know more than you had to. He was like that. Even to his own detriment. If he'd told you how the trick worked, he might not be dead."

"I don't know about that," I said, louder than I meant to. "I did see the word 'safe' before I moved to the top of the guillotine. I saw it. And Marvin did, too. We both saw the word safe, or we wouldn't have gone through with the trick."

This time he shook his head. Then he looked at me and seemed to come to a decision.

"In that case, I'd better show you how it works. I had to show the police on the real one that did the dirty deed. So, the secret's out. Or will be. I've got the miniature one over here. My prototype. I always do one of these first. Work out the bugs."

He crossed to a small table on which a ten- or twelve-inch-long guillotine sat, one that could probably lop off the tip end of a cigar. Or a finger.

He lifted the small-scale guillotine up and turned it around. Then he removed the one-piece back cover made from metal. There the inner workings of the guillotine were on display. He ran a soft finger, almost lovingly, over the exposed, intricate machinery. He may have been a big man, but his fingers were slim and delicate, an artist's fingers.

"You see this?" He pointed to a tiny, button-like lever. "When you push that in, it shows green, which means safe. The prototype is too small to print the word 'safe' on it, but the color green means the same thing."

"How do you make the same lever read danger at one point and safe at another?"

"I'm glad you asked that, you clever girl, you. And this is why they pay me the big bucks." He winked at me good-naturedly. "On this prototype, when the lever is out and in the danger mode, the top half of the lever lights up red, picking up the LED light behind it through the one punch hole at the top. If you look closely at this small lever, you will see the red color is at the top half of the lever. Conversely, when you push the lever in, it connects with the bottom light, which is green, showing through a punch hole at the bottom. Both lights can never be on at the same time. Circuit overload. On the life-size guillotine, it's a little easier. The words 'danger' and 'safe' are punched out of the metal, so the LED light shows through the characters depending on which mode it's in."

"But these levers control what, exactly? Like the green one. What does it do?"

"Another good question. That little lever holds up one side of a thick bar, a metallic alloy made of chromium, cobalt, and nickel. Scientifically, if you remember from your science classes—"

"Probably not."

"Too bad. Anyway, the combination of chromium, cobalt, and nickel, or CrCoNi, has been found to have the highest toughness ever recorded on Earth. It has impressive strength and ductility, with outstanding damage tolerance."

"And that's what the bar built inside the top half of the pillory is made of?"

"Yes. That's what keeps the real blade from descending all the way down. When you pull the lever out and into the danger mode, the bar which is on a hinge on one side, drops into a hollowed-out side of the framework of the guillotine. This action allows the blade to slice through anything and everything in its path before it stops at the bottom. See?"

I did see. On the prototype, Swan's CrCoNi bar had fallen out from somewhere inside the pillory in a flash, fitting into a small recess at the side of the frame. If you weren't looking for it, you probably wouldn't see it. I sure hadn't.

"Del Vecchio knew to stand in front of it for just that moment," he said, "preventing anyone else from seeing the bar drop into the framework. Then he'd cut the cabbage head in two, just to prove the danger. After that, he had to put it back into the safe mode. What that means on the life-size guillotine is you have to manually lift the bar up with one hand and back inside the pillory. But it's done in an instant." He demonstrated with his forefinger on the prototype, still talking. "Then you push the lever back inside to the 'safe' position with the other hand. When you do that, it not only physically goes underneath that side of the bar, but the hinge on the other side connecting it to the framework is released."

"The bar becomes its own unit inside the pillory?"

"Precisely. The safety lever not only releases the bar's hinge, but goes underneath the other side of the bar and locks into place. You can hear the click. The magician waits for the sound."

"So, wrapping this up, the CrCoNi bar is inside the pillory to prevent the real blade from dropping all the way down. But when you want it to, the bar drops free, slides into the framework of the guillotine, and allows the blade to come all the way down."

"Exactly. But when that happens, there is a digital sound of the blade continuing to drop. That's what makes the audience *think* it's dropping all the way down. I created that sound effect. It's all part of the illusion."

"But how does the audience see what they think they see? Even from where I was standing it looked like the blade went all the way down."

He leaned into me, even though there was no one else around, and whispered,
"There are other ways to do this trick, but 'Take the less complicated route', that's my motto."

Ah! Another motto. And a good one. Swan went on.

"The split second the blade hits the top of the pillory, two partial blades from below are triggered to thrust up from the bottom of the platform about an inch away from either side of the magician's head. From a distance, even a short distance, it looks like the blade continues all the way down. You know what they say, 'At twenty feet and heavily splattered.'"

"That's not a motto; that's a quote, right?"

"Right."

"Well, it somehow got by me. Shakespeare?"

"Theater tech-speak. It means things look one way close up but another way from where the audience is sitting. It's about deception or, as magicians like to say, illusion. But back to the two bottom blades. Once again, they're triggered to come up, but only when the bar is inside the pillory and in the 'safe' mode. They stay in place beneath the platform when the blade comes down all the way. That's also what costs the big bucks, making all these things work when they should."

"Speaking of big bucks, I understand Del Vecchio had an argument with you about money on the phone at the theater the other day. Several people overheard it."

I phrased it that way because I wanted to see if he got defensive. He didn't.

"I'm not surprised. He was yelling his head off. Our original agreement was it would cost eighty-five thousand dollars for me to build the guillotine and he agreed. Then the cheap SOB called me the other day saying if I didn't give him back ten thousand dollars, he'd report me to the Better Business Bureau. He thought it was only worth seventy-five."

A look of disgust came over Henry's face. "But he was like that. Always trying to nickel-and-dime you. A cheapskate and not a nice man. Sailor left the room whenever Del Vecchio came here, so that shows you. Sometimes I would refuse to make him an illusion, like the two boxes for sawing the woman in half. He gave me trouble right from the beginning on that one and I told him to go elsewhere. Any work I do, it's going to be the right way or not at all," he added firmly. "Going back to the guillotine, do you want a demonstration on this prototype? This does everything the big one does, even the sound effects, although you have to strain to hear them."

"No thank you. The real event was enough for a lifetime." I thought for a moment. "It can't be one hundred percent foolproof, though, Mr. Swan."

"Call me Henry." He grinned. "After all, we're revealing home truths now."

"And call me Lee." I smiled despite how I was feeling. "Then truth time, Henry. In my experience there's always a flaw."

"Not in this case. This is so simple in its structure, there are no flaws, Lee. I showed the police that. That's why people come to me for their illusions and pay top dollar. The person's head never gets near any of the blades due to machine error. Too many stop guards. The setting up of the bar and its deconstruction—the safe to danger— has to be done by a person's hands. The only thing built into the guillotine is the exact moment someone pulls the cutting blade back up to the top by the rope, the lower blades retract into the bottom of the platform. Anything else has to be set up

106

deliberately. Either Marvin committed suicide, or somebody killed him."

"I never thought of suicide, Henry." I paused for a moment, running through the possible scenario. "Nah. Doesn't read. He just bought season tickets for the San Francisco Playhouse and planned a vacation next month on the Costa del Sol."

"I agree. Too mean," Henry said. "That type likes to inflict themselves on the world for as long as possible."

"You're a sage, Henry."

"It's living with a cat. They teach you these things."

"They do, indeed. Going back to the guillotine, you're saying the lower blades are triggered to go back into the base by the upward pull of the rope?"

"You got it. You must have seen that happen when you pulled on the rope. No, probably not," he contradicted himself. "It happens instantaneously. And it's a good illusion."

He smiled again. This time I got a whiff of stale cigarette breath. Not my favorite odor, but it gave me an idea.

"Did you find anything different this morning when you went through the real one for the police? Maybe you need a cigarette to think about it," I suggested.

He thought for a moment. "Maybe I do. Let's go out the back. I never smoke inside. Sailor is sensitive."

I followed him behind the counter and watched him pull the washed-out red velvet curtain aside for me to enter. This was where the real work took place. Fragments of motors, plastic and metal gewgaws, electronic gadgets – all undefinable in their current condition – were strewn about. I recognized an iron maiden from my memory of an old Vincent Price horror movie I once saw. This one had been taken apart, spikes laid out on the tabletops. A large cat cage sat in a corner, empty, even too big for the likes of Sailor.

"Where's the tiger?" I asked, gesturing to the cage.

"Disappeared. That's why the cage is here. Needs to be fixed. And it was a lion."

"You mean there's a lion wandering around here, Henry?"

"Not here. Reno. And Elmer only wandered back to his dressing room, but it did spoil the trick. Spooked the audience, too." He gave off an easy chuckle.

Even though he wasn't giving me the answers I wanted to hear, Henry Swan seemed to be a nice guy with a sense of humor. I relaxed a little and followed him through the maze of works-in-progress to a door that led outside.

A shaded patio with a canvas overhang sat directly against the building. A six-foot-tall wood fence stood on the perimeter of the remaining three sides, apparently to keep visitors out. Or maybe a rambunctious cat in. There was a gate with a lock that led out to a cement driveway. Two large, comfy-looking lawn chairs, one yellow, one blue, on either side of an aluminum table looked inviting. Several cat toys lay scattered about on the carpeted part of the cement. Well-tended potted flowers and plants dappled the area here and there and some hung from the fence. Against the wall of the building was a refrigerator. Next to the fridge, was a low counter with two shelves. The top shelf held a small microwave. Below, plates, flatware, and cans of cat food were neatly stacked. Henry and Sailor's own private oasis.

"Want a beer, soda, iced tea, lemonade?" he asked.

"No thanks."

He opened the fridge door, and I heard the clanking of bottles hitting against one another. The fridge was filled to capacity with them. He grabbed a bottle of lemonade and looked at me questioningly, extending it toward me. I laughed and took it.

"Sit down anywhere," he said.

"Thanks." I sat down in the blue chair, twisted off the cap, and took a long drink of lemonade. I was thirsty and hadn't even known it.

He got one for himself and put the bottle on the table. He pulled a pack of cigarettes from his shirt pocket, extracted one, and lit it. He inhaled deeply and blew out in the other direction, away from me. I appreciate thoughtful smokers.

"My one vice." He gestured to the cigarette, lowering his bulk into the sturdy canvas-and-wood yellow chair. "I don't drink anything but an occasional beer. My downfall is ice cream." He laughed again.

Suddenly, Sailor appeared through the cat door, ran over, and leapt up on Henry's lap. He butted the man's stomach again, hopped atop the table, and crossed over to me, jumping into my lap. He settled down, turned over, and showed me his white tummy, apparently ready for a good rub. Supporting the hanging-over part of him, I obliged.

"He's only allowed out here when I am, and then only on the patio. There's too much traffic. But he's a good boy and listens to me." He ground his hardly smoked cigarette into a nearby ashtray. He looked at me with a grin. "I don't smoke out here when he's around. Nor in the house, neither. My world pretty much revolves around him. And my wife," he added.

"I know what you mean. We've got two cats, Tugger and Baba. I call Tugger, 'My Son the Cat'. Baba is really Gurn's cat, but I adore her."

"Gurn's your husband?" I nodded. "My wife's name is Grace. Sailor is really my cat, but Grace adores him, too."

We grinned at each other, suddenly old pals. Then the mood changed. His smile vanished.

"So, let me think. Was there anything different from when I handed the guillotine off to Del Vecchio to when I checked it over yesterday with the police?"

I would have leaned forward in the chair but didn't want to disturb Sailor who was spread out over the entirety of my lap and then some. Relaxed, his head was thrown back and dangled off the side with all four legs in the air. The rubbing continued while I asked, "Anything at all, Henry? Please. Something that didn't feel right or sound right?"

He thought for a moment, then shook his head slowly. "To be honest, not a thing. Everything worked as it should. Although I did notice the safety lever slid in and out a little smoother than it normally did. But I checked that. I tried to see if it could have slipped out of the safe mode and gone into the danger mode on its own. If it was my error, I wanted to know; this is my livelihood. I did it several times. One of the detectives tried it, too. The only way it would move from safe to danger or danger to safe was if you moved it manually. I'd like to help you, little lady, being you're a new friend of Sailor's and all, but I think we're clutching at straws."

I sat for a moment, drinking lemonade and rubbing Sailor's tummy, not even bothered the man called me "little lady." Sometimes you have to let things go and look at the bigger picture. Because one thing for sure, us being mutual friends of Sailor's, I sensed Henry would help me if he could.

But he couldn't.

Chapter Eleven

From South San Francisco, I headed north toward the Marina. I hit the speed dial on my phone, sitting in its holder in the air vent to the side of the steering wheel. Gurn answered on the first ring, as if he'd been waiting for me to call.

"Hi, sweetheart," he said. "How'd it go?"

"Not so great. Henry Swan is a nice guy. Seems to know his business. He says there's no way for someone to rig the guillotine from safe to danger without it being done manually."

"You believe him?"

"I would if I didn't know I didn't do it and there was no one else around. It had to be rigged. There's an unknown fact here."

"What fact is that?"

"I don't know. That's why I'm calling it unknown. But maybe I phrased it wrong."

"There's an undiscovered fact; is that what you mean?"

"Exactly. And our conversation only serves to reinforce that Henry Swan comes across as knowing what *he's* saying, whereas I come across like an idiot. He's going to be a credible witness for the other side."

"It's not a court case yet, and we're going to make sure it doesn't get to that."

"From your mouth to God's ears. How did it go with you?"

"It didn't. I got to Madison's house in Sea Cliff only to be told she'd gone to the tennis club, and I was to meet her there."

"She's playing tennis less than forty-eight hours after her husband was decapitated?"

"She's playing doubles right now. Her secretary told me if I wanted to talk to her, I'd have to wait until they finished. It's forty-love, two sets down. I should be able to talk to her soon."

"She has a secretary?"

"His name is Johan. And he looks exactly like a Johan. White-blond hair, pale blue eyes, and a heavy Swedish accent. Ah! Sweetheart, I see their game is over. We'd better hang up. Where are you going now?"

"I thought I would go back to the theater, pick up the makeup I left there, and nose around a little. And I'd like to personally apologize to Billie for ruining her costume."

"You're going to try to go into that tunnel again, aren't you?"

"You know me so well. I even wore sneakers. But if Fenner's men are hanging around, I might not be able to do much."

"Good luck, sweetheart."

"Thank you."

"And be careful."

"I will."

"Gotta go. Madison's walking over. I'll text you with an update when I'm done." He hung up.

Keeping the car at a steady sixty-five, I hit another number on speed dial. Richard didn't answer on the first ring, and when he did, he seemed out of breath.

"Hey, Lee. I was hoping you would call."

"You sound out of breath."

"I am. I was under my desk looking for a WiFi booster. I keep a spare or two under there."

"Don't we have our own server?"

"It's been compromised. Sunspot issues. Doesn't happen often, but when it does, a booster helps."

"The world of an IT guy. Any luck with the stick?"

"All kinds. DI is off the hook. Steven put everything, and I mean everything, on that stick. It was like a journal. Details about his sabotage job on Heart's Desire hoping for a bonus of a hundred grand from his employer. Nowhere does he say True Love Forever hired him to do the job, though, so he was probably freelancing."

"Maybe he just forgot or neglected to write it down."

"Not a chance. The man loved to write things down. He even wrote where he stashed the money he took periodically from his wife's and father-in-law's bank accounts. Nearly half a mil. It's in a numbered bank account in the Cayman Islands. Then he wrote about giving Donna a real sob story about how he lost the money in the stock market. He even mentions what he said to her. Donna seemed to believe anything and everything he said. He was a real con man."

"From what you're saying, I don't think Donna and Steven worked together on her father's death. Doesn't sound in Steven's character."

"I don't think he could work with anybody on anything. He was a user, a true grifter. Interesting, if not sick, individuals. According to my brief research, he could have been a narcissistic sociopath."

"Doesn't sound good. Or fun to be married to."

"Taking from people who trust them is something that makes them feel good about themselves. From what Steven wrote, the more he scammed people, the more he liked it. Even his wife was fair game."

"Wow, I'd probably have to take a shower after reading all that."

"I went on my phone and looked at all the pictures I could find of Vicki and little Steffi."

"Even better. On the bright side, if Donna ever reappears and wants her money back, we know where it is. Any skinny on the two twin nephews?"

"Wyman and Winston Del Vecchio. They can sure use the money, Lee. Their pastry empire is going south as we speak. Apparently, they hit Marvin Del Vecchio up for an advance on their inheritance a few months back. He said no. Winston called him a lot of nasty names on social media."

"So, they are possible contenders?"

"I'm going to say 'possible' even though there are issues."

"Issues?"

"Wyman Del Vecchio is running for city council. His brother is his campaign manager. Both men were in the middle of a campaign rally Saturday night in the Marin auditorium with hundreds of eyewitnesses."

"Witnesses don't always see everything at all times, even though they think they do. And large crowds sometimes mean people can disappear for a short time. Mill Valley isn't that far from the Marina, is it? It's only about twenty minutes."

"I hadn't thought of that," he said, surprise coloring his voice. "Maybe."

"Okay, moving on. Is there enough evidence on the stick for us to bring to Heart's Desire?"

"Definitely. Lila plans to work on the presentation as soon as she gets back from San Francisco with her car. So, all we have to do now is clear you. How did it go with Swan?"

"Dead end."

A deep breath and then more false bravado along the lines of Gurn's. "Well, now I can concentrate totally on you. We'll just keep at it. Where are you?"

"In my car. On my way back to the theater."

"Going to try to go into the tunnel again?"

"Everybody thinks they know me!"

"And they do. Listen, Lee, on another subject, Carl is overdue on his check-in call."

"How overdue?"

"Nearly forty-five minutes. He should have arrived in North Tahoe by now or at least reported in."

"Can you track his phone?"

"Tried. No signal. Might be sunspots. Of course, he could be in a dead zone. Some areas are like that despite what Sprint says. But that's why I was looking for my booster."

"Does Lila know?"

"Yes. I texted her. Our Lady says not to panic yet."

"Then let's go with that. But keep me posted."

"Will do."

I hung up, troubled. Carl was diligent. He knew the rules and followed them. He should have called. Okay, maybe sunspots. I tried to put it out of my mind. At least, for now.

The rest of the drive to the Lithuanian Theater on the Marina wasn't too bad. A half an hour later, I parked the car, locked it, and started the two-block walk to the theater.

The largest population of Lithuanians in California is in the San Francisco Bay Area. They built this theater in 1952 and have been doing live performances or renting it out to other organizations since the seventies. It's a large theater, colorful, and well-kept up.

I knew of it through my Lithuanian American friend and skiing buddy, Janina Babonas. Her father was the manager of the theater, her mother the bookkeeper. On the rare occasion there wasn't anything live going on there, they would show movies from all over the world.

Mom and Janina's mother, Sofjia, became friends as well. When Mom's committee was looking for a venue for the Sons and Daughters of Fallen American Heroes fundraiser, the theater was the first place she called. And lo and behold, it was available. I smiled at the thought. Then something suddenly dawned on me. I did an internal monologue as I traipsed down the street.

Wait a minute. I haven't spoken to Jan since this happened. She and her family are on their usual one month a year in Palanga. Palanga. What a darling town. And the beach was just the best. And that hunky guy. What was his name? Viktoras. My first major crush. Oooh, to be fifteen again.

Wait a minute. I'm getting sidetracked. I'd better call Jan later today with some sort of explanation about what's going on.

Wait a minute. And this was my third minute waiting. This isn't a missing box of Cracker Jacks. This is the death of a performer in front of an entire audience. The show was canceled, and all those tickets had to be refunded. And the press was there, too. It's been in all the papers. I'm sure the assistant manager, Mr. Saxe, called the Babonas in Palanga. If not, someone else did. But in that case, I'm sure I would have heard from Jan. Unless…

I paused en route, sat down at a bus stop, and called my mother who answered on the first ring, highly annoyed and not afraid to show it.

"Liana, this is *not* a good time. If this is *unimportant*, please call me back *later*. I'm *next* in line to pay for the car. Over three *hundred* dollars. It's *outrageous*."

"Sorry, Mom. This is a necessary call."

"*Very* well," she huffed.

"Listen, did you call the Babonas and tell them what happened at the theater?"

"Of *course* I did. I called them that *very* night. When I went upstairs to bed. It was afternoon *there*. I *didn't* want them to hear it from a *stranger*."

"Okay, that explains a lot."

"They wanted to fly back *early*, but I told them it wasn't *necessary*, and I would keep them *updated*, which I have been. I also *told* Sofjia to *tell* Janina you would call *soon* with your own explanation. You should *do* that, dear. It's only *polite*."

"With all that's going on, Mom, the whole theater thing got by me until just now. But I'll call her the first minute I can. Maybe Jan or her parents know something about the tunnel. Carl check in yet?"

"I received a *voice* mail not fifteen minutes ago, *quite* brief and, if I *might* add, *somewhat* disturbing."

"Why disturbing?"

"He *usually* has more to say. He gives me more *details*."

"What did he say? Can you send the VM to me?"

"I don't *have* to. It's *three* words. **Everything's fine. Carlson.**"

"That was it?"

"Yes. I'm not sure *if* anything is wrong, but if I *don't* speak with him in *person* by *tomorrow* morning, I will *alert* Francis. *Hopefully*, this is just me being *overly* cautious. I must *go* now."

We hung up with me thinking she wasn't being overly cautious. Carl never calls himself Carlson. Lila's the only one who calls him by his given name. Her and the DMV. Maybe Carl was trying to tell us something. Or someone else had read his driver's license.

Chapter Twelve

The backstage door was locked. I knocked several times and waited. *Rats. I should have called to make sure someone was going to be here.* Just as I finished berating myself, the door sprung open.

A surprised wardrobe supervisor, Billie, stood holding the door halfway open. I didn't know Billie personally, but through the Babonas. They spoke highly of her skills and work ethic. Unless there was a movie showing, Billie was backstage to make sure everything went smoothly with costumes, whether she built them or not. Even the smallest of productions were enhanced by her being on-site. Jan mentioned once Billie received a yearly salary, modest but livable.

"Just the person I hoped to see!" I exclaimed. "Although, I wasn't sure if you would be here."

"Why, hello, doll," she said, a smile lighting up her face. "I'm here trying to get ahead on the costumes for Octoberfest. But you're right. It's hard to say when I'll be here. Most of the time, I can choose when I show up. When we're working on a new show, I'm here around eight thirty, nine o'clock in the morning, and put in at least twelve-hour days. But when a show is up and running, I come in around six or seven at night." She winked at me. "That's one of the perks of the job, flexible hours. But come in, come in, doll."

Billie stood back and opened the door wide enough for me to enter. Known as the theater's lovable character, she was probably in her late fifties, and around my height, five foot eight. Dyed, frizzy blonde hair came off a two-inch salt-and-pepper growth, the apparent natural order of things. It was hard to tell her body type as she always wore a muumuu, colorful but shapeless. Billie also sported huge, gypsy-style dangle earrings with lots of sparkle. The rest of her sparkled, too. Iridescent blue eyeshadow, hot-pink lipstick, and toenails painted in hot-pink holographic nail polish. Those were hard not to notice on feet wearing rubber flip-flops, no matter what the weather.

Billie shut the door and drew me into an embrace, saying, "How are you, doll? What a horrible thing you've been through. And to think the police think you might have done it on purpose. Why would you? You didn't even know the man. Did you?" She studied my face, looking for answers.

"Not before meeting him here the other day."

"Well, it's all horrible. Just horrible. Can I do anything for you? A cup of tea, doll? You look like you could use one."

"No, no tea, but thanks, Billie."

"Well, never mind. Come down to my parlor, said the spider to the fly, and then tell me why I'm the person you wanted to see."

She pushed me toward stairs leading down to the wardrobe room. Once in the basement, a long hallway led to ten dressing rooms, the props room, greenroom, and at the end of the hall was Billie's fiefdom, the wardrobe room. We entered the large room with racks of costumes hanging in rows, twenty, thirty feet deep. In a corner was Billie's workspace with an industrial-sized sewing machine and tables filled with bolts of fabrics for the never-ending next production. Billie was considered an institution, having been the theater's wardrobe person for decades.

I walked through the door ahead of Billie and turned back to her. "Well, I came to pick up my things from the dressing room. But I also wanted to apologize to you for ruining the costume when I ran off and got trapped in the tunnel. You worked so hard to get it ready on time. You weren't even finished sewing it until after the half hour call."

"That happens a lot in the theater. Sometimes things aren't ready until the performer is going onstage. Adds to the drama," she said good-naturedly.

"It would make me feel better if you'd let me pay you for the costume."

She inhaled a sharp breath. "Absolutely not, but you're such a doll to offer. I'm just glad you weren't hurt. It was an old costume out of stock. I can't remember the last person who wore it. Don't even worry about it. Throw it in the trash. Promise me you'll do that."

"I already have. It was practically in shreds."

"But you aren't in shreds. That's what counts. Listen, doll, I locked your dressing room with my master key. I didn't want any of your things to 'take a walk' until you came back for them."

"Thank you, Billie. That's so thoughtful."

She reached inside the folds of her lime-green muumuu and took out a large brass key on a silver ring. After handing it to me, Billie patted my cheek before crossing to a table holding an electric kettle, cups, a small carton of milk, and a bowl of sugar. Very homey. Turning to me, she said, "Are you sure you don't want any tea, doll? Water is always boiling for tea in the wardrobe room."

"No thank you, really. But could I ask you something else?"

"Ask away." There were several different flavors of tea, but Billie chose her favorite, Earl Grey. She put the bag into an empty cup and poured in hot water from the electric kettle.

"Billie, you're usually down here during a performance, but I was wondering if you might have been wandering the wings that night. You didn't happen to see any stranger backstage when… uh… the accident happened, did you?"

Billie picked up a spoon and thought. "You mean, someone who didn't belong here?"

"Something like that."

Billie scooped up a teaspoon of sugar, stopping midway before putting sugar into the steeping tea. "No. Nobody. If I had, I would have told the police." After she put the sugar in the cup, she laid the spoon down and stared at me. "Why? Did you see someone?"

I backpedaled a bit. "No. It's nothing. I was just curious, that's all. Thanks. I think I'll go check out my dressing room, if you don't mind. Anyone else here?" I asked casually, thinking about the police.

"No, no one. I wouldn't be here myself if I didn't have the Octoberfest on the books. There will be one hundred people in the production, fifty men, fifty women, dancing and singing. I have to make generic black pants for the men, and red skirts for the women, and white aprons for everyone. It's a long-term project." She let out a laugh.

"But one you seem to embrace," I said.

"Well, I've got nothing else in my life right now. Even my dog died last winter."

"Oh, no! I'm so sorry."

She shrugged. "Well, Fifi was seventeen. What can you expect?"

"Right." Small talk done, I turned around and headed for the door. "I'll return the key to you before I leave," I said, waving goodbye. I paused and turned back to the older woman. "It doesn't bother you, being in this big theater by yourself?"

"Been here over twenty-five years. It's home to me. But lest you think my life is only this theater, I'm taking a few days off. Flying to Delaware for my niece's graduation. She's a full-fledged architect."

"Good for you! And congratulations to your niece."

I left thinking kindly thoughts about her unnamed niece starting life out as an architect, and went down the hall to my former dressing room. As I unlocked and opened the door, my nose involuntarily wrinkled from the stale air in the windowless room. It smelled unhealthy and like old tennis shoes. I left the door partially open for ventilation, sat down, and studied all the makeup, creams, and lotions sitting forlornly on the table. Then I looked up and saw the clothes and shoes I'd been wearing before I changed into the costume. They were still hanging in the closet along with my raincoat. I should have brought a shopping bag, I thought. Maybe Billie had something I could use to get all the stuff back to the car.

I stood with plans to return to the costume room when the phone rang. Gurn. I sat back down and grabbed the phone so fast, I whacked myself on the ear with it.

"Ouch! Darling, how did it go?"

"Not too well."

"Uh-oh."

"Now, don't get upset, sweetheart, but there's no other way to say this. Madison says she saw you coming on to Del Vecchio numerous times, and when he didn't reciprocate, she believes you killed him in revenge. And that's what she told the police."

It's a good thing I was sitting down because I quivered all over like a bowl of raspberry Jell-O. I was speechless, too. A rare condition for me. I even found it difficult to breathe.

"Honey, are you there?" Gurn's voice was anxious.

"Wow," I managed to get out. "Do they still hang people? Because I feel the noose tightening around my neck."

Chapter Thirteen

"Listen, *mi cielo*, I can be with you in about fifteen minutes. You're still at the theater, right? Sit tight and I'll be right there."

First of all, when he calls me his heaven or sky in Spanish, I know I'm in deep doo-doo. Second, I couldn't have moved from the chair at that moment, even if I'd wanted to. And third, him saying he would come and pick me up like I was a first grader was the worst sign of all. He must have seen me swinging from the same rope I did.

Sudden indignation coupled with outrage turned gelatinous me into a flaming flambé. I didn't smolder. Veritable flames shot out of my mouth. I think they heard me screaming in Oakland.

"Of all the fat nerve! Madison told the police I was coming on to that scuzzbucket Del Vecchio? I couldn't stand to be in the same room with him. Even so, is that any reason to cut off his head? What is she smoking?"

"Calm down, sweetheart."

"I will not calm down!"

"And that's another valid approach," he said, shifting positions. "You don't have to if you don't want to. But let me tell you, the reading I got was that she's jealous of you. I'm sure the cops got pretty much the same reading. They're not stupid."

"Jealous? Of me? Why?"

"Because you're as gorgeous, if not more so, than she is. Women who live by their looks don't like any competition."

"Are you saying that to make me stop shouting into the phone?"

"Not really, although it would be appreciated. For the record, you are gorgeous."

"You're prejudiced, but thank you."

"I'm not prejudiced, but you're welcome."

"Here's *my* reading. She's *trying* to throw *suspicion* off *herself*." Oh my gawd! I was starting to emphasize words like my mother does. Could things get any worse?

"Hmmm. I hadn't thought of that," Gurn said.

"She has a strong motive. Money. And she had access to the guillotine more than anyone else, save Del Vecchio or his daughter. Maybe that's why she was around the theater so much. Waiting to rig it to fail."

"Yes, but how?"

"I don't know. But I've got to find out before Wednesday. According to Henry Swan, it can't be done. But it *was* done." I heard a ping from my phone. I removed it from my ear and looked at the incoming message. "I just got a message from Frank. Hold on a sec; let me read it. I switched to messages and saw the longish text from my godfather, probably dictated on his phone.

Lee, I suspect you are heading back to the theater to crawl around in that tunnel again if you're not already there. If so, don't bother. Fenner's men searched through what was left of the tunnel last night. He tells me all they found

were the remains of your shoes and part of the hull of a ship. When they gave the all-clear, the city filled in the remainder of the tunnel and sealed off any entrances. They finished around six this morning.

Well, rats. But I wasn't surprised. The land that is now the Marina neighborhood was originally part of the Bay and filled in for the 1915 Panama-Pacific International Exposition. At the time, they used debris and rubble from the 1906 earthquake. Consequently, the Marina District was the part of San Francisco most heavily damaged in the 1989 Loma Prieta earthquake. Liquefaction and foundation failures happened right and left. Not only is much of the Marina built on a bunch of junk, but the rest is nothing but sandy ground with a shallow water table. "Never put your full weight down around here," is my motto.

I switched the phone back to my call with hubby. "Frank says the tunnel has been filled in. He says they found nothing except my shoes. In a way, that's good news. I was afraid Donna's body might have been in there. So, after I pack up, I may as well leave. But meanwhile, why don't you head on home, or maybe you need to check in with the business? Ever since you came back, I don't think I've given you much time to do that."

Gurn is a certified public accountant when he isn't giving advice to the Pentagon or being my sleuthing sidekick. Besides all that, he owns his own CPA firm and has seven people working for him. He hadn't checked in with them since his return that I knew of. My job as his wife was to nag him a little. It's not written down anywhere, but it felt so right.

"I already called," he said. "They're good. When you hire the best, you never need to be there except to write their weekly paychecks. You're sure you're okay now?"

I laughed. "Darling, I was initially shocked by what you told me, but I'm fine. I'll see you at home in about an hour and a half."

"We'll have some takeout, then head over to Milpitas to see David's act, and talk to him. Sound good?"

"It's a date."

Chapter Fourteen

Musing, I sat back in the chair. Okay, so as of now, there is no more tunnel. But if no one was found in it, and I know I chased someone into the tunnel night before last, where did that person go? Time to call Jan.

I went into my phone numbers, found Janina's mobile number, and gave her a call.

"Hello? Lee, is that you?" My friend sounded concerned.

"Yes, it is, Jan. Sorry I haven't called you sooner."

"Never mind that, how are you? Has this been cleared up yet? Mom said your mother called to let her know there had been an accident onstage, and a magician was beheaded when you were acting as his assistant. Your mom has been calling with constant updates, and of course, we hear from Mr. Saxe, the assistant manager, daily. I mean, did I get this right?"

"Right. That's right."

"Oh, Lee, I'm so sorry." Her voice was warm and sympathetic. "They don't honestly think it was you, do they? Mr. Saxe called right after Lila did, and he told Mom you'd been arrested. That can't be right, is it? Why would anyone think you would do something like that?"

"It's all being sorted out now, Jan," I said vaguely. "Listen, I wanted to ask about—"

"Dad wanted to come back right away," she interrupted, "but it's *didžioji močiutė's* birthday."

"Let's see if I get this right. That's your great-grandmother?"

"You remembered! Mom said we shouldn't leave, and everybody else said we should stay here, too. We don't know how much longer great-grandma will be with us. Palanga is so gorgeous right now. And it's the once a year the entire family gets together."

For those not familiar with Palanga, it's a famous resort town on the Baltic coast of Lithuania and a worldwide tourist destination. Lithuania is a beautiful country whose citizens are generous, friendly, into food, music, family, and flowers. My kinda people.

"What could we do once we got there, anyway?" Jan asked.

"Stop acting so guilty," I laughed. "Of course, you should stay. And you're right, there's nothing you can do if you did come back. Moving on, how is your great-grandmother?"

"For ninety-nine, she's doing surprisingly well. Her birthday's tomorrow."

"Good, good. Now that we've got that out of the way, Jan—"

"You're sure you're okay, Lee? These despicable charges have been dropped, haven't they?"

"Almost." Vague again, but why have the conversation? I'd been having enough of them with my family. "Jan, I need to ask you about the tunnel."

"The tunnel?" My friend sounded surprised. "The tunnel off the theater? You know no one's allowed in there. It's been closed off for decades."

"But let's say someone did go in there; where did it lead?"

"Lead? For heaven's sake, why? Don't go in there, Lee. It's way too dangerous."

"Not a problem, Jan. The city filled it in early this morning. No more tunnel."

"Thank God. Why are you asking about it, then?"

"I need to know where it went. And, if you could tell me, it would be great. It's important."

"Okay," she relented. "Let me think. It was dug long before the theater was there, when it was connected to a saloon during the gold rush. You know, the coastline was different then; the water came farther in before all the landfill was added. I remember being told when I was a kid, the tunnel used to lead to the harbor. The saloon was famous for drugging men and shanghaiing them through the tunnel and into waiting ships. Five dollars a head, I think. An absolute fortune then. I remember hearing it was one of the few tunnels that didn't cave in during the 1906 earthquake. But that doesn't mean it was safe. The theater owners wanted it filled it in, but talk about a fortune—"

"Okay," I said, my turn to interrupt. "Great history lesson, but where did it lead?"

"Nowhere. At least, not anymore. Originally, it went from the saloon, under the empty lot next door, and continued beneath the lot across the street to what a hundred years ago was the shoreline. But I understand the street and parking lot were filled in back in the thirties. Something about city ordinances."

"This doesn't make any sense," I said more to myself than Jan. "How could someone go into the tunnel night before last and disappear if it doesn't come out anywhere on the other end?"

There was a knock at the door. I turned around and saw Billie standing in the doorway holding a cardboard box.

"Jan, I've got to call you back. What time is it there? I'm never good at international date lines."

"Almost eleven," she said with a laugh.

"P.m., right? It's getting late for you. Maybe I should call you back tomorrow."

"Don't worry about the time. Call me anytime, day or night. I'm keeping the phone by my side. I'm worried about you, Lee. Call me whenever."

I hung up with Jan and turned to Billie who was beaming at me, still clutching the cardboard box.

"I was in here earlier today," Billie said, "and saw all you had to take home with you. I thought you could use this empty box." She set it down on a chair by the door.

"Thank you so much, Billie."

"You're welcome, doll."

"Billie, before you go, do you know anything about the tunnel that was filled in this morning by the city? You've been here twenty-five years. You must have heard something."

"Only that when this place was a saloon, they used to kidnap young boys and men by drugging their drinks. Then they'd take them through the tunnel and sell them to ships in the harbor. Terrible business. Terrible."

"But you don't know anything more recent? Maybe somebody using the tunnel these days?"

"For heaven's sake, why? All you have to do is go outside the door and cross the street. Why go down into a dirty, dangerous tunnel? What an imagination you have, doll. One would think you were more than a magician's assistant."

I smiled brightly. That's right. No one at the theater knows what I really do for a living. They just know me through the amateur theater group as Lila's daughter. "Oh, just curious, Billie. Theater ghost stories are so thrilling, don't you think?"

She looked at me as if I had a screw loose, a look I've received many a time. "If you say so, doll."

Chapter Fifteen

After returning the key to Billie and giving her a quick hug, I walked the two blocks back to the car, carrying the cardboard box full of my stuff and junk. Every now and then I looked down and wondered just what I was stepping on. Someone's settee? Or the contents of their medicine cabinet? Having a vivid imagination is not always a good thing.

After I put the box in my trunk, I got into the car and reached for my phone. Richard, God bless him, had given me everyone's phone numbers in one neat file on my phone. I called Mrs. Claudia Del Vecchio, ex-wife number two of the dead magician. I'd noted she still lived with the man she left Del Vecchio for fifteen years previous, yet never married him. Having more or less a live-and-let-live attitude about life and the people I share the planet with, I personally didn't give a hoo-ha. But her reasons might be interesting to know. If it was because of elder Del Vecchio's will, that would tell me a lot.

Claudia herself answered the phone and agreed to meet me in forty-five minutes or so. Her Italian accent, soft and pleasant, was easy to understand. And she herself was very pleasant. Maybe this wouldn't go so badly. Maybe this case was turning around. Maybe I was just hungry.

It had been a long time since Tío's quesadillas. As fabulous as they were, they can only go so far. I unlocked the glove compartment and grabbed one of my stashes of Milky Way bars. Warm and gooey from the heat of the sun, I managed to get chocolate all over my face and hands. Messy but worth it. As I cleaned up with wet tissues, I faced the fact that chocolate was a girl's best friend. No point in mentioning it to her cat or hubby, but the truth was the truth.

I arrived at Claudia's Redwood City address within fifty minutes. On Whipple Street, it was one of those adorable thatched-roof homes reminiscent of the Cotswolds. Set back from the sidewalk, it had a sweet little garden filled with budding and blooming white roses with a cobblestone walkway leading to the house. It wasn't a grand house, maybe only a three-bedroom, two-bath, but I knew from real estate values, it was worth over several mil.

I hurried up the walkway, and then the three steps to a front door painted in a faux variegated green and copper veneer. Spectacular. I lifted the old ironwork metal rapper on the door and rapped three times, feeling as if I not only stepped back in time but into jolly old England.

The door swung open immediately, and a stunning woman, dressed in a multicolored, flowing caftan stood before me. *Come September*, a movie with Rock Hudson and Gina Lollobrigida, is one of my favorite go-to movies when I'm feeling sad or depressed. Barbara Stanwyck is my number one favorite actress, but Gina Lollobrigida is in the top twenty. And here she stood. Or a younger, living replica of her. And she looked camera ready, too.

"Hello," she said, displaying a beautiful smile and beautiful teeth. "You are Miss Alvarez?" If I didn't already know how to pronounce my last name, I would have chosen the way she said it, soft rolling r's and all.

"Yes, I am."

"And I am Claudia Del Vecchio."

"Please, let me say, Mrs. Del Vecchio, I am sorry for your loss. I realize he was your ex-husband, but nonetheless."

She shrugged in a noncommittal way. "*Così è la vita.* Such is life. Why don't we go into the living room?" She turned and glided away. Yards of lightweight fabric floated behind her.

I followed her through a short hallway and into a high-peaked-ceilinged room reaching up twenty feet or more. The space was done entirely in white, from ceiling to floor, with accents of primary colors in throw pillows, small bric-à-brac, and scatter rugs. One wall displayed a row of lead-lined, small glass-paned windows. Opening from the side, they were cranked halfway open. The result was light, airy, and welcoming. She indicated a white cushioned sofa where I should sit. She dropped down into a matching chair across from me, crossing her legs at the ankles. So ladylike. So Mom. So not me.

In between us sat an oval, dark wood coffee table. A silver coffee service for two was sitting on the table, complete with cups, saucers, and a dish of pastries. I began to drool.

"Let me offer you some coffee and pastries, such as a brioche, cannoli, or cornetto. There is a wonderful Italian pastry shop not a mile from here in downtown Redwood City. It is like a visit home. I must warn you, though; the coffee is strong. I make it my mama's way."

She beamed at me. I beamed back. There was a lot of beaming.

"I'd love some coffee, but I'll pass on the pastry. Thank you." Why did I say that? Oh, right. Take-out dinner waiting at home.

She took her time pouring coffee from the silver coffeepot into two white porcelain coffee cups. The cups and saucers were of a sleek, modern design. She looked up at me with another toothy smile. "I hope you don't mind if we speak softly. My parents are sleeping, and I don't want to disturb them. This is not a large house, and sound travels."

Her English was flawless, her manners impeccable, and her demeanor charming. I didn't trust her as far as I could throw Jumbo the elephant and his trainer.

But I kept right on smiling. "That's right. You have your parents with you now."

"Yes. It is a blessing and a challenge. But Paul, he is so good that way." She gave off a dramatic sigh as she handed me the cup of coffee. "What is your need of me, Miss Alvarez?" She leaned forward, almost in a conspiratorial way. "Why don't I call you Liana? And you must call me Claudia. Oh," she added as an afterthought, "milk? Sugar?"

"Nothing, no." I usually don't drink coffee black, but playing the tea scene between Gwendolyn and Cecily from *The Importance of Being Ernest* was getting old. "Actually, Claudia, I have a few questions."

Her entire body tensed up. She sat back, clasped her hands together, slender fingers grabbing at one another.

"Oh?"

"For instance, when you divorced Marvin Del Vecchio, why didn't you take the children with you? Most mothers do that."

If the impertinence of the question bothered her, she didn't show it. She reached forward and picked up her coffee cup with a shaky hand. Claudia took a delicate sip before answering.

"When I divorced Marvin, my children were eight and ten. He told me I could have them, that he wouldn't stand in my way. It wasn't until after I moved in with Paul and filed for divorce did I find out Marvin had persuaded the judge — a friend of his — that I was an unfit mother. Marvin cited two occasions on which I raised my voice in a restaurant — we Italians do that — as an indication of a bad temper. Also, the fact I had moved in with Paul, unmarried. I did not think that would be reason enough for the children to be taken away from me, but it was."

"And remaining unmarried meant you still qualified as one of the heirs in Lionel Del Vecchio's will."

She set the coffee cup down and looked down at her fingernails, long and bright red. "You know about that?"

"I know a lot of things."

"Then you should know Marvin has… had… something on this judge. I don't know what, but… " She broke off talking.

"You're saying the judge was pressured by Marvin into doing what he asked?"

"Yes. I was only allowed to see my children once a week until each were sixteen years of age."

My eyes narrowed on her. "That was a heavy price to pay for a man."

She would not be goaded. Smiling, she said, "But what a man."

Her answer, while flippant, had a ring of truth to it. Outwardly, she came across as one cool number, somewhat like the image Lila projected. But there the resemblance ended.

There was no way my mother would have left her children behind, no matter what the scenario. I knew that in my very being and had it proven to me time after time.

When something happened to one of us kids, Mom was one hands-on mother. When Richard went missing at a class picnic in junior high, she formed a search party, even called out the hounds. My brother was found before he knew he was lost. As for me, a few years back when I'd been abducted, literally shanghaied, Mom scaled the pirate ship to rescue me, ruining her best Jimmy Choos in the process. That's mother love.

I felt a pang of sorrow for Donna and David Del Vecchio. When something like this happens, young children often feel their mother has deserted them, no matter what rationale is given.

"Did you fight for your children?" I asked, hoping to make Claudia lose her cool.

She did and with a capital C. "How could I fight for them? I had no money, no way to hire a lawyer. And against a judge? Marvin didn't want them. He hated me for leaving him, so he took my children. *La vendetta*. He said he would not take them if I married Paul, but why should I do that? And would Marvin have honored his word? A man who broke his word time after time? He was filled with hatred. He hated his father for writing the will in such a way he could claim none of it. But Lionel knew his son was a bitter, dislikable man filled with hate. Marvin hated his own son for being a better magician than him and threw him out of the house. He treated Donna like a slave. She married the first man to come along just to get away from her father. I'm glad he's dead, although I had nothing to do with it. How I managed to stay with him for as long as I did, I do not know."

Wow! And this was said almost as a run-on sentence. "And is meeting Paul Renkin what prompted you to finally leave Marvin?"

She pulled herself together, shrugged her shoulders, and picked up the cup and saucer again. "I fell in love. Real love. Something that made me feel good about myself. I sacrificed everything for it, and I don't regret one day."

Her words hung in the air for a moment. I digested the certainty of them.

"Did you know your daughter has disappeared?" I watched her closely.

She didn't look me in the eye, and once again, studied her fingernails. Pretty, but not that engrossing. And the gesture told me something.

"You know where she is," I stated. "Where?"

"She is safe." This time she looked directly at me. Then she put down her coffee cup again and stared at me in what one could only say was a dismissive way. "I think you should leave."

I stayed seated. "When did you last hear from her? Because I don't think she's safe anymore, if she ever was."

For the first time, a frown crossed her lovely face. "Of course she is."

"You know your son-in-law, Steven, is dead. Murdered. You know that, don't you?"

Her face blanched, leaving what looked like a clown-like application of makeup. "Yes. I… I received a phone call from the police. But he was not a nice man. I never liked him."

"When did you last hear from Donna?"

"Last night. No, the day before yesterday. But she said—" Claudia broke off. She looked confused but rallied. "Please leave. It's time for my mother's pills." She rose and left the room.

I let myself out, got into the car, and thought about my meeting with the magician's second wife. I wrote a quick text.

Richard, High Priority: 1 - find judge in Marvin/Claudia Del Vecchio custody battle for children. 2 - what possible secret could Marvin hold over judge to win custody?

The phone rang just as I pressed send. Gurn.

"Hi, darling," I said before he could utter a word. "I'm close by. Redwood City. I decided to pay a visit to Claudia Del Vecchio. It was on the way home, and she agreed to meet with me."

"Learn anything?"

"She was more revealing than she meant to be. She's a romantic but loves money just a little bit more. She admitted Del Vecchio tried to blackmail her into marrying Paul Rinken and giving up the inheritance in order to have her children with her. She refused. She also knows where Donna is. Or was. She believes her daughter is safe. However, the last time Claudia heard from her was the night Del Vecchio was killed."

"You think that's significant?"

"I do. There's a part of her that's as gullible as Donna seems to be. Initially, she believed her husband when he told her she could have the children when she left him, even though she says Marvin broke his word to her repeatedly."

"It could be she chose to believe him, so she could do what she wanted to do, be with Paul Rinken."

"And even though Marvin would be true to his nature, it wouldn't be her fault. Yes, I can see that. The art of self-deception."

"Well, now that we've psychoanalyzed her into oblivion, I have some updates myself, courtesy of Richard, on Miss Italy. He and Andy found out a few interesting things. Should I wait until you get home to tell you? I picked up club sandwiches and barbeque chips."

"Good idea. I'll be there in about fifteen minutes. Is there iced tea in my future?"

"Ask and ye shall receive."

"I'm askin'."

"You're receivin'."

Chapter Sixteen

I arrived back at the apartment to find Gurn sound asleep in the easy chair, head thrown back and snoring softly, Baba curled up in his lap. Tugger lay on the armrest, doing his imitation of the sphinx. Upon hearing me tiptoe in the room, cardboard box in hand, Tugger leapt down and came running to me with a silent meow.

I put the box down, lifted My Son the Cat in my arms, and kissed his little white forehead, brushing one soft, orange ear with my cheek. He began to purr. My blood pressure dropped about fifty points. I carried Tugger to the sofa and lay down myself, him still in the crook of my arm. I fell asleep in an instant.

Forty-five minutes later, I awoke to sounds in the kitchen. I looked around me. Gurn and the two cats were gone. That could only mean one thing: dinnertime. I sat up, stretched, and headed for the kitchen. Gurn was setting our small kitchen table with compostable, eco-friendly paper plates and napkins, and utensils, two unwrapped sandwiches, and two bottles of chilled iced tea.

When Gurn heard me enter the room, he turned to me and smiled. I hurried over and went into his arms. We kissed long and languorously. For that moment, there wasn't anything or anyone else in the world but the two of us.

Then Tugger let out a yowl. We broke free and looked over at him sitting in front of his empty cereal bowl. Baba was sitting in front of hers giving us a mournful look that said she hadn't eaten for a week. This was even though Tío had fed them in the morning and left a bowlful of kibbles for the rest of the day.

"Why don't you continue setting the table and I'll feed the cats?" I asked, laughing.

"Sounds good," he said with a chuckle.

I opened an overhead cabinet, reached in for two cans of deluxe cat food, and locked the first one in the electric can opener. *Whir, whir, whir* went the blade, completely cutting the lid from the can. The lid lifted off when I raised the blade, and I put the canned shrimp into one bowl. Repeating the procedure, both cats were fed in nothing flat, and I didn't even get my hands dirty. Modern appliances. You gotta love 'em.

I sat down opposite Gurn, and we dug into our own dinners. Club sandwiches with extra avocado, just the way I like it. I crunched down on a potato chip, then asked, "So, what did Richard tell you about Claudia?"

"Not Claudia, but Paul. But in a way, it's the same thing. Let me consult my notes. I scribbled down a few things while Rich was talking." He picked up a small pad sitting on the table beside him. "Apparently, Paul's health club empire is on the verge of bankruptcy. The pandemic didn't do anyone any good, and he borrowed some serious money just to stay afloat during that time. A balloon payment is due in thirty days of nearly two million dollars. If he can't pay it, which, according to his bank statements he can't, the bank forecloses on his business."

"Richard got into his bank statements? Of course. There is no firewall too high. But are there other assets? What about the house in Redwood City? Whose name is that in?"

"Hold on," he said, grabbing his notepad again. "The house is in his name. But it has two mortgages on it already. The only other thing he owns outright is a ten-year-old BMW."

My brain went into overdrive. "Del Vecchio seems to have died at a very convenient time for the two of them. Now that he's dead, couldn't Claudia take a loan against her share of the inheritance? She could cosign a loan for Paul or something like that, couldn't she?"

I looked at my CPA husband and waited for an answer. For this he didn't have to look at his notepad.

"It all depends on how the trust is worded, but with a good lawyer or accountant, more than likely."

"Offering your services, Mr. CPA?" I teased.

"I'll pass." He smiled, then winked at me. Becoming serious again, he said, "Essentially, if the bank wants their money and not a chain of health clubs, they'd probably cooperate."

"Or Claudia could borrow the money from one of her kids, now that they will be getting over fifty million each. Especially Donna. From everything

I've heard, she's a pushover." I took a healthy bite of my sandwich and mused while I chewed. I swallowed quickly, then said, "Unless she's already been done away with, which means everyone in the tontine splits her share of the money. In that case, it might be better for Claudia if her daughter was dead."

"Boy, you don't think much of her maternal instincts."

"Going to worst-case scenario. Who came up with this ghastly tontine idea, anyway? It just appeals to the baser part of human nature."

"Sobering thought," Gurn said, taking a slug of iced tea.

"When's the reading of the trust slash will, anyway? Did Richard find out?"

"Wait a minute." Notepad time again. "Friday, 3:30 p.m."

"When are they releasing the body to the family for burial?"

"Not set yet. The postmortem hasn't been completed. More tests."

"The ME is unclear on the way he died? Big clue: no head."

"Protocol, I suspect."

"Another way of saying bureaucracy. You know," I said, downing some iced tea myself, "if we didn't need to have our wits about us when we go to see David's act tonight, I'd be drinking a martini right now."

"And I'd be joining you. Want some good news?"

"Yayyy."

"Andy found Elizabeth Hofsted and Marvin Del Vecchio's marriage certificate in Sofkee Lake, Florida, population four thousand and thirty-three."

"They were married there?"

"Yes. The San Francisco Police found a postcard in the back of a drawer of Del Vecchio's desk. It was from Elizabeth's mother and dated decades ago. She lived in Sofkee Lake."

"She still with us?"

"No. Gone since 1990. As the postcard didn't have anything to do with their investigation into you; Fenner passed the tip on to Frank, who passed it on to Richard, who passed it on to me."

"Well, God bless. That means Fenner knows we're looking for the beneficiaries."

"Not officially, but yes. Rich passed the info to Andy who followed up, as there was no record of Elizabeth Hofsted and Marvin Del Vecchio being married in California. He called the one and only church in Sofkee Lake. And sure enough, Reverend Handler, age ninety-one, searched his files and found the original marriage certificate dated November 14, 1985. It had been filed at the Sofkee Lake county seat, but the administrative building for the county and all its records were destroyed when Hurricane Kate hit the Panhandle a few weeks later. It's not like today. The 'cloud' only began to take shape in 2002. According to Rich, the only place the certificate could have lived after the hurricane was where the marriage was performed."

"Good ol' Mother Nature."

"Andy asked the reverend to make a copy of the license and email it to him. At least that can happen."

"Did it get sent yet?"

"No, the rev promised to do it as soon as possible, maybe tonight. He was scheduled to do a baptism this afternoon."

I sat back, thinking. "Does Richard know what the postcard said?"

"I have the answer to that, too," he said, swiping his phone. "Rich sent me an image of the postcard. Here's what it says: 'Dear Beth and Marv, thought you would like to know Beth's old boyfriend, Harlan, is running for mayor. Love, Mother.' Not much info there."

"Actually, quite a lot. First of all, Elizabeth was called Beth. And if she had a boyfriend in Sofkee Lake, odds are she had some sort of life there. When did Mrs. Hofsted move there?" Gurn shrugged. "Is there any date on the card?"

"I'll zoom in as much as I can," Gurn said, pushing a few buttons on his phone, then shook his head. "Nope, can't make it out. Too blurry."

I picked my phone up from the table, called Richard, put the phone on speaker, and set it back down on the table. When my brother answered, I said, "You're on speakerphone, Richard. Sorry to bother you at home, but—"

"I'm not home, Lee," he interrupted. "I'm still at the office and was about to call you. Found the judge. And in less than five minutes. You know, say what you will about AI, but when you know how to use it, it's a powerful tool and faster than any real person could be."

"Spoken like a true IT guy."

"Thanks."

"Wasn't necessarily meant as a compliment."

"Hardy har har. His name is Judge Matthew Macleay. Several years after handling the Del Vecchio custody hearing, his wife divorced him when she found out about his visits to underage prostitutes."

"That could be what Del Vecchio had over him."

"Probably. Macleay liked to drink and play poker with his cronies, of which Del Vecchio was one."

"And spilled more than whiskey at these games, I'm guessing."

"Then he was impeached."

"Impeached?"

"All judges must comply with the California Code of Judicial Conduct, which contains standards for ethical conduct. Judges or justices that violate any of those standards may be removed from office, making them no longer eligible for election by the voters. Visiting underage prostitutes falls into that category. That's probably why he's living in Tennessee now, running a tackle shop."

I let out a huge sigh. "I don't think there's anything here that helps my case. So, let's get back to the postcard Fenner found in Del Vecchio's desk and why I called. Is there any way you can see the date and year the stamp was canceled?"

"Way ahead of you."

“I hate it when you say that.”

“Sorry,” he chortled. “But that’s another reason why I’m here and not home. I enhanced the card as much as I could. Still can’t make the day out, but the year is 1988. And before you ask, this Harlan’s last name is Steiner. Easy to find since he ran for mayor. He didn’t win. And Andy had to hear five minutes on why him not winning ruined the entire town.”

“Andy spoke with him?”

“Yes, but I got a verbatim report. Elizabeth Hofsted — or Beth as she was known then — was the new girl in town in 1983.”

“So that’s when she moved there.”

“But Harlan didn’t know from where or couldn’t remember. They went together a couple of months their senior year in high school.”

“Does he know where she is now?”

“Nope. He was a bit of a player back then. He said she was something to pass the time. Andy had to remind him who she was.”

“Did Harlan have any pictures of her?”

“Not one. His wife is on the jealous side, and he had to get rid of every picture of every girl from his past. From what Andy says, Harlan probably had to hire a U-Haul truck to take them all away. And another hardy har har.”

“What did she look like?”

“All Harlan could remember was she was tall, brunette, and always wore pink accessories.”

“Did he know what color her eyes were?”

“Not sure. Maybe hazel, maybe not.”

"What about the high school itself? Do you think there's anything there?"

"Lee! I don't know how we let that get by us. Didn't think about checking with the schools. I'll get on it right now. Sorry about that."

"Don't worry about it, Richard. We're all tired. Go home now. You've been pushing yourself like crazy."

"No more than you, and we're on a time crunch. I'm not going anywhere. Vicki understands."

"You're just the best, brother mine. What you've done so far is outstanding." We hung up, and I turned to Gurn. "You heard all that?"

"I did. Do you think you should talk to this ex-boyfriend yourself?"

"No, Richard and Andy pretty well covered it. This is so frustrating. Where is this elusive first wife of Del Vecchio? Maybe the marriage certificate will give us something."

"I wonder if she was as good looking as the other two wives?" Gurn asked.

"Don't be such a man."

"Sorry," he laughed. I joined him, then sobered.

"Actually, she probably wasn't. You heard Richard say this Harlan couldn't remember what she looked like, not even the color or her eyes."

"Well, that's sad, but then she probably didn't have twilight-colored eyes like you. Large, deep, and memorable." He leaned across our small table and kissed my nose.

"You talked to Frank, right?" He nodded. "I take it police didn't find any pictures of Elizabeth with they did the house search." He shook his head. "Nothing else?"

"Unfortunately, no, *mi cielo*," hubby said. "Frank said Del Vecchio seems to have destroyed everything from his first marriage."

"Guilty conscience. He dumped her the way his mother got dumped by her first husband."

"If the postcard hadn't been shoved to the back of the desk drawer, we wouldn't know about Sofkee Lake."

I slumped down in my chair. "Boy, I could sure use that martini right about now." I sat bolt upright. "Wait! Idea. They had a formal wedding. Maybe they hired a professional photographer. People usually do. Maybe we can track him down and find some pictures of Elizabeth or people attending the wedding. It was nearly forty years ago, but it's better than nothing."

"And here comes the bad news."

"Uh-oh."

"Reading from notes: Wedding photographer retired in 1996 and died in 2004. His wife had a garage sale and sold everything off. Anything left of his work or where it is now, is anybody's guess."

"Make that a double martini."

Chapter Seventeen

After a quick shower and a change of clothes, Gurn and I headed out for Milpitas, almost directly across from Palo Alto but in the East Bay. Milpitas, Spanish for "little place where corn grows," is a city in Santa Clara County, and has become home to numerous high-tech companies, as part of Silicon Valley. But what it's really famous for, in my opinion, is the Great Mall, Northern California's largest indoor outlet shopping center. "If you can't find it there, you can't find it anywhere"– another one of my mottos. I got a million of 'em.

Just as we entered California Highway 237 East, I got a phone call from Richard.

"Hi, Richard. Don't tell me you've got something so soon?"

"That was a good idea about the schools. There are only two, Sofkee Lake Elementary, grades one through eight, and Ponce de Leon Senior High, nine through twelve. So, I went directly to the high school. Being it's ten p.m. on the East Coast, they're closed, but I got into their mainframe."

"Richard! For shame. But go on."

"Listen," he said defensively, "they should have better firewalls if they want to keep people like me out. Anyway, Elizabeth Hofsted graduated from

156

there in 1985. Not much about her is online, but it did mention she was an honor student in science."

"Any school photos?"

"Not online. They probably have their yearbooks in the school library. I'm going to send Andy down there in person tomorrow morning to have a look. We can't keep doing this online because we get virtually nothing."

"Well, we don't think she went to college, because she married Marvin Del Vecchio the same year she graduated, moved to California, and there's no record of her here. Was anything about their wedding in the local papers?"

"Yes, but the pictures are fuzzy and far away. Not one close-up of the bride. Even when I try to enhance her face, I don't get much."

"So, we still don't know what she looks like. Jeesh, I've never known a person to be so elusive."

"We'll find her. Don't worry."

But I did worry.

Bo's Ale House was off Town Center Drive. It was fairly new, and from what I understood, still trying to compete with established wine and beer places for the patronage of the eighty or so thousand of the Milpitas population. If all the cars I saw crammed in Bo's parking lot meant anything, Bo's Ale House needn't have worried. Not only was their parking lot full, but so was nearby street parking. Gurn finally found a place three blocks away, and we walked back to the ale house.

Plastered on walls, signs, and streetlights were posters advertising David Del Vecchio, winner of this year's *Magicians and Their Magic* television show. In equally large letters was the announcement of his last two-weeks' appearance at Bo's Ale House. I paused mid-route and looked at his smiling face on a poster, playing cards flying through the air from open hands.

David Del Vecchio's features were similar to that of his mother, Claudia, only more masculine. There was no doubt about it. He was a handsome young man and came across as very likable. In short, he didn't look one thing like his father.

Loitering around outside the ale house were dozens of people—mostly young—laughing, chatting, and having a grand old time. Several of them stood in front of the door but stepped aside to let us enter.

We went into a dimly lit room, smaller than I thought it would be, with a couple of tables and chairs scattered around. The room may have been underwhelming, but not so with the décor.

The walls and ceiling of Bo's Ale House were painted a flat black. This was done to set off the multitude of neon signs hanging on three of the four walls flickering in intense, vivid colors. Depicting images of anything alcoholic, some had sayings such as, "It Must Be Five O'Clock Somewhere" or "It's Always Beer Time."

A few were even animated. A turquoise waterfall cascaded into a sky-blue pool surrounded by head-bobbing pink flamingos and lime-green palm trees with bright orange trunks. Another neon tableau was the outline of a tipped, crimson-colored wine bottle. A dazzling yellow cork tumbled from its mouth, arse over teakettle, followed by blindingly scarlet-red wine pouring out of the bottle. The scene repeated endlessly.

Feeling a headache coming on, I was about to whip out my sunglasses when I noticed the fourth wall where the bar stood. Less dramatic, the backlit shelves glowed in a soft white behind rows of beer and wine bottles. In front of this presentation, sat a long, carved, mahogany-wood bar contrasting with the flat black paint. Draft beer dispensers with tap handles displaying brands, most unknown to me, took up an area of the back counter, along with glasses, mugs, and steins. Two dozen or more tall stools surrounded the bar with enough people sitting on them drinking beer to prove it was the beverage of choice.

Near where we stood was a long line of people holding tickets or their phones. The line snaked from the front door to the back of the room where another door led somewhere. Standing next to this "somewhere" door was young woman in a black T-shirt with the Bo's Ale House logo written in neon green and blue. She was taking tickets or scanning phones as fast as she could. I later found out the other room was larger, containing a stage surrounded by small tables and chairs.

The waiting mob was talking and laughing at the top of their voices, so if I had anything to say to Gurn, it'd have to keep. He gestured for me to follow him to the bar. A thin guy with a green waxen look to his face, thanks to a nearby neon sign, moved over to an empty stool and let us have the last two seats together. I smiled a thank-you and he nodded.

A redheaded, bearded man in his mid-to-late twenties stood behind the bar. He also wore one of the logo T-shirts stretched over a beer belly. He came in our direction, leaned over the bar, and grinned at us.

"It'll quiet down in a minute," he shouted. "As soon as everyone gets inside to see the show. What'll you have?"

"We wanted to see the magic act," I yelled, cupping my hands in front of my mouth.

He said something neither one of us heard. He tried again, louder this time. "You got tickets?"

We both shook our heads. Then he shook his, pulled at his beard, and shrugged. The line behind us began to peter out, and the din lessened to a dull roar.

"Too bad," he yelled, then lowered his voice a notch or two. "Show is sold out for the next two weeks. Then Dave goes to Vegas for a two-year contract."

Gurn leaned forward and called out, "He must be pretty good."

"The best." He made the statement with a lot of pride.

"He a friend of yours?" I asked. Most of the audience was inside now, and we could actually have a conversation.

"He is. He's been doing us a favor by appearing here for free for the month. We've been trying to settle in, and it hasn't been easy."

"You Bo?" Gurn asked with a smile.

160

"Bo's my wife. Short for Bonita. I'm Phil. Bo and I went to Cal with Dave, and we all became friends. What'll you have?"

"I'll take whatever's on tap," Gurn said.

"Got stout, lager, wheat beer, pilsner, ale, India pale ale, porter, brown ale, and bock. Take your pick."

"Surprise me."

"Don't do that to me, man." His tone was friendly and good-humored. All three of us laughed.

"In that case, brown ale," Gurn said.

"Good choice. How about the lovely lady here? he asked, turning to me.

"What kind of chardonnay do you have?"

"We got eighteen."

"Now it's my turn to say surprise me."

"This is not a problem. I'll bring you Bo's favorite, a crisp chard out of Napa."

Phil walked away to get our orders, and Gurn and I looked at one another.

"Okay," Gurn said, "how do we get to see David Del Vecchio?"

"I vote we tell Phil the truth. When in doubt..." I shrugged.

Loud cheering, a drumroll ending with the crash of a cymbal, followed by a round of applause came from the other room.

"The act must be starting," Gurn said.

Phil returned with a large glass of a dark-colored ale and a frosty wineglass filled with a pale gold liquid. I waited until he set them in front of us.

"Phil," I said, "I'm going to tell you the truth."

"People usually do. I'm a bartender."

"You heard about David's father?"

The smile left his face. He reached for his beard again. "Sure did. His father died in a pretty gruesome way. But he was a pretty gruesome man."

"You knew him?"

"Sure. Last time I saw him was when he came here the first day of Dave's act. Made a scene right before Dave went on. It was almost like he was trying to throw him off his game, you know? But Dave's a professional, through and through. Went on like nothing happened. Besides, he was used to his father trying to destroy his life."

Gurn didn't say anything but took a healthy swig of beer.

"How do you like it?" Phil asked.

"It's good," Gurn replied.

Phil had a smile of satisfaction on his face, then turned to me. Even though I hadn't tasted the wine yet, I gave an obligatory, "Yum, yum." I leaned forward and lowered my voice. "Listen, Phil, my name is Lee Alvarez. I'm a private investigator, and I've got to talk to David about a few things. It's important." I pulled one of my cards out of my clutch bag and handed it over.

"Your name sounds familiar." He looked at my card, then studied my face as if trying to link the two together.

"You've probably seen my picture in the papers. I was acting as Del Vecchio's assistant when he died. It's a long story."

"You're the one that cut off his head," he said, pointing a finger at me.

"No, she didn't," Gurn put in. "She happened to be onstage when it occurred."

Phil took a step back and looked at me. "But you're tagged with it."

"I am," I agreed. "But I didn't do it."

He studied my face again. I saw him reach for his beard, but he stopped midway. He leaned on the bar in between the two of us and studied a water ring on the wood.

"You want the truth? There's about ten people I know who would have liked to see him end up the way he did. I'm one of them, if I could've figured out how to do it," he added, raising his head and looking me in the eye. "You know, Dave had to work his way through college. All that family money, and he was a waiter living off tips and student loans. Bo fed him spaghetti and meatballs for years. He couldn't afford a car, so I drove him wherever he needed to go. Sometimes when he didn't have rent money, he crashed with us."

"Sounds like you three are tight," I said.

"He likes to say Bo and I are the family he can count on. And in case you think it's him, Dave was right here doing this act when the axe fell. We'll both swear to it."

"I don't think he did it, Phil. But he might be able help me find out who did."

Phil thought again, tapping my card with the tips of his fingernails. "Tell you what. I'll send Dave a note, tell him you're here. If he wants to see you, you'll have to wait until the show is over, go backstage, and talk to him there. He's an easygoing guy, always willing to help. That's why he's working here free for us, when he could already be in Vegas making ten thou a week. Ever since he won that *Magicians and Their Magic* TV show, his career went through the roof." He leaned in again. "I'll tell you, though, on the QT, he's a little shaken tonight. We all are."

"Why?" I asked. "What's going on?"

"Dave nearly got killed crossing the street this afternoon. A car came out of nowhere and nearly ran him over. Fortunately, Dave is quick on his feet, but I saw the whole thing, and that car looked like it was coming right at him. I don't know how some people get their driver's license."

"What kind of car?" This time Gurn asked the question.

"I don't know. Big. SUV. It happened so fast. But he's all right, though. You never know what life's going to throw at you, do you? 'Live for today', that's my motto."

And another great motto surfaced.

"Listen, back to his father's death," Phil said, taking in both of us. "If you try to take Dave down for it, Bo's going to come after you. And you don't want that."

He grinned. I grinned back. We both looked at Gurn.

"She doesn't sound like anyone I'd want coming after me," Gurn said with mock seriousness.

"You'll meet Bo after the show. She's the stage manager. And the house manager. And the stage-door johnny." He looked at his watch. "You've got about an hour to wait. Want some fries?"

Chapter Eighteen

Nearly an hour and a half later, Bo showed up. I was not prepared for Bo. Her straight brown hair was short and no-nonsense. She wore no makeup but had about four or five pierced earrings in each ear and each finger sported a ring. She wasn't quite my height but probably had a good seventy-five pounds on me. Not fat. Muscle. Her arms were as thick as tree trunks, as was her neck. Everything about her screamed muscle. If Phil had included the title "bouncer" in her list of credits, I would have believed it. Even with my karate skills, I wouldn't want to meet her in a dark alley.

Then she smiled at me. Her whole persona transformed. Her blue eyes sparkled, and her features softened. She became a sincere and friendly person.

"Hi," she said, and reached out a hand to shake. "Sorry to keep you waiting, but sometimes Dave's fans just won't leave. You must be Lee Alvarez." She shook my hand briefly, then turned to Gurn.

"Are you a marine, mister?" Still smiling, she reached her hand out to him.

He took it and shook. "Navy."

"I knew it! I thought you looked familiar. I saw you at Cal. Officer. You teach NROTC."

"No longer, but I did."

"I was on the ladies weightlifting team. I used to watch you and the cadets do warm-up exercises on the field. I liked to do the jumping jacks with you. See if I could last longer than you or your men."

"And did you?"

"Sometimes." Her laugh was wholehearted and honest. "After Cal, I was going to join the marines, but I married this hunk right here, instead."

She walked over to Phil and wrapped her arm around him, squeezing him tightly. He took on a slightly pained expression.

"Easy, babe," he said, kissing her on the cheek.

"Sorry, honey," she said releasing her husband. She turned back to us. "Now I run a powerlifting gym during the day and work here at night. But enough about me. I talked to Dave. He wants to see you. I'll take you back to his dressing room."

We followed Bo into the other room, weaving in and out of small tables and chairs until we came to the small stage. Bo hopped up from the floor to the stage not using the three steps. Gurn followed suit. I thought about doing the same thing just to be one of the gang, but it had been a long day.

"Dave," Bo yelled out. "I have those people to see you."

"Come on in," a voice said from behind a closed door. "But open the door slowly. I don't want you to scare anyone."

Anyone? I thought. Gurn took his time opening the door, but gestured to me to enter first. I stepped inside a tiny space that looked more like a supply room than a dressing room. A folding chair sat in front of a small desk being used to hold a mirror on a stand. Two gooseneck lamps were on either side of the mirror, more or less for light. Two more folding chairs sat facing the small desk.

David Del Vecchio was sitting on a small sofa against the back wall spoon-feeding a floppy-eared puppy. Two more puppies were lying in a cardboard box cuddled up next to one another and sound asleep.

"Come on in, and sorry I couldn't come out to greet you." He glanced up at us and then back down to the tan pup. "But they have to be fed every three or four hours. They're on soft food now. I give them Gerber's. They love it. I'm almost done with the last one."

My eyes filled with tears. That's what puppies and kittens do to me. "Oh, they're adorable. Where did they come from?"

"Their mother was hit by a car, so here they are. I'm their foster daddy until we find them a home. I work with the ASPCA. But if I have to take them with me to Vegas, and find them a home there, that's what I'll do. Right, Buddy?" David picked up the puppy who yawned the answer in his face. With a laugh, David returned him to the cardboard box, where the puppy cuddled with the others.

"We hear you had an incident yourself, with a car today," I said, watching his expression.

"Phil mentioned that, did he? It was no big deal. I was crossing the street against the light, and I just didn't see him."

"It was a man?" I asked.

"No idea. Man, woman, something. It was totally my fault. As I said, I was crossing against the light."

"That's not quite how Phil described it. He said it looked like the car came out of nowhere and headed directly for you." I studied his face, waiting for the answer.

"Phil reads too much crime drama. I'm the one that came out of nowhere." That done, David changed the subject. "So, you're Lee Alvarez?" he asked.

"I am. But I want you to know right up front, I did not kill your father."

"Of course you didn't," he said with finality, screwing the lid on the jar of baby food and standing. He crossed to a small fridge sitting on the floor. He went on talking while he opened the door and put the jar inside. "When the police were here to tell me about my father, and what happened, I knew it couldn't be his so-called new assistant. Anyone who knows anything about these tricks knows how complicated they are. In order to sabotage one, you'd really have to know how they work. How could you do something like that after only being with him for two days? And if I know my father, he gave you as little information about the guillotine as possible. Take a seat. Who's this, your husband?"

"Oh, yes," I said. "I'm sorry. David Del Vecchio, my husband, Gurn Hanson."

The men shook hands while I sat in one of the metal chairs as tenuously as possible.

"I think I read about you, too." He looked at Gurn.

"You flatter me," he said. "But Lee and I have had our share of adventures."

Gurn also sat down on a metal chair but didn't look like he put his full weight down. The chair let out a groan anyway. David noticed and smiled.

"Sorry about my 'dressing room,'" he said, emphasizing the last two words. "It's really for storage. I'll be fixing it up for the next act before I leave. The whole cabaret thing was Bo's idea, give them wine or beer and a good show for an extra twenty bucks. I'm being followed by a country-and-western singer. So, what can I do for you?" he asked, sitting back down on the small sofa, looking directly at me.

"First of all, condolences about your father."

It was his turn to study me. "Thank you, but I think you know we were estranged most of my life. My father was not always the nicest person sitting at the dining room table. I'm sorry he died the way he did, but frankly, I don't feel much, other than sorry for Donna. She took his death hard."

"Did you tell her about it? How else would she have known?"

He became a little guarded. "No, she knew."

"I'm hoping you can tell me where your sister is." An emotional wall shot up between us. "I'm asking, David, because I'm worried about her safety. I know you two are still close, despite the impression you tried to give your father. I've seen her emails or, rather, our IT guy has. We know you're in contact with her almost daily."

David's demeanor changed. The cordiality disappeared, and he became serious and withdrawn. "I really don't have anything more to say. Forgive me, but if that's all you came for, I think you should leave."

"Oh, fer cryin' out loud," I said, exasperation filling my voice. "Your mother said the same thing when I asked her. What's going on? I believe Donna to be in danger, but you two seem to know something you're not saying."

He thought for a moment, then looked at Gurn. So did I. Taking his cue, Gurn said, "If you think you're protecting her by being silent, you're not."

David leaned over and stroked a sleeping puppy. I could tell he was thinking. I felt my phone vibrate inside the small bag my hand rested on. I ignored it and watched the young magician. He sat back again, shaking his head.

"Four days ago, Donna received a phone call from Steven. The way she tells it, he sounded scared. And she'd never known him to be scared before. Usually, he's cocky. I never liked him. The way I saw it, when Donna married him, she married a man like our father, abusive and controlling. People often do that. We tend to gravitate to what we know, even if it's painful." He paused. "I think you can tell I've been in a lot of therapy. I only wish Donna had done the same thing. I'm not a psychiatrist, but I think Donna suffers from BPD or borderline personality disorder."

"I've heard of that, but what is it exactly?" I asked, looking from one man to the other.

Gurn jumped in. "If someone has BPD, they usually have a lack of sense of self, or loss of identity. It sometimes happens to soldiers in the field."

"People with borderline personality disorder," David said, "may experience intense mood swings and feel uncertainty about how they see themselves. Their feelings for others can change quickly, and swing from love to hate in an instant." He added, "The result in Donna's case is, she can sometimes be persuaded to do things she doesn't want to do by people with a stronger personality than hers. Like marrying someone she doesn't want to marry."

"Or talked into killing someone?" I asked.

He shook his head vehemently. "No, never! At least, I don't think so." David looked sad and lost in thought.

"Let's go back to four days ago. What happened?"

David seemed to come out of his trance. "One of the men Steven testified against in the bank swindle broke out of jail. Just jumped over the fence and walked away. When he went to jail, he swore to get Steven for what he did to him. Not only Steven, but his wife, too. Of course, Steven took off, leaving Donna to suffer the consequences. But maybe he had a twinge of conscience later on, because he called her the next day and told her to leave the Bay Area. They have a cabin in North Tahoe, really off the grid. Not even electricity. That's where she went."

"Who did she tell about this?" Gurn asked.

"Mom, me. She might have told Madison. They were close, but she'd never tell her father. He probably would have called every news station in town and used it to advertise the show. He was like that."

"So," I said, "Donna is at their North Tahoe cabin, hiding out?" He nodded. "When did you last hear from her?"

"Night before last."

"The night your father died," I said.

He nodded again. "But I can't call her. No service. When she needs to make a phone call, she drives four miles to a public phone off the highway. Her carrier doesn't even have service there."

"Did you expect to hear from her yesterday or today?"

"I did, yes, but then I read on the news feed earlier today they captured this guy outside of Arizona. He never even came into California. But I wish Donna would call. I don't think she knows any of this unless she has a portable radio with her."

My phone buzzed again. Two times at ten o'clock at night? Had to be important. I rose. "Excuse me for just a moment; I have to take a call."

I went for the door while Gurn, always a master at filling in time said, "Tell me about your big win on *Magicians and Their Magic.*"

I was back in about five minutes. As casually as possible, I said, "Something's come up, and we have to go, David," I said, standing in the doorway. "Thanks for your help."

Gurn had a look of surprise on his face but covered it. He unwrapped himself from the metal chair and stood. "Yes, thanks. And good luck in Las Vegas."

David, also surprised by the abrupt ending to our conversation stood as well. "Of course. Anytime," he said, looking from Gurn to me.

"Where are you staying?" I asked, seemingly out of the blue. "I know you've been touring for the better part of a year. Do you still have an apartment in the Bay Area?"

"Ah… no. I'm staying—" He looked down at the puppies in the cardboard box and corrected himself. "We're staying with Bo and Phil. Up in the Oakland Hills." He grinned. "Just like the old days when I crashed on their couch in college. Only now I have my own room." He looked at me, curiosity written all over his face. "Did you want to… send me something?"

"No, no. Just being nosy."

I let out a light laugh along the lines of *aren't I amusing?* David joined me, polite guy that he was. A silent Gurn came and stood by my side, apparently waiting for me to take the lead.

"Well, thank you again, David, and as Gurn says, good luck in Vegas."

I turned and left the small room, followed by Gurn. He whispered in my ear, "What was that all about?"

"Later," I whispered back.

When we were outside and clear of anyone overhearing us, I turned to him. "That phone call was from Frank. Madison Del Vecchio was found locked in her car in her garage about two hours ago. Carbon monoxide poisoning."

Chapter Nineteen

"Oh my God! Is she—?" He broke off there.

"No, but it's touch and go. Madison would be dead if the maid hadn't forgotten her phone and went back for it. Frank says the maid tried to go into the house via the garage. The garage door was locked, but she could hear a car running and smelled the carbon monoxide. She ran into the house and tried the inside door. It was also locked, so she called the police on the landline. They were there in less than three minutes. It doesn't take much carbon monoxide to kill a person, but the doctors are hopeful she'll pull through."

"I wonder if this means what I think it means?" He looked at me.

I looked at him. "That someone tried to kill her because she's one of the inheritors of the will?" I asked. "To be open-minded, it could be a suicide attempt."

"Does she strike you as the suicidal type?"

"Not as long as there's a plastic surgeon plying his trade. That's why I wanted to know where David was staying just in case someone is trying to eliminate the competitors. The fact he's staying with friends makes him safer."

"Especially if one of those friends is Bo. Phil wasn't kidding when he said you don't want to be on the bad side of her. But, sweetheart, don't you think we should have told David about Madison?"

"He'll know soon enough. Frank told me Fenner's men are on their way to talk to him now. I can't help but wonder, where was Madison's secretary, i.e., watchdog, Johan? Doesn't he live in the house?"

"He does," Gurn said slowly. "So, where was he?"

"And after that question, is Donna as okay as her family seems to think she is? I've got a bad feeling about this."

By this time, we had arrived at the car. He beeped the doors open and we got in. I shut the passenger side of the car before going on.

"You know, darling, I've been thinking," I said, clicking my seat belt on. "When all this first happened Saturday night I was so shocked I wasn't thinking clearly. And then I was put on such a tight time frame to clear myself, I went into a panic. But I've calmed down now. A lot of what has happened doesn't make sense unless someone very close by is responsible. And whoever it is, has to have help."

He started the car and pulled out before asking, "You're kidding. You're saying we're looking for a murderer and a helper? Who? Donna?"

"Don't know yet. But either way we need to find her. She might not be as safe as everyone thinks she is."

"So, you *don't* think she killed her father?"

"No, she could have done that."

"So, you *do* think she killed her father?"

"Possibly. That said, she could have just been in the wrong place at the wrong time."

"I'm confused."

"I suspect that was the plan all along. The art of confusion and misdirection. We need to get to that cabin as soon as possible. Can you fly us there tonight?"

Gurn's latest plane, a Cessna Citation M2 was capable of night flying, but I knew there was more to it than just getting into the plane and taking off.

He didn't take his eyes off the road, but I could see him processing this request by the expression on his face. "You want to fly to Tahoe? Right now?"

"I think we need to, yes."

"Okay, easier said than done. First of all, I'd have to file a flight plan, and I don't even know where we're going."

"Richard gave me the cabin's address and the coordinates."

"Then I'd have to see if any small airports nearby are open," he added, almost as if I hadn't spoken. "Most of them shut down at ten p.m. except for emergencies. Which means we'd have to land in Reno and rent a car. If you think we should go, fine, but it might be quicker and easier to drive."

"You're probably right. It's about four and a half hours from here."

"Four, if I put the pedal to the metal, and there's no one on the road," Gurn interjected.

"Okay, Speedy Gonzales, let's get home, change clothes, and leave." I looked at my watch. "That should get us there at about three a.m."

"The element of surprise," he said with a grin. "Love it."

"While you drive us home, I'm going to read my texts. I think everyone in the world was trying to reach me over the past two hours."

The first text was from my friend, Janina:

Hi Lee. I'm not sure if this is important, but Dad says that the tunnel used to have two separate entrances when the saloon was there. One was off the saloonkeeper's office and the other was at the back of their taproom. They would take the shanghaied men out from both places. The two tunnels joined about fifteen feet away from the building and continued to the wharf. When the theater was built, one tunnel was at the end of the dressing rooms hallway. That's the tunnel you chased whoever into. The second tunnel was originally off the greenroom, but when they redid the theater back in the seventies, they switched rooms around, and Dad can't remember where the second entrance is now. But he does remember it was on an outside wall. He says he doesn't think it can be used since the remodel.

"But that might be wishful thinking," I muttered.

"What did you say?" Gurn gave me a quick look, then his eyes went back to the road.

"Just thinking out loud about that stupid tunnel, darling. Not to sound Shakespearean, but it vexes me." I went to the second message, which was from Richard. It was so long, I knew immediately he'd dictated it, same as Frank does.

Andy received copy of marriage certificate from Florida. Not much help. Elizabeth Hofsted

married Marvin Del Vecchio on November 14, 1985, two weeks before Hurricane Kate hit, destroying the courthouse records. I'd give you the names of both witnesses, but no point. They've passed on. The reverend doesn't remember anything about the wedding, it being nearly four decades ago, but he does keep notes from each event. He'd made a note in the margin of the vows he read at the ceremony to wear his lifts. He's around five foot four and self-conscious about it. Other than that, nada, but we'll keep searching for Elizabeth. People can't stay off the grid forever.

I thought about when he wrote for a minute, then texted back.

I don't understand this. I thought everyone was on the internet one way or another. I can understand before 1985 because the internet was just starting, but after that, how could it happen now? Please explain.

My brother sent back a message only seconds later.

If someone knows what they're doing, information can be rerouted or deleted. But I'll find something eventually, don't worry.

Hurriedly I wrote back.

So, you're saying that someone has deliberately deleted or rerouted information about her?

His answer came almost immediately.

You can erase info from most places if you know what you're doing, and that seems to be what happened. But not everything. There's always one thing people forget about. I will find

Richard's remark about the grid made me stop reading and think about Donna and the Tahoe cabin. I turned to Gurn.

"Darling, do you have the pedal to the metal?"

"I'm behind a sixteen-wheeler. Not happening."

"Oh well." I heard a ding and found there was another missive from Richard.

"Wow!" I exclaimed after reading that.

"What?" Gurn asked.

"Let me read you this last part Richard wrote about Madison's watchdog, Johan Nilsson." And I did.

"A total change of identity, down to the accent," Gurn said, after giving off a soft whistle. "Something about him didn't seem real. Remember when we watched *The Farmer's Daughter* on TCM with Loretta Young? Most of the actors were doing a Swedish accent. Some were good, some were a little forced. When I talked to Johan at the tennis courts, his accent seemed a little too Hollywood to me."

"Putting his acting skills aside, darling, that begs the question, just what was he doing in that household being a secretary to Madison? Hiding out?"

"It begs another question, too, sweetheart. Did the lady of the house know?"

"Not to jump ahead of myself, but if it wasn't an attempted suicide by Madison—which I don't think it was—is he the one who tried to kill her?"

"But why?"

"She could have discovered his true identity."

"Or, as I say, she may have always known."

"Darling, are you going to play the devil's advocate for everything I say?"

"Yes," he laughed. "And you wouldn't have it any other way."

I laughed, too, but stopped when I heard another ping on my phone announcing a new message. This one was from Frank, short but not so sweet.

Madison Del Vecchio was no attempted suicide but attempted murder. Contusion on back of head. Hit from behind. Still touch and go. Don't do anything stupid.

I read the message to Gurn, leaving off the last sentence. No point in stating the obvious. We both became lost in thought for a moment. Gurn was the first to speak.

"So where does this leave us, sweetheart?"

"With a lot of suspects and not a lot of facts. Here's what we know so far: Less than forty-eight hours ago, Marvin the Magnificent was murdered onstage and very dramatically. A couple of days before, his daughter, Donna, went missing with her dog. The day before that, her husband, Steven, disappeared. Then last night I found his body at the family cabin in Tahoe." I let out a long sigh. "Was it only last night? It seems like a century ago. And it's possible Steven's death isn't connected to his past life as first thought."

"And now an attempted murder on Marvin's widow, Madison."

"All of this has to be tied into elder Del Vecchio's strange trust. Has to, has to. But why now? It's been in place for decades."

"Hmmm. That's an interesting question. Why now? Someone's sudden need for money?"

"We know that's true for Claudia Del Vecchio, ex-wife number two. The man she's devoted to, Paul Rinken, is about to lose everything if he doesn't get a large influx of cash. And Mr. Wong, with his grandchild at death's door, needs money for the operations to save the baby's life. It's a now-or-never scenario for both of them."

"What about the other heirs? Have a gut feeling about anyone in particular?"

I shook my head. "No. I just plain don't know enough. Was Donna in Tahoe when her father died? Or is her family covering for her? And, though it's unlikely, is she the one I saw in the wings right after the blade fell? And if not her, who? And while David Del Vecchio seems like an upright guy, he had a lot of reasons to want his father dead."

"About fifty million of them. But he was nowhere near the theater when it happened. That said, he, Phil, and Bo might be in this together. Maybe he rigged the trick sometime during the day before the performance. Could he have done that?"

"Maybe," I mused before adding, "because I don't have any idea how Marvin's death was rigged to happen. With David being in the same business, however, he could figure a way. If he wanted to."

"Can you rule anyone out? Like the Mill Valley nephews?"

"I don't see how. They need money to expand, and there's bad blood between both sides of the family."

"And then there's Marvin's three wives."

"Now I'm starting to get depressed. We can't locate wife number one, but she was divorced from him twenty-eight years ago. What would trigger vengeance on her part this late in the game? Besides, she may be dead for all we know."

"Well, there's a thought that should cheer you up."

"You'd think, wouldn't you? But it doesn't."

"I believe we can rule out Madison," Gurn said, pulling into the driveway and around to the back of the small complex to our garage apartment. "She seems to be one of the victims."

"I hope so. Or she's a complete dunce. If she was guilty and wanted to throw suspicion off herself, a smart person would have chosen another method."

"You are saying she's not too smart?"

"I don't see Mensa sending her a membership application anytime soon. However, that said, most people know carbon monoxide kills in a very short amount of time. You can read about it on the internet. The Great God Google spares no details."

"That's true. If the maid hadn't forgotten her phone, Madison wouldn't have been found when she was."

We exited the car, shutting the car doors as quietly as possible, so as not to disturb Mom and Tío only yards away in the big house. Keeping his voice down, Gurn continued.

"But how is Johan, aka Edgar Smith, tied into this?"

"Not a clue," I whispered. As we climbed the stairs to the apartment above the garage, I continued in a more normal voice. "And here's a long shot. Is Henry Swan involved? If anyone knows how to rig that trick, it would be the creator. And no one would have thought a thing of him being backstage and checking the guillotine out. I'll have to check that out."

"How does Swan become a suspect?"

"He might have had to refund ten thousand dollars to Marvin, had he lived. People have killed for a lot less money, especially if they feel they're being cheated. He's got a great cat and all that, but he could have done it."

"And the list ever lengthens," Gurn said.

"You ain't kidding. I've got suspects coming out of the woodwork. Everyone but the tooth fairy."

"That puts us back to the number one question: who rigged the guillotine trick to turn deadly?"

"And equally important, why now? Into this conundrum, darling, we need to put Carl. After his stilted three-word message, he still hasn't reported in. For all we know, he may be in trouble. Mom left me a voice mail. She's worried about him. She called Frank for help. She's never done that before."

"We need to get to that cabin, Lee." Gurn's expression was grim.

We opened the door to find the cats curled up on the sofa sound asleep. It didn't take us long to change city clothes into something dark, comfy, and warm down to the boots. After that, I went into the kitchen with the intention of giving the little darlings enough food to last into the next afternoon in case we were delayed coming back. But Tío had already fed and watered them, even topping off their dry food bowl. A quick rush to clean out the litter pans, a kiss on top of kitty noggins, and we were off.

Gurn and I'd had a brief discussion about whether or not we should tell the family where we were heading. My vote was no. Putting aside it was after 11:00 p.m. and Mom, Richard, and Tío were probably sleeping, I had three big reasons: 1 - Mom would probably insist on coming along because of Carl's silence. She has a way of doing that. 2 - Richard would load us up with all types of electronic gear for going "into the wilderness," and 3 - Tío would probably pack all the coffee, sandwiches, and snacks that would fit into a small suitcase. Between the three of them, we wouldn't get on the road until sunrise. I elected to call them in the a.m., once we knew what was what.

As it was my family, Gurn acquiesced. That's another way of saying you give in to the person even though you know they are wrong. And man, was I wrong.

Chapter Twenty
Tuesday

Even though this was my bright idea, four-plus hours on the road at three o'clock in the morning after a long day felt more like ten hours. Gurn and I took turns driving, while the other one dozed in the passenger seat. Once we arrived in North Tahoe, we had to leave the main road for a dirt road and then onto what was little more than a wide trail. And, oh, lucky us, it was also pitch black, no moon. When we got to the approximate location, trying to find the spot met with a series of dead ends. Even with four-wheel drive, the trip was an absolute nightmare. And thus, I groused my way to the cabin.

Fortunately, Gurn wears a watch that not only tells time in every zone of the world, the nautical depth to which the wearer dives, and everyone's birthday, but if you put in the coordinates, it will guide you to the longitude and latitude of any place, no matter how obscure. I was driving at this point when Gurn looked at his watch and said, "Pull over. The cabin should be about a quarter mile ahead. We'll go on foot from here."

I stopped the car next to thick brush and scared a jackrabbit half to death. He came leaping out of a bush and ran like he had someplace better to be. I could sympathize.

"Okay," Gurn said, once we alighted from the Jeep. "Let's get organized."

It was a cold night, having dropped down into the mid-forties. But I stopped wrapping a scarf around my neck and concentrated on his words. I often bow to his experiences in Afghanistan and other tours of duty when we're on reconnaissance.

He grabbed a large bag and pulled things out, setting them on the hood of the Jeep. "Here is a flashlight, nighttime goggles, hunting knife, and a Glock."

"When did you have time to get all this stuff together?"

"When you were cleaning out the cats' litter pans."

"For the record, I brought Lady Blue and my own flashlight." I tapped the two front pockets of my jacket with its large, deep pockets. "In this case I think my Detective Special might do the job. Small and convenient."

"Not as accurate as the Glock, but if that's your weapon of choice, we'll go with it. I'll throw the extra Glock in the trunk."

"Although I am glad to have the nighttime goggles," I continued, taking them from his hand. "Could I dispense with the hunting knife? It's uncomfortable in the pocket of these jeans. They're a little tight."

"Even though we're hoping none of this will be necessary, attach it to your belt or stick it in your boot. It's in its own sheath."

"Okay." I didn't bother telling him I wasn't wearing a belt, so I stuck the sheathed knife in my boot and maneuvered it around until I could walk comfortably.

"So, now what?"

"Put the goggles on. This way we don't have to use flashlights. But keep your flashlight handy." After putting on the goggles, he went over to the dirt trail, and squatted down. "These are fresh tire marks. They'll probably lead us to the cabin. Let's go."

Nighttime goggles are weird. Everything has a green, surreal look. I wouldn't want to try to apply makeup with these things on, but it is amazing how you can find your way in the dark. Gurn followed the tracks, and I pulled up the rear. In about fifteen minutes, a clearing came into view with a small cabin dead center. A faint light came from one of the windows. In front of the cabin sat two cars; one looked like Carl's Tesla. My heart skipped a beat.

I would have said something to Gurn, but he was in scouting mode and already at a side window of the cabin, the one that showed the faint lighting. He pulled off his goggles. I joined him, pulled my goggles off, and looked inside.

The shadowy lighting came from a kerosene lamp sitting on a narrow table next to the window. Sitting next to the lamp, Johan/Edgar was absorbed in a *Superman* comic book. I took my time scrutinizing him. As with his pretend name, he could have been of Norwegian stock. His pale skin and straight white-blonde hair fairly shimmered in the soft illumination of the kerosene lamp. In one ear, a small, gold hoop earring reflected light as he moved his head from side to side, looking at the pictures. He was not a large man, maybe my height, slight and with delicate features. It gave him the look of an artist. But looks can be deceiving. Here was a young man who was known to be dangerous.

As if I needed any more proof, my eye caught the Beretta 92 sitting on the narrow table next to the kerosene lamp. It lay accessible and within easy reach. I withdrew Lady Blue and continued assessing the cabin.

This was a true, rustic cabin, one Abe Lincoln might have built back in the day. Maybe twenty by twenty, everything including the—ha-ha—bathroom was contained in the one room. The bathroom consisted of a commode and small sink, angled in a corner off the minuscule galley kitchen. A curtain on a clothesline hung nearby. Obviously, it was pulled in front of the commode when necessary for privacy's sake.

Part of the kitchen was a stone fireplace with a kettle hanging on a swinging hook above the remnants of a fire, a few glowing embers still visible. In front of the hearth, a small table was littered with dirty mugs, plates, plastic flatware, a jar of instant coffee, tea bags, and leftover take-out food. On one side of the fireplace, Carl was sitting slumped over in a kitchen chair, his hands and feet tied. A makeshift bandage was wrapped around the back of his head, blood showing through the fabric. He was either asleep or unconscious. Either way, he didn't look good.

On the other side of the fireplace was Donna. While her feet were tied, her hands were free. In her lap the small Pomeranian, Honey Boy, lay curled up and sleeping. Donna was not asleep. Every now and then she would swipe at her eyes and nose. She was crying, silently crying.

I felt outrage hit me, the likes of which I've seldom felt. Gurn tapped me on the shoulder. He indicated he was going to the front door, probably to kick it open. He gestured for me to stay where I was, keeping Lady Blue aimed at Edgar. I didn't have to be told that if their captor reached for his gun, I would fire at him through the glass. I'm a good shot, even though I hate firearms. I have to put in a certain number of hours at a firing range every year to keep my PI license. And it's for moments like these.

I nodded to Gurn and off he went, Glock in hand. As for me, I hoped not to have to shoot Edgar, but if he reached for his Beretta with the man I loved at the door, I'd do what had to be done. I released the safety and took aim.

The night was deathly quiet, so the sound of Gurn kicking the door in, practically breaking it off its hinges, was deafening. Out of the corner of my eye I could see Carl stir at the noise. But Donna screamed and instinctively tried to stand up. With her feet tied, she fell over to one side, the little dog leaping to safety. Honey Boy began to bark furiously, running halfway to the crashed door, then back again to his mistress. But I concentrated on Edgar, my finger on the trigger.

Edgar also leapt up, but instead of reaching for his gun, he backed up against the far wall, holding his hands in front of his face and body, as if for protection. Gurn was across the room and on him in an instant. He threw Edgar to the floor facedown, forced his hands behind his back, and wrapped a black nylon tie around his wrists. Then pivoting around, Gurn sat on the backs of his legs to keep Edgar from kicking, then tied his ankles together. Pulling the knees up into a bent position, Gurn took a third tie, swung himself to the side of Edgar, and tied the man's wrists and ankles together. All done in less than fifteen seconds. If this ex-SEAL were in a calf-tying contest, he would have won first place.

I ran around to the entrance and pushed aside the splintered door hanging by the bottom hinge. Once I saw Gurn was on top of things, literally, I ran to Carl's side and bent down, calling his name. He opened half-dazed eyes, trying to focus on me.

"Lee?" he muttered.

"Carl," I said. "Talk to me. Can you do that?"

But he shook his head. Head lolling to the side, his eyes closed.

Meanwhile, the dog continued to yap, sixty yaps per second, standing at his mistress's feet. Having untied herself, Donna stood up but was crying and wailing loudly into her hands. She showed no signs of stopping.

Between the two of them, I couldn't even think, much less talk to Carl. I left Carl's side, went over to Donna, grabbed her by the shoulders, and shook her. Shocked, she stopped crying and stared at me. Honey Boy stopped yapping, too, and stared up at both of us, his small head turning from one to the other.

"Donna, talk to me. What happened to Carl?"

"Who... who are you?" She looked at me with red and swollen eyes. "You look familiar. How do you know me?"

"We met at the theater. But we can talk about that later. How long has Carl been like this?"

Donna's voice came out loud and strong. "Too long. Ever since Johan... uh... Edgar hit him over the head. Edgar shouldn't have hit him so hard. I did what I could, but—"

"Shut up," Edgar said, nose on the floor, his voice slightly distorted. "Just shut up. He'll live."

"He has a concussion," she answered back, stronger than I would have thought. "He needs medical attention. I told you that."

"Lee, go get the car," Gurn said to me, now standing at Carl's side and checking his vitals. "Drive it as close as you can. I'll carry Carl out. We need to get him to a hospital as soon as possible."

"What about me?" Edgar spat.

"I'd make myself comfortable on the floor," I said, heading to the door. "Until the police arrive for you." I turned back to Donna as Gurn untied an unconscious Carl. "Come on, Donna."

Donna tapped her chest three times, and Honey Boy leapt up in her arms. She followed me to the door but literally swooned when she stepped over the threshold.

"Oh my God, Donna," I said, grabbing the dog from her and setting him down. As she leaned against the doorframe, I wrapped an arm around her and guided her to a rickety chair on the small front porch. "Sit down. I'm so sorry. I was so worried about Carl, I forgot you've been kidnapped for nearly four days. Do you need some water? I think I saw a bottle of water on the table in there."

"No, no. I think I'm just a little weak from hunger. I'll be all right."

"You mean he didn't give you any food?" Outrage ran through me again like a rogue wave.

"He brought me a sandwich now and then, but truthfully, I gave most of it to Honey Boy. He was starving."

I looked at the small dog panting at her feet. Truth be told, that's what I would have done had I been in the same situation and the cats were dependent on me.

"What's going on out there?" Gurn demanded. "We need to get Carl to a hospital."

"I'm on my way," I yelled back. In a quieter voice, I said to Donna, "You stay here while I get the car. And I have a Milky Way bar in the glove compartment. That'll hold you over till we get to the hospital."

She gave me a faint smile. "I love Milky Way bars."

Chapter Twenty-One

Gurn and I stood in the doorway of the small hospital room. Donna was sitting up in bed, but her head lay back on the pillows, and her eyes were closed. Even her youth couldn't hide the fatigue and strain that showed on her face from the past few days. A saline bag with fluids led into one hand. Across from her, a television hanging on the wall had a commentator giving a blow-by-blow of a soccer game. I turned to Gurn.

"Do you think she knows? About her father and husband?"

"A good question. I was careful not to say anything in the car and she didn't ask."

"No, she didn't. And that makes me wonder. But now that we're back in civilization, if she doesn't know, do we tell her or wait for the police to do it? Or is she going to hear it on the news first?"

"We'll have to play this by ear. If it were me, I'd rather hear it from someone like you than the police. Although, if she's sleeping, we shouldn't wake her up."

I nodded in agreement, knowing he was right. But there were questions that needed to be answered, and some couldn't wait.

The rustling sound of my jacket as we tiptoed in made her eyes pop open. "How is he?" she turned her head to us and asked. "The man, how is he? I've forgotten his name."

"It's Carl," Gurn said. "He's in surgery now. We'll know more in a few hours."

"Oh God," she said, running her hand across her forehead. "I knew it was bad. When I was allowed to check him, his pulse was weak, and his lack of response bothered me. I worried he might slip into a coma at any time."

"You sound like you know what you're talking about," I said.

"Not really, but I wanted to be a nurse, an RN. I finished the first year's courses when Father told me to give it up to be his assistant. His last assistant quit, and Father said he didn't feel like training another one. But nursing is all I've ever wanted to do. To help people get better when they're sick." Her voice was filled with such yearning, I felt my eyes well up.

I sat down on the edge of the bed and took her free hand. "Well then, that's what you'll do as soon as you get out of here. The doctors say they'll release you tomorrow morning. They want to keep you overnight for observation and to get your fluid levels up. But first, the police may want to question you about what happened and... other things." I paused. "Donna, you've been through a lot, but I would like you to consider hiring me to investigate, among other things, your kidnapping. You don't have to pay me anything, but it will give me greater access to find out what's going on."

"Investigate? I thought you were a showgirl or something."

"I'm something, all right. But I make my living as a private investigator. I'm also the lead suspect in—" I stopped talking. I didn't want to throw anything at her she didn't know yet. "Donna, how much do you know about what's been happening in the outside world while you were kidnapped?"

She leaned so far back into the pillows, it was as if she were trying to become part of them. "You mean that my father and Steven are dead? Edgar told me. Again and again, he would tell me. He bragged about it."

"I'm sorry. What an appalling way to learn," I said.

She looked down and grabbed a piece of the blanket with her free hand, twisting and turning it with trembling fingers. "At first, I didn't believe it—him. But then he brought me online printouts for both, describing their murders. I was terrified. He told me I would be next if I didn't—" She let out a sob, then turned anxious. Donna leaned forward, grabbing my hand. "Mom's all right, isn't she? And David? He didn't hurt them?"

"No, he didn't hurt them," Gurn stepped in to say. "In fact, they're on their way here now. You'll see them soon."

She looked at him, searching his face for the truth. Apparently, she believed what she saw and relaxed. Donna turned back to me.

"Your name's Lee, isn't it?" she asked.

"Yes, Lee Alvarez."

"And you say you're a private investigator?"

"Yes, for Discretionary Investigations. My mother, Lila Alvarez, is the CEO. We were at the

theater undercover, looking into Steven's part in…
something else."

"Do I want to know what this something else
is?"

"Not right now," Gurn said.

"Your mother's got a nice singing voice for a
detective," Donna commented after a beat.

"Thanks. I'll be sure to tell her. That's why we
were there. And then when you didn't show up for
rehearsal, I filled in as your father's assistant."

She reflected for a moment. "He was not a nice
man," she said with a shaky voice. "But he didn't
deserve to die the way he did."

"No, he didn't. And because I was onstage at the
time, I'm being blamed for his death."

Her eyebrows rose and astonishment showed
on her face. "But Johan… er… Edgar—I keep
forgetting his real name was Edgar—Edgar told me
he did it. He said it again and again. Why would
they think you did?" She looked at me, then at
Gurn. "Thank you for rescuing me. I didn't think
they were ever going to set me free, not from what
he was saying."

"They?" I jumped on the word. "Who is 'they'?"

"W-what?" she stuttered.

"You said you didn't think *they* were ever going
to set you free," Gurn said, coming closer.

She became agitated. "I don't know. I never saw
anybody but him, but… there was something…"
Her voice dropped off and we gave her time to
think. After a moment, she shook her head. "I guess
I don't know why I said it. If you hadn't come
along… Of course, I will hire you to investigate

what happened if you think it will help. Are you sure you don't want money or something?"

"Just a handshake will do," I said, reaching out my hand. She took it and we shook hands on it. "Now that we've got that settled, do you feel up to calling Mr. Wong and then handing the phone over to me? It's important or I wouldn't ask right now."

I handed her my phone. She dialed the number of the mansion in Sea Cliff. A man answered, probably Mr. Wong.

"Mr. Wong? It's Donna."

"Miss Donna! Are you all right? Where are you? Are you all right?" His response was so loud, we heard it from where Gurn and I were standing. And very un-butler-like.

"I'm fine, Mr. Wong."

"Praise be to God!"

From the sound of his voice, he cared about her. She looked at me. I nodded and reached out my hand for the phone. Before she handed it over, she said, "Mr. Wong, forgive me for making this short, but when I come home, you and I will have a nice long chat. I'll explain everything then."

"I look forward to that, miss."

"But meanwhile, Lee Alvarez is here. She is investigating… things… for me and wants to talk to you. I want you to give her all the help you can. Please."

"Of course, miss." His voice became more formal and businesslike.

I took the phone from Donna's hand. "Good morning. Mr. Wong."

"Good morning, Ms. Alvarez. How may I help you?"

"My associate, Gurn Hanson, and I need to see Johan Nilsson's room."

"I understand, Ms. Alvarez."

"Has anyone been in there besides the police?"

"No, ma'am. They were in his room this morning, and I locked it after they left."

"If I drop by sometime tomorrow, would that work? I would do it this afternoon, but we're still in North Tahoe."

"I understand. Anytime you and Mr. Hanson want, Ms. Alvarez. If I'm not here, I will arrange for someone else to let you in. Meanwhile, I will keep Johan's room locked until you arrive."

"Thank you, Mr. Wong."

"My pleasure, Ms. Alvarez." I hung up from my trip to Downton Abbey and turned to Gurn. "Being I'm not sure what tomorrow brings, if I can't go, will you?"

"Sure. What am I looking for? Or will I know it when I see it?"

"Go with that," I said. "I think it's vague enough."

We both laughed. Donna gave us a shy smile.

"I wish I'd had the relationship with Steven you have with your husband. The only thing he liked about me was my money."

"Well, that was his loss," I said.

"Why don't you tell us how you wound up in the cabin," Gurn said.

"When I got the phone call from Steven that morning at the theater, Johan—that is, Edgar—

overheard my end of the conversation. I was pretty freaked. I was shaking so much I knew I couldn't drive a car. Edgar offered to help me, drive me to the cabin. I was so grateful. He was Maddie's secretary. I knew him for months. I thought I could trust him. Maddie said I could."

"So, she knew where you were going?"

"Yes, I told her. And she promised to make it seem like I'd showed up eventually."

"Who else knew where you were?"

"I called my mother and David from the pay phone near the cabin to tell them what I was doing."

"Did you tell them Edgar was with you?"

"No, I just wanted to get to the cabin. I thought they might ask a lot of questions if I mentioned it. But when we got to the cabin, I wished I had said something. Everything changed. He—" She broke off and covered her face with her hands. "He scared me, threatened me."

"Donna, a little earlier when he said you would be next if you didn't do something, what was Edgar coercing you to do? Can we talk a little about that? Do you have the energy?"

She nodded but looked down and didn't say anything. We gave her all the time she needed. Finally, she said, "He wanted me to give him the numbers to a bank account in the Cayman Islands. I didn't know what he was talking about. Then he told me about Steven, what he did with all my money. That he'd even embezzled some of Father's money. Over a half a million dollars! He'd sent it to the Cayman Islands. Steven told me he lost it in bad investments. He lied to me. But Edgar wouldn't believe I didn't know anything. Last night he said if I didn't tell him soon, he would kill Honey Boy, the way he killed Father and Steven." She fought back sobs, then grabbed at my hand. "You're sure Mom and David are all right? It seems like everybody around me is dying. Even that man, Carl. What's going on? What's going on?" she repeated, her voice rising in pitch and in volume.

"Easy, you're safe now," Gurn said.

"Was Edgar at the cabin with you all the time?" I asked. "Or did he come and go?"

"He came and went, but he would be gone for hours at a time. That's when he would tie me up. Then, and when he was sleeping. When he was gone, I would scream my head off, but nobody could hear me. Steven was so paranoid. He built that cabin in the middle of nowhere. He'd go there all the time. I hated it, but he said it was his refuge."

"Then yesterday morning Carl showed up, right?"

"I thought he was going to save me. But Edgar hid behind the door and hit him with something when he walked through. So hard. I could hear the crack. It was terrible." She paused for a moment, then almost whispered, "I'm worried about Maddie."

"Madison?" Gurn asked.

"Yes. Last night he also said something about hurting Maddie. He's like the Grim Reaper. He kills everyone he comes near."

Gurn and I exchanged looks. We silently agreed not to tell her about the attack on Madison. It might be too much.

"He's not going to hurt one more person, Donna. I promise you." I stood and straightened the bedcovers around her. "Why don't you try to get a little sleep before your family gets here?"

"But what about Honey Boy?"

"He's fine," Gurn said. "We've got him. Try to let the sedative they gave you kick in. Try not to worry."

"Honey Boy's down in the car playing with one of the cats' chew toys as if it were his own. Fortunately, he can't read, so he didn't notice Tugger's name on it," I added. I deliberately made the small joke, and she smiled more than laughed, but at least, her face took on a little color. "We'll keep him with us until you're released. And he had his dinner and breakfast. Have they fed you yet?"

"Yes, a little while ago. Food never tasted so good. What time is it? Edgar took my phone."

"Nearly eight a.m.," Gurn said. "Try to rest."

"I'll try. Other than being tired and a little dehydrated, the doctors told me I'll be fine."

"And you will. Here's another Milky Way bar in case you find the need for it." I pulled it from my pocket and handed it over. "The worst is over, Donna. At least for you," I said. "You're going to be all right. Your mother and brother are fine. You'll be together soon. Probably within a couple of hours."

"You're so sweet, Lee. Thank you." She took the chocolate bar, but her hand dropped to the bed as if it weighed a ton. "I'm so tired." Donna's head lolled to the side, and she was fast asleep.

I watched her for a moment, then heard the sound of a woman clearing her throat. I turned to see Police Chief Dabuda Lel Ti standing in the doorway, gesturing for us to join her.

Once she knew she caught our eye, she backed out into the hall. We hurried over to her. I quietly shut the door to Donna's room. Without any kind of fanfare, Chief Lel Ti looked at me and said, "He's gone."

Chapter Twenty-Two

"Who's gone?" Gurn asked. "Edgar Smith?"

"I don't believe it," I said.

Chief Lel Ti turned to Gurn. "And you would be?"

"Oh, sorry, Chief," I jumped in with. "This is my husband, Gurn Hanson. Gurn, Chief Dabuda Lel Ti."

The two shook hands with a somberness people often do when trouble's the main reason they're meeting. The chief of the North Lake Tahoe Police studied the man in front of her.

"This is the Lt. Commander Gurn Hanson into whose custody you've been released? They neglected to mention he was your husband."

"Slight oversight, I'm sure," Gurn said with ease.

"No doubt," the chief said with the same amount of ease, fighting off a smile.

"I don't understand," I said, going back to Edgar's escape. "When Gurn hogties them, they stay tied."

"Not when someone cuts the ties," the chief said, waving the cut tie in front of us again.

Gurn took the tie from her and studied it. "It's been cut, all right. What time did you get to the cabin?" he asked.

"Your call came in at four-ten a.m. My people got there at four thirty-five."

"A twenty-five-minute window," Gurn said. "That has to mean someone was waiting nearby. Maybe a lookout?"

"No," I said, shaking my head. "We were followed."

"You sound very sure of that," the chief said. It wasn't exactly a challenge but close enough. Before I could say anything, Gurn turned to me.

"I never saw anybody. And I checked continually."

"We were driving from the Bay Area," I said. "If someone was following us, it wouldn't have taken long to figure out where we were heading, especially if they made it their business to know. Then they either beat us there or took another route."

"Who is 'they'?" Lel Ti demanded.

I let out a defeated sigh. "I wish I knew. Donna told us she didn't think *they* were ever going to set her free. Even if she didn't realize what she said, if it came from her subconscious, I think there's validity to it. And it confirms what I've been saying. There are two people involved in this: the one who calls the shots and the one who obeys."

"Two of them? So, which is Edgar Smith?" the chief asked. "The leader or the lackey?"

"He didn't strike me as leader material," Gurn said. "Hasn't the brains or guts."

"I totally agree," I said. "There's someone else."

Frustration erupted from Chief Lel Ti. "Then who? I've got one dead body, a kidnap victim, a man who was beaten into a near coma, and an escaped suspect. And it's not even nine a.m. yet." She took a deep breath. It seemed like she was willing herself to relax. "Every available officer is searching the woods for Smith. If he's there, we'll find him."

"Chances are," Gurn said, "whoever cut Edgar free took him about as far away as they could get."

"Nonetheless, it's protocol," the chief said with a shrug. "I have to search. Meanwhile, let's go back to the station. You two need to make a statement." She turned and took fast strides toward the hospital's elevator, Gurn right behind her. I loped along. As we waited for the elevator, I asked, "Is there any update on how Steven Kutner died?"

She hesitated slightly before answering me. "Well, I don't see any harm in telling you. Besides, if I don't, someone else will." The inference being Frank. "The ME says his lungs were filled with chlorinated pool water. He looks like he was struck with a blunt instrument and was unconscious when he went into the water. Oh, by the way, I found a special-delivery package on my desk today from a Richard Alvarez, Discretionary Inquiries, Inc. Any relation?" She looked at me.

I was so startled, I tripped over my own foot. I tried to recover and smiled. "Yes, he's my brother and the director of Information Technology at our agency."

"Uh-huh."

I got the big stare but kept smiling. When it was evident I wasn't going to say anything more, the chief continued. "In his note, he said you came across the enclosed flash drive on the ground near your car after you and Chief Thompson discovered Steven Kutner's body. You brought it to him to see what was on it. Once he opened the files, he discovered files belonging to our victim, and thought he should send the drive on to us."

She scrutinized my face, searching for the truth. I continued to smile while thinking of something, anything, to say. The elevator arrived. A male nurse studying a chart was already on board. That gave me more time to come up with something as we descended to the lobby. By the time we reached the outdoor exit, I had that something.

"That's right. I found it near the car, which as you know was hundreds of feet away from the pool area so, naturally, I didn't think it had anything to do with the crime scene."

Lel Ti stopped walking and turned to me. "What made you pick it up and bring it all the way back to the Bay Area and your brother, the tech guy?"

"Oh, that's just me." I gave off a jolt of embarrassed laughter that was so high pitched, it made my ears ring. "I was more or less curious about what could be on it."

"She gets like that," Gurn corroborated.

"And you never thought it had anything to do with the dead guy in the pool?" the chief asked, her tone conveying total disbelief.

"No, I didn't. Why would I?" I challenged. That part felt right, even though I was lying through my teeth.

"I can't help but wonder, Ms. Alvarez, why Chief Thompson didn't tell me anything about it. We agreed to share information."

"He didn't know," I ad-libbed. "He didn't see me pick it up, and I didn't show it to him. I just put it in my pocket. Frankly, I didn't think much about it until later that morning when I saw my brother at breakfast. And I thought, Oh, goody. Let me show this to Richard and see what's on it. Maybe there will be some games or something. Richard loves… games," I finished lamely.

"Uh-huh."

Translating the above, that meant liar, liar, pants on fire. Chief Lel Ti continued to stare at me. I continued to smile until I thought my face would break.

"Well, I've got the disk and files now," the chief said, obviously deciding to move on. "And from what I understand, your Richard broke through the coding, so we should be grateful to him for saving us time."

"Good, good," I said, my relief almost making me drop to the ground. "I'll be sure to tell him."

I wiped my brow that had become quite dewy. Actually, sweaty. Mom likes to say, "Horses sweat, men perspire, and women glow." If so, I was glowing like a football field at halftime.

Gurn leaned in and said in my ear, "If you should ever decide to give up your day job to go into acting, don't. You'll starve to death."

"Oh, hush," I said a mite too loudly.

"How's that?" Lel Ti asked.

"Hush… puppy. That small, deep-fried round ball made from cornmeal. Delish, delish. I think I'll have a hush puppy for lunch today. Really hungry for one."

"Whatever floats your boat," Lel Ti said, stepping back, literally, and taking a neutral position. "From what I understand, you've been helpful down in the Bay Area from time to time. And I hear your father was something of a legend when he was on the force."

Once a police officer, always a police officer. A special club with loyal members. You and those around you put their lives on the line every day. I made a mental note to never abuse the position I apparently held, if for no other reason than to honor my father's memory.

The chief said, "Let's head for the station. I want to hear more about this tontine-like will. You two want to come with me or drive your own car?"

"We've got Donna's dog, Honey Boy, in the car," I said. "Even though the car's in the shade and the windows are cracked, I don't want to leave him alone for that long a time."

"In that case, why don't you follow me back to the station? You can bring the dog inside. He can meet Bowser, our hound dog rescue. Big but harmless. One more thing, I got a call from Inspector Fenner. He wanted me to tell you that Madison Del Vecchio is out of danger."

Without another word, she left us, walked toward the parking lot, and got into a waiting police car. We were heading for the Jeep when I stopped in my tracks as the realization of Fenner's words hit me. I turned to Gurn.

"Wait a minute. How did Fenner know where I was? I didn't tell anyone."

"That would be me, sweetheart," Gurn said. "I called Frank from the car when we took a pit stop. You don't undertake operations like this without alerting someone." He paused and winked. "Protocol."

Chapter Twenty-Three

"What have you got to say for yourself?" Frank asked when I answered the phone several hours later.

The interview at the North Lake Tahoe police station with Chief Lel Ti seemed to go on forever. I mean, how many ways can you say how you came through a battered-in door at three thirty in the morning? We handed over all weapons, which included Edgar's Beretta, to have checked for legality. Ours were legal; Edgar's was not. Then we were fingerprinted. My PI status was checked, Gurn's credentials were checked through Washington, and we wound up back in the parking lot of the hospital about three hours later. Our handguns were back safely in the trunk of the car.

Having been awakened by Frank's phone call, I pulled the lever on the passenger seat from a reclining position to sitting, and looked at the clock on the dashboard. I'd been asleep for two hours.

"And while we're on the subject of what you have to say for yourself," Frank said, "remind me to kill you."

"Will do," I said, stifling a yawn.

"Taking off like that after I told you that you couldn't leave the Bay Area unless under my supervision."

"I know. I promise not to do something like that again. Honest. It wasn't planned; it just happened. I hope you can forgive me."

"Is that from the it's-better-to-seek-forgiveness-than-ask-permission school of thought? That doesn't mean I'm not going to let you have it when I see you."

"Then you may as well know the rest."

"The rest?"

"Remember that disk I found on Steven Kutner's body? Well, I gave it to Richard, and after he extracted the files, he sent it on to—"

"To Dabuda. Yes, I know. Richard told me, and it was the right thing to do. But if you ever pull a stunt like that again, messing with evidence, I'm going to kill you."

"Absolutely. I deserve no less, but moving on—"

"Moving on?" His voice had the incredulous tone he often takes with me. "That's all you have to say is 'moving on'?"

"Yes. How many times can you kill me?"

"I'm working on that."

"Meanwhile, how is Madison Del Vecchio doing? I understand she's out of danger."

"Awake and talking."

"Was she able to say anything about what happened?"

"Fenner tells me all she remembers is going into the garage and walking toward her car. The next thing she knew, she woke up in the hospital. But she did say one thing. She said she heard what sounded like someone coming up from behind her. Then whammo. But she didn't see anyone."

"So, she was little, if any, help at all."

"It looks like Smith did all three, although how he managed the guillotine trick is beyond me. But according to the transcript Dabuda just sent me of her talk with Donna Kutner—and my God, Lee, you keep us hopping—Smith admitted to killing Marvin Del Vecchio."

"But it's *not* Edgar. Frank, he's a fanatic. I don't think he rigged the guillotine. I don't think he's capable."

"Have you lost your mind? Your saying that, puts you right back in the picture. Why would he admit to something he didn't do?"

"He's covering for the real murderer."

"Why?"

"Protecting them? Honor among thieves? Trying to feel worthy? How about love? I'm scatting here, but people do strange things for love."

"Love? You have to stop reading all those romance novels."

"I read Jane Austen, fer cryin' out loud! Those aren't romance novels. Well, yes, in a way they are. But really, they're about manners, and the mores of the time. Take *Pride and Prejudice*—"

"Let's not and say we did. My turn to move on. How's Carl Reed doing? Any good news there?"

Carl came to DI straight from twenty years on the Redwood City police force, having reached sergeant status. While he and Frank didn't know each other during that time, they'd chatted once or twice when Carl joined DI as an investigator. But as I've learned, "Once a cop, always a cop" is the motto. It's not my motto, but a good one.

"He's in a medically induced coma until the swelling on his brain recedes. They've already done surgery to relieve pressure," I said. "We'll know more tonight or tomorrow. Mom's on her way here to stay with him, as I've got to get back to meet with the judge in the morning."

"No, you don't. Donna Kutner's witness statement saying Edgar Smith told her he killed her father and husband has gone a long way to appeasing the judge. I just got off the phone with Plenca. While you're not completely off the hook, Judge Plenca has postponed your hearing in her chambers until more evidence comes in. I also lied about you being AWOL in Tahoe, and told her I had released you into the recognizance of one Lt. Commander Gurn Hanson, US Navy. I failed to mention he was your husband, as you never took his name. But I'm warning you, Liana Margaret Alvarez, you keep this up, and I'm going to throw you in the clink myself."

"Frank, you are just a prince among men."

"Never mind all that. What's going on up there? Dabuda is so busy she can't even talk to me. I hope she knows most of what she's going through is your fault."

"You don't really mean that, do you?"

"No, I don't. But it felt good to say."

"Because your words went through me like a knife."

"Oh, Lee, honey, I'm sorry." He paused. "How do you manage to do that? You take off, break the conditions of your release, endanger your life, Gurn's life, and Lord knows who else's, and I wind up apologizing to you."

"Well, I'm sorry, too, Frank. But we're both just trying to do our jobs, right?"

"Listen to me. Slow down. Seriously. You've done good so far. But whoever this is, he or she is one merciless killer. They're even making me nervous. And so far, they've been one step ahead of everyone, including you."

"I know, but I'm close to figuring this out. I can see something waving at me in the distance. Something I haven't quite gotten ahold of yet."

"I'm going to get ahold of something. And when I do—" He deliberately stopped the sentence there. "And with that, I'm ending this conversation."

"Love to Abby."

I disconnected and leaned back, closing my eyes. Then it dawned on me I was alone. No hubby, no dog. I looked over at the driver's seat, finding a note. I picked it up and read his neat, cursive handwriting, now nothing more than a dead art. When I think of the years I practiced to make my b's and p's legible only to have it come to this. But I digress. His note read,

Sweetheart, took Honey Boy for a walk and will search for some take-out lunch along the way. I'll also call Lel Ti to see if there's an update on anything and how much longer she intends to keep us

here in Tahoe. If it's overnight, we need to get a motel room. I'm too old to spend another night in the car. ∞

He always drew the infinity sign at the end of his notes to indicate his eternal love. One time he drew a heart. It looked more like a teardrop, which I found a little disconcerting.

The phone rang again. I looked at the incoming number. My brother.

"I've got a bone to pick with you, Richard," I said. "Why didn't you tell me you were sending Steven's flash drive to the Tahoe Police?"

"Well, what did you think I was going to do with it? Keeping it any longer would have been tampering with evidence."

"Which we already did."

"Yes, but this way, it looks like a chance encounter. You merely found it far away from the murder scene."

"If only I had known all of this when Lel Ti was asking me what the hey."

"Oh, pshaw —"

"Pshaw? You're pshaw-ing me?"

"Lee, I knew you'd think on your feet. You always do. My smart-cookie big sister."

Well, there's not much you can say after that, so I was quiet. Richard went on.

"Listen, I have a bone to pick with *you*. Why didn't you tell anyone you were returning to Tahoe? And in the dead of night? Our Lady is livid. And you know the Isle of Mad Mom is not a place you want to visit."

"Uh-oh."

"And Tío couldn't believe you would go away and not let him know he needed to take care of the cats."

"I already called Tío and apologized. I thought we were going to be home by morning. That nobody would be any the wiser."

"How's that going for you?"

"Boy, there's nothing like being told off by your kid brother."

"If I had only known where you were heading," he continued as if I hadn't spoken, "I would have given you one of the sat phones. There's no coverage for cells in that area. A satellite phone, as you know from your past adventures, is the only way to communicate from most geographic locations on the Earth's surface, as long there's either an open sky or a line of sight between the phone and the satellite. Both kinds of phones have their limitations, but between the two of them, you should be able to communicate from pretty much anywhere. I asked Mom, and she's bringing you one now. Carry both with you at all times. This way if you just take off again, at some point we can reach you."

"Mom is on her way to Tahoe?"

"Yes. Driving her Jag and all by her lonesome."

"Thanks for the heads-up."

"You're welcome."

"Richard, hurt feelings aside, if we hadn't left when we did, Carl might be dead. Every second counted with him. As it is, he's not out of the woods yet."

"Hmmm."

"Hmmm, what?"

"When you're right, you're right."

"Thank you, Richard. Huge relief."

"Here's what I have to add: first, be sure to tell Mom that and in those same words. It will go a long way to pouring water on milady's dragon flames that have been known to singe eyebrows at twenty paces."

"You're being very poetic. That's unlike you."

"Second, Andy took the red-eye to Florida. He's at the school now. He found the yearbook Elizabeth Hofsted is in and her photo."

"Finally!"

"Don't get your hopes up. You'd never know who she was today by this photo. Worse, the features simply aren't there to do a then-and-now recognition process."

"You're sure?"

"Yeah. You'll see when I send you the photo. Hold tight, on its way."

A split second later, there was a ping on my phone. I opened it feeling as if I'd won the lottery. But I hadn't.

"Yowzah," I said.

While in color, the picture was of a girl with long, dark hair in need of shaping, and thick bangs covering her forehead and eyebrows. Horn-rimmed glasses sat on her nose, leaving no way to tell what color her eyes were. In fact, you couldn't see much of her face at all. But what could be seen of her expression was dead serious, as if it was a mug shot instead of a senior high school photo.

"Disappointing, right?" Richard asked.

"The exact word. Were there any other photos of her in the book? She was in the chemistry club, wasn't she?"

"Science club. The only other photo in the entire book. I'll send that one on, but it's in a lineup with other members of the club, and she's standing in the back row. Compared to the other girls, she looks tall. That's about all I can tell."

I heard another ping. I studied the image. It was even worse than the first. "And still no recognizable features. So that's it, Richard?"

"That's it. Andy also checked the junior yearbook. She's not even in that one. Might have been sick that day. There's just her name in place of a photo. But while Andy's there, he's going to see if they'll give him any information about what school she transferred from. Don't hold out much hope, though. He was told a lot of the records from then were lost or damaged by Hurricane Kate. I say a pox on all hurricanes."

"What's with all these classical or poetic references?"

"If you must know, Vicki and I are taking turns reading Byron, Kelly, and Sheets out loud. I have become a poetic person."

"That's Byron, Shelley, and Keats."

"Whatever."

"About the sat phone, Richard... While I'm willing to carry it at all times, if it's not too cumbersome—"

"They're no more cumbersome than a cell phone," he interjected.

"And I thought they were way too expensive."
"Sis, be not a piker."
"The Bard?"
"The brother. Gotta go, Lee."

Chapter Twenty-Four

I laid my head back on the headrest and tried to figure out what was going on. In the past thirty-six hours—nearly forty-eight—I had made little, if any, headway. It felt like I was doing a five-thousand-piece puzzle. The one you should have never bought, have been working on for weeks, and wind up throwing across the room in frustration, box and all.

I picked up Gurn's note and flipped the paper over to the clean side. After taking a pencil from the glove compartment, I tried to marshal my thoughts as I wrote.

Marvin Del Vecchio, death by decapitation. But how was it done?

Steven Kutner, death by drowning. Are the two deaths related?

<u>Suspects for Del Vecchio's death, possibly inheritance driven:</u>

Wife #1—Elizabeth Hofsted—Whereabouts unknown. Is that deliberate?

Wife #2—Claudia Gracioso—Never married longtime lover. Money above all?

Wife #3—Madison Cartwright—Suddenly a victim. But did she set that up?

Child #1—David Del Vecchio—Estranged. Magician. Did he kill his own father?

Child #2—Donna Kutner—Kidnap victim or in league with kidnapper? All a ruse?

Nephew #1—Wyman Del Vecchio—Politically ambitious. But at what cost?

Nephew #2—Winston Del Vecchio—Needs money to expand. How far will he go?

Staff—Wong Chen—Faithful butler. What would he do for granddaughter's health?

<u>Suspects for Del Vecchio's death, non-inheritance driven:</u>

Staff—Johan Nilsson/Edgar Smith—Villain, yes, but who is he working with?

Guillotine creator—Henry Swan—Monetary troubles with deceased. Did he snap?

Assistant—Me—Idiot pawn. Rats.

I examined the list. Should I add in all the possible motives, time frames, etc.? I decided not to, I wanted to keep it simple. I studied all the names and wondered at any links between them. Then an idea popped into my head, and I grabbed my phone. Richard answered on the first ring.

"What's up, Lee?"

"How much info do we have on Edgar Smith? I'm going to check out his room in Sea Cliff tomorrow, but more of a background might be helpful."

"The kidnapper, right?"

"Right."

"Wait a minute, let me bring him up. Let's see, let's see," he muttered. "Okay, Edgar Smith, born in Boise, Idaho, twenty-six years ago. Went to grade school, high school, junior college. Nothing unusual other than him being in trouble with the law as a radical extremist and racial bigot. He does have a juvenile record, but I can't get into that."

"Richard, dig as only you can do. I want everything about him from the moment he was born—and tout de suite."

"I know you're serious when you start speaking French."

"Also, find out why Madison Del Vecchio hired him. What are his credentials as a secretary?"

"Okay. Second and third layers coming up. Sorry I don't have it on hand, but it's been a little busy. Want me to call you back when I know more?"

"Please."

"Please?" he repeated. "Now I really know you're serious."

We hung up just as I saw Gurn rounding the corner. He was accompanied not by Honey Boy but my mother. Fair enough trade. I got out of the car and stretched, then stood tall as my mother came closer.

"I ran into Lila as I walked across the hospital parking lot," Gurn said. "She's checked into the motel nearby."

"Yes," Mom said. "You can *see* it from here. It's *very* convenient."

I jumped in with, "Hi, Mom! How are you? Now, before you start yelling, let me—"

My mother looked shocked. "*Liana*, I do not *yell*. It is not *necessary* and *certainly* isn't ladylike. May I *remind* you, you were not raised in a *barn*."

"No, no, I meant… I'll start again."

"Yes, *do*."

"Hi, Mom! How are you? Let me defend my actions of last night."

"There is *no* need. Gurn has explained *everything*, and I understand *completely*. You took the *only* course *open* to you at the time and you very *well* may have *saved* Carlson's life."

I looked at Mom in wonderment and then to Gurn, who gave me his famous lopsided grin. I rallied. "Exactly. What he said. So, Gurn, where is Honey Boy? Powdering his nose or something?"

Gurn said, "After finding your mom, we met up with David Del Vecchio coming out of the hospital. Honey Boy jumped right into his arms and that was that. They are old friends. David booked a motel room with the puppies in the same motel as Lila. Pet friendly. After seeing Donna, David was on his way back to the motel and took Honey Boy with him."

"If Honey Boy's as sweet with the puppies as he was with Bowser," I remarked, "they will have another new daddy. Was Claudia with him or is she staying with Donna?"

"She *chose* not to come," Mom sniffed. "It seems *she* was needed at *home* and David came by *himself*." Lila Hamilton Alvarez can sniff with the best of them, and I could feel her disapproval at the decision Claudia Del Vecchio made. "However, *I* am going to make that *child's* welfare *top* priority along with Carlson's. It will be *incumbent* upon me to *represent* her mother. The *fragility* of this *abandonment* must be *minimized* as much as possible."

And another Charles Dickens moment descended upon us.

"Claudia Del Vecchio does have her elderly parents to take care of, in all fairness, Lila," Gurn said. "I'm sure she was torn between where to be: with her parents or her daughter."

"When I *spoke* with her and *offered* to drive her up with me, she *mentioned* she had to stay because *Paul* needed her. Well, it is *not* for me to *judge*," Mom added, in her most judgmental tone.

The phone rang just as I was searching for something neutral to say. Do not toy with Mom's judgments. I reached for my phone through the open car window, aware that Gurn and Mom were watching me.

"Hi, Richard. That was fast. What have you got? Hmmm. That's what I thought. This is our first big break. Go with it." I hung up and turned to my mother. "Mom, I'm so sorry, but Gurn and I have to head back to San Francisco."

She was aghast. "For *heaven's* sake, right *now*?"

"Right now. I don't have time to explain, but I'll call you in a little while with an update, okay? Meanwhile, please let me know how Carl is doing and give my best to Donna." I turned to Gurn. "You might want to drive, as we need the pedal to the metal. Or I will. Your call."

"I'll drive," he said.

"I *thought* we were going to have *lunch* together," Mom said, as I opened the passenger door of the car and climbed inside.

"Sorry, Mom, but duty calls, and we need to get back to the Bay Area as soon as possible," I said.

"Just a *moment*, young lady," she said. I froze. Her hand went inside her handbag and drew out a small black sat phone around the same size as my cell. "Be *careful* with this, *Liana*," she said, reaching through the open car window and handing it off to me. "*Need* I tell you it cost twenty-five *hundred* dollars?"

"Wow. Lookee here. It goes right into the side of my boot like the hunting knife did. These phones sure have gotten smaller over the past few years."

"*What* hunting knife? What are you *doing* with a hunting knife?" Mom demanded, glaring at me.

I thought on my feet. Recent events had caused lying to become easier for me. "The hunting knife I had when we went fishing a few months back. You know, for cleaning fish? I put it in my boot to keep both hands free for casting."

"I *thought* you *hated* fishing," she said.

"You know, Mom, we've really got to go."

"I *see*."

That was another version of Lel Ti's "Uh-huh." Nobody believes a thing I say. Hmmm.

"And don't forget the *solar* charger," Mom added, giving me the slim rectangular accessory. "Twenty-five *hundred* dollars, Liana," she repeated.

"Got it," I said. "Twenty-five big ones. Kind of like what some of your shoes cost," I added under my breath. Fortunately, Mom didn't hear me, she was so wrapped up in her lamentations.

"Well, I suppose if you two *must* go, you *must* go. I'll have *luncheon* on my *own*."

She looked from me, then over to Gurn, standing at the driver's side of the car. Gurn looked back at her, smiled and shrugged, then opened the driver's door.

"Theirs is not to reason why, theirs is but to do or die," he said to my mother, while starting the car.

"Shakespeare?" I asked, waving goodbye to Mom as we pulled away.

"Tennyson."

We stopped for some takeout and were on the road for about a half an hour when I remembered. We hadn't been officially told we were free to leave Tahoe yet by Chief Lel Ti. But luck was with us. I was in the process of dialing her number when she called and told us the department was satisfied. I'd have to try to remember this particular moment when everything went wrong. As usual.

Not fifteen minutes later, Richard called.

"Long time, no hear," I joked when I answered. "What's up?"

"Something not good." His voice was dead serious.

"I don't like the sound of this. What?"

"I just heard on the Marin Police scan that Winston Del Vecchio was killed in a hit-and-run accident. Not twenty minutes ago."

"Oh my God." My voice was barely audible. "One of the twins is dead?"

"Yes."

"Who's dead?" Gurn demanded to know, not quite hearing what I'd said.

"Winston Del Vecchio was killed in a hit-and-run accident about a half hour ago."

"Where did it happen?" Gurn asked.

"Where did it happen?" I repeated, then put the phone on speaker. "You're on speaker, Richard."

"Right outside his store. He was crossing the street on his way to a haircut appointment. People heard the crash and came running, but by the time they got there, Winston was lying in the street and the car was gone. Dead at the scene."

"No witnesses?"

"None that have come forward yet. But it's only just reported. I wouldn't have known anything about it if I hadn't decided to tune my scanner on to Marin to see."

"Good thing you did, Rich," Gurn commented.

"This is escalating, gentlemen," I said. "I don't think I told you yet, Richard. David was nearly run down by a car yesterday."

"In that case, Winston Del Vecchio's death doesn't sound like such an accident," my brother said.

"Two attempts on heirs in as many days. One successful and one not," Gurn said.

"I have to say," Richard said, "the Del Vecchios are dropping like flies."

"Not dropping, brother mine. Being killed off."

Chapter Twenty-Five

"You're sure about this?" Gurn asked, as he parked the car on the street.

"Well, darling, I've been thinking. Another one of the heirs might die at any minute, and I would feel terrible if I hadn't done something to prevent it."

"Time to call Fenner in."

"Not yet. I don't have any proof, and I don't want to alert anyone that I'm looking in their direction. Let's find the door first."

Being the Lithuanian Community Theater was dark with no performances for the next two weeks, it was easy to find a spot right in front of the theater. We got out of the car and headed to the closed box office. Looking though the plate-glass window, we could see it was shut up tight and dark inside.

"Where did Janina say the emergency keys are kept?" Gurn asked, following me to a corner of the exterior. There, a mural of the country of Lithuania was done in mosaic tiles. Below the mural, yellow, green, and red subway tiles representing the colors of the national flag, covered the lower wall in rows going down to the cement floor.

"Third red tile, third row down," I muttered. "Keep a lookout. Make sure no one is watching us."

He turned around to face the street, standing between me and the rest of the world.

I went to the designated tile and gave it a slight push. It popped open on hinges revealing a small tin box within a recessed hole. Inside the tin box was a key ring with two keys to the theater. I removed the keys and returned the box to the recessed hole. I closed the hinged tile and came up behind Gurn.

"Voila," I said in a stage whisper.

He turned around to face me. "Which doors do they open?"

"One for the stage door, and a master key for every room inside the theater. Very convenient. Let's go around to the back."

With a jiggle here and there, I opened the backstage door, and we went inside. It was dark and cool, but musty smelling. I reached for the light switches near the entrance, but Gurn covered my hand with his.

"Let's use the lights from our phones, sweetheart, just in case," he whispered. "No need to announce ourselves if we don't have to."

I whispered back, "You think someone might be in the theater?"

He shrugged noncommittally. "Let's keep this on the down-low."

"Okay," I hissed back, reaching inside my pocket for my phone. "Maybe we should have brought one of the weapons."

"Let's just find that door to the tunnel, get out of here, and call Fenner, if need be."

"I think this empty theater is making you nervous. It has that effect on people."

"Reminds me of a few Al-Qaeda camps I've been in."

We turned on our phone lights and headed for the stairs. Down we went, and it was the eeriest feeling I'd had in years. Pitch-black, the air so heavy you almost couldn't breathe, and deathly quiet.

At the bottom of the stairs, I turned and played the phone's light down the length of the hall toward the entrance I'd used to the now-filled-in tunnel. The light faded after several yards, and all I could see were shadows of what I imagined to be the sealed-off door.

I turned in the opposite direction and walked past two doors, the props room, then the greenroom, and stopped in front of the costume room. I tried the door handle, but it didn't turn.

"It's locked," I said, reaching inside my pocket for the master key on the ring with the stage door key.

The door creaked open, adding to the feeling I was in the middle of a 1940s' horror movie. Not the Bob Hope kind, the Bela Lugosi kind. Gurn stepped over the threshold, and I followed. I shut the door behind me and reached for the light switch. But before I switched it on, I said, "We're not going to be able to do much without some light, darling."

"With the door closed," he replied, "it shouldn't be a problem."

There was a heartbeat of a wait for the overhead fluorescent tubes to obey, but they finally fluttered on. I stood still and took in the surroundings. It all looked the same. The racks of costumes, boxes of folded clothing on shelves lining the walls, the heavy-duty sewing machine, now covered, sat exactly where they'd been. I crossed to the small table holding the plug-in teakettle sitting beside a box of tea bags, and sugar bowl. The small milk pitcher was not there. I opened the small fridge and saw the pitcher filled with milk on the top shelf. In the wastebasket, several still-wet tea bags lay.

"Someone's been here recently, Gurn," I said.

"Then we'd better get a move on," he said. "That's the outside wall, right?" He pointed to what could be seen of a wall behind racks of costumes.

"Right. Behind all that."

"These costumes are packed pretty close to one another. We're going to have to get them out of the way before we can find the door."

"I've got an idea," I said, looking to the right of the room. "I'll open the curtains to the changing rooms, and we can push the racks partway into them."

"That should do it."

The curtains swooshed open when I gave them a tug. Then I went to the first long rack, maybe twenty feet in length, and looked for the foot brake that locked it in place. Laden with dozens of hanging costumes, some quite heavy, the combined weight had to be several hundred pounds. "The brake must be on your side. We can't move it, otherwise."

"Got it. You pull and walk backward as far as you can, then get out of the way. I'll push it as far as it will go. This is a pretty big room. I think we can clear the door."

As we approached the tenth and last costume rack, I was a mere shell of my former self. Side by side, about half the length of the first four had fit into the men's and women's changing rooms, still leaving us room to maneuver. But the last five were bears to find open space for. No wonder they'd been crammed so closely together.

"After all this," he said, "I hope you're right."

"We'll find out soon enough. Let's just pull this one away from the wall, darling, not move it anywhere," I said. "Maybe we can go behind it and look for the door."

"I don't know, sweetheart," he said. "I think we need as much light from the room as we can get once we open the door. These costumes block most of it."

"Yeah, I guess you're right. In that case, why don't we go sideways with it? Cram it as near as we can to the other five."

"Okay," he said. "Lock coming off. I'll pull my side toward the front door. You try to keep your side from moving at all. Or going over."

"That's all we need," I said. "Dozens of costumes on the floor."

After several minutes of huffing and puffing, we finally got the rack to where we wanted.

"You know," I joked, "this could be a new category for the summer Olympics. The push-pull of costume racks."

But he wasn't listening. He was staring at the wall behind me.

"There it is," Gurn said, almost with reverence. "You were right."

I spun around and looked at a door dead center in the wall, looking as if it was used often. "You know, I sort of hoped I wasn't."

I ran to the door, followed by Gurn, and turned the knob. The door opened with ease. Stifling air greeted me, not cold or damp as it had been when I entered the tunnel a few days before. Of course, that was before the collapse and over 90 percent of it being filled in. The remaining tunnel was much smaller and didn't go anywhere now. I screwed up my eyes to see inside. Even with the light from the room, you could barely see a thing; the blackness was all-consuming. I pulled my cell phone from my pocket and turned on the light. Gurn did the same.

"The second entrance to the tunnel, at last," I said. "Let's do a quick peek, and then get out of here, darling, in case she comes back."

"It's too late for that, doll," a voice said from the front of the costume room. "I'm back."

Chapter Twenty-Six

I froze in place. "Hello, Billie," I said, then turned slowly to face her.

Standing beside her was Edgar, smiling an evil little grin. I'd been concentrating so hard on the find, I hadn't heard them come in the room. Gurn's look of surprise said the same thing for him.

They walked inside the room and stood halfway between the hall door and us. Even though she had a handgun aimed at my heart, I feigned a casualness I wasn't feeling. "I wondered if you were on a plane to Delaware, Billie, or if that was all part of the ruse. Or should I say, Beth? Beth and son."

"So, you're Elizabeth Hofsted," Gurn said, taking a step closer to her. "You've been tough to find."

"You both think you're so smart," she laughed. "The two of you. I've been in the greenroom listening to you struggle to move those racks for over twenty minutes now. You know what I did when I wanted to go into the tunnel? I go to the middle of each rack and push the costumes aside enough to step through."

"I guess we're more tired than we thought," I remarked. Out of the corner of my eye I saw Gurn take another imperceptible step toward Billie.

"They're a couple of dummies, Mama," Edgar said. "Even though they got the drop on me. Sneaky dummies, that's what they are."

"Enough, Edgar. Be still for Mama." Billie looked at Gurn and me. "Now, I want you both to drop those phones to the floor, and kick them to me. Not that they work inside the tunnel. But let's have them. Don't do anything stupid," she said to Gurn. "If you take another step closer, Big Boy, she gets shot, and I couldn't miss from here."

My phone has an impact case that was supposed to be good for up to six feet so, I dropped the phone from a standing position. It hit the floor with a *thunk*. Gurn bent halfway down, almost setting his phone on the floor. Was he going for a weapon in his boot? But he rose and kicked his phone toward her.

"Now you, doll. Kick the phone to Billie." I did. "Thank you," she said with false politeness. "Put those hands high in the air. Good. Edgar, honey, go over and check Big Boy's pockets. Be careful. As you say, these two are sneaky."

"I know how to frisk people down, Mama. I did it back in Boise." He moved toward Gurn, and I noticed a decided limp in his right leg.

"Wait a minute," I said to him. "You're the one who was backstage. You're who I chased into the tunnel. It wasn't a woman running with hip action, it was you with a limp."

He paused, licked his lips, and stared at me, almost embarrassed. "I fell off a garage roof when I was seventeen and broke my leg. It never healed right. But shut up. Just shut up."

"Don't let her get to you, Son," Billie said to him. "Go on with what you started. Search the man."

Taking a frustrated breath, Edgar continued on to Gurn, searched his pockets and down his legs, and found his sheathed hunting knife attached to the back of his belt, as well as his wallet. "Look what I found." Edgar displayed the knife and wallet with pride. He opened the wallet and pulled out the cash. "There's two hundred dollars in here, Mama," he exclaimed, pocketing the money and throwing the wallet with its remaining contents, across the room.

"Do you have a knife, doll? A gun?" Billie asked of me. I shook my head. She cocked her head at me. "Are you telling me the truth?"

"Yes, just the phone. No knife, no gun, no wallet."

"I believe you," Billie replied.

Edgar pouted. "Don't I get to search her, Mama?"

"I don't think that would be wise, Edgar. The female is deadlier than the male. Always remember that." She turned her attention back to me. "How did you know who I was? I've been pretty good at covering my tracks. But I may need to do more. So, before we move on, tell Billie how you knew, doll." She may have been smiling, but her voice was anything but friendly.

"I pieced things together. You were the right age, on the scene, everyone's friend, with no past before 1995, around the time Elizabeth Hofsted fell off the radar. And then there's the teakettle and the tea bags sitting on the table, both here and at the cabin. Earl Grey. The only kind you like. And I knew that tunnel had a second entrance in the theater. And it was Edgar I saw in the wings, not Donna. Probably making sure the rigging of the trick worked and then reporting back to you."

"Off with his head," Edgar said with his evil little smile.

I swallowed hard and went on, "When I chased him into the tunnel at the end of the hallway, he went to the left, circling back around to here. I went to the right and straight into a cave-in. Did you engineer that?"

"No," Billie said. "You could call it good timing on Mother Nature's part, at least for me. Well, I have to admit you're on the smart side, doll."

Gurn made a move toward the wardrobe woman. "Uh-uh-uh, Big Boy," Billie said to him. "If I have to tell you not to move one more time, I swear I'll shoot your wife. And don't think I won't. Now stay back." Gurn obeyed, backing up a foot or two.

"But then you found your son," I said, trying to continue with the thread of our conversation.

"He found me. Last year. My son was the result of a chance encounter with a traveling musician whose last name I didn't know. He took off the next morning and that was that. As usual, I was screwed. No pun intended."

"Ah, Mama," Edgar said. "You shouldn't say things like that."

"Edgar, honey, the truth is the truth. But he gave me one beautiful thing, you. Even though I had to give you up for adoption." She turned and looked at me. "I had a breakdown after I gave birth to him. No family, no money, no one to help me take care of a newborn, so the doctors coerced me into signing papers, and took him away to the waiting arms of a new mother. Never giving a thought to helping me. Just doing what profited them."

"No one can blame you for feeling the way you do," Gurn said, his voice firm, "but this is not the way—"

Suddenly, Billie turned on Gurn. She looked like she might shoot him. "Shut up, Mr. Know-It-All," she shouted. "You're just like all the other men. Think you know everything. I don't like you," she added.

"And then you remembered the will," I said in a loud voice, hoping to take her focus off Gurn.

It worked. She swung the gun back in my direction, instantly calmer.

"Exactly. Lionel's will. Where all the ex-wives get a share of the fortune once Marvin went to his great reward. All that lovely money. When Edgar found me, I came up with a plan for the both of us. Why wait for that piece of garbage to die in his own good time? Why not make it happen? I had a lot of flexible time working here, and his mansion is not that far away. So, I started watching his house. I followed his new wife, that horny little numbskull, always rubbing up against anything in pants whenever she went to the tennis courts. I overheard her say she was looking for a live-in secretary. Knowing what was going on inside the house would be an extra benefit for me. So, I forged a résumé for Edgar, even gave him a new identity, courtesy of a few people I know in the Tenderloin: Johan Nilsson, private secretary, complete with green card. At a ridiculously low salary, too. And there we were."

"I did a good Swedish accent, didn't I, Mama?" Edgar preened.

"We're a good team, Son." Billie glanced his way, her smile changing from cruel to loving.

"And then what?" I asked, hoping to keep her talking.

She faced me again. "I waited for my opportunity."

"*We* waited, Mama," Edgar said.

"Yes, *we* waited. Then last month I heard Marvin the Magnificent was booked into this theater to do his act — if you can call it that — along with others for a charity for fallen heroes. As you couldn't get more fallen than me, I knew my time had arrived."

"So how did Steven fit into all of this?" I asked. "You did kill him, didn't you?"

"No, she didn't. I did," said Edgar, jumping in. Pride covered his face.

"It was his own fault, Lee," Billie said smoothly. "The man was a blackmailer and a thief. Always snooping around backstage. He overheard me call the person he knew to be Johan as Edgar. He was a computer hacker, you know. Tracked Edgar back to Boise and then to here. He liked to mind everybody else's business so he could find a way to make some money off them. He figured out what I was doing and wanted to be our partner."

"But he got greedy," Edgar said. "And I didn't like him. Thought he was smarter than me."

"He had his moments of service, though. Just to prove he had something to offer, he went online and deleted everything about me he could find." Her face darkened. "But then he wanted half of everything. Half!"

"And he called my mom a few names he shouldn't have."

"So, you fixed him," Gurn said.

"My hero," Billie said. "Yes, I'm afraid that one is on Edgar."

"Ah," I said, trying to keep this easy-breezy conversation going. "But how did you rig the guillotine to fail?"

"How do you think?"

"Haven't a clue," I confessed.

"Then I guess it's for me to know and you to find out."

"Oh, come on." I smiled. "Why don't you brag a little?"

"Let's stop talking and kill them, Mama." Edgar glanced at her and licked his lips again.

"We can't kill *everybody*, Edgar," she said in a pragmatic tone, looking his way. "You need to learn to slow things down. But we have time in Rio to work on that." After Billie's teachable moment with her son, she turned her focus back on me. "What we need to do is stage an accident."

I didn't like the sound of that. Time to keep her talking.

"Rio. Of course," I said. "That's why you kidnapped Donna. You hoped she had the account number to the money Steven had in the Cayman Islands. Your plan was to go to Rio de Janeiro and live off that money. Once there, you'd lose weight, change your hair color, and get back as close as possible to looking like the young woman in the yearbook photo of nearly forty years ago."

"Then you'd show up for your share of the inheritance as Elizabeth Hofsted, ex-wife of the deceased," Gurn said.

"After all, you have six months to make a claim on the will," I added.

"Nick and Nora Charles strike again," she said with a sneer.

"I thought their name was Alvarez," Edgar said, a look of puzzlement covering his face.

"Never mind, Son," Billie said.

"During which time the woman known as Billie Evans disappears," I said.

She looked at me again. "Correct. Billie Evans supposedly flew to the East Coast yesterday. She's going to write a letter to the Babonas family soon, and announce she's staying in Delaware and moving in with her niece. Goodbye Billie Evans, hello Beth Hofsted. Eventually."

"All very neat," Gurn said. "Well thought out. But what about us?"

"We'll get to that," Billie said, smiling.

I could see where Edgar inherited his evil little smile from. I involuntarily shivered.

"Here's what's going to happen with you two. You're going to discover the tunnel, go inside, the door will slam shut, and you'll be trapped. The theater is closed for the next two weeks, and no one will be here. Any screaming or pounding you do will echo into the night. The thing I've discovered since the cave-in is there's hardly any air in there now. You'll use up what's inside within less than an hour. By the time anyone comes into the wardrobe room and discovers this mess with your fingerprints everywhere—and thank you for doing that—they'll find you both suffocated inside the tunnel. An unhappy accident."

Chapter Twenty-Seven

"You know what I love about you, darling?" I asked as I reached out and searched for his hand in the dark. "The fact you never say 'I told you so.' I should have told Fenner where we were going."

"Never mind that, sweetheart," he said, giving my hand a squeeze before releasing it. "Let's concentrate on getting out of here."

We'd been in the dark for fifteen minutes, breathing in the thin, putrid air of the tunnel. I knew the span of time because Gurn turned the light on from his watch. Not bright enough to do any good, other than read the correct time. We'd been leaning against the door trying to hear what was going on in the outside room. After some chitchat between them, we heard Billie and Edgar leave the wardrobe room. They slammed the door behind them and noisily went up the stairs. Straining our ears, we finally heard the banging of a distant door. Had they left the building?

"It's been awhile, I don't think they're coming back," I said, after a time.

"I agree. Let's get a feel for this door. Maybe I can break it down."

"Hold it. I was reluctant to pull it out before in case they returned, but I've still got the sat phone in my boot."

"That's right! And you didn't hand it over to Billie when she asked you if you had anything else on you. Good for you."

"I have my moments." I leaned down to the outside of my left boot, slipped my fingers inside, and pulled the phone out.

"Too bad we can't call anyone from underground," Gurn said. "You have to have a line of sight between the phone and the satellite."

"At least we can use the flashlight on it," I searched around on the phone trying to find the button for the flashlight. It slipped out of my hands and fell to the ground. "Oh, criminy, I dropped it."

I squatted down, groping the ground with my hands. I felt Gurn do the same thing beside me. "Got it," he said. "When Lila handed it to you, I noticed it looked similar to the one I use or used on missions," he said. "I think I know where the flashlight is."

I could feel him stand. I did, too.

"Here we go," he said as the flashlight came on. I felt a surge of hope run through me, though it was becoming increasingly difficult to breath in the tunnel, even in the short amount of time we were in it.

He turned slowly in a circle with the light, both of us surveying the inside of the tunnel. Maybe six feet deep, eight wide, and six and a half feet high, the cavern with its crudely chiseled stones looked foreboding and claustrophobic in the scant lighting. On one side, the tunnel had newly fallen rocks and dirt, where the cave-in had been. On the other side, a dead end. Then Gurn focused the light on the doorknob and its keylock dead bolt.

"The doorknob looks like an older one to me, sixties or seventies," Gurn said. "They still did the job, though. Hopefully, there are no surprises with it."

"Come again?"

"Like a bomb that's triggered to go off if you try to break it down."

"Darling, sometimes more information is not necessarily a good thing. Especially when it's a tad on the pessimistic side."

"Just speaking from experience, sweetheart."

"Precious mine, this is a theater and not a high security place. I would say it's an ordinary knob and dead bolt, and looks like it came straight from a hardware store."

"I bow to your reasoning, beloved. Mind out of Iran and Afghanistan and back to reality. This is no doubt an ordinary door, not a booby trap."

"And that's the good news. The bad news is, the door looks like solid wood to me, not a hollow core," I said.

"Still doable."

"That's the spirit."

"How do you want to do this? I go first? You go first?"

He was talking about doing a sidekick on the door, sometimes called the twist kick. It's the same thing he'd used to knock down the cabin door. To be technically accurate, Gurn uses the tae-kwon-do move and I use karate. Similar execution but not quite the same. The bottom line was, they were both powerful moves providing you knew what you were doing. Each should get the job done.

The problem was the air was thin. I could already feel the burning in my lungs from a lack of oxygen. Gurn's breathing sounded labored, too. And we were exhausted from lack of sleep. We had to do this right, and we had to do it fast.

"Both of us at the same time," I said. "A double whammy."

"We should do a couple of stretches before we attempt this. We're going to need some room."

The space being as tight as it was, I moved as far behind him as possible. We both dropped into the Cossack-squat mobility exercise. After five or six of them, I felt limber enough not to pull any muscles.

"Ready?" he asked.

"Ready."

"Okay," he said, obviously thinking. "Why don't you take the light back and shine it on the doorknob?" I did. Standing to my left but slightly behind me, he raised his right leg. I raised mine. We did a practice run, needing to test where each foot would land so we wouldn't get in each other's way. Keeping our legs straight, we locked our knees, making the leg like a battering ram. As I am five eight and he six one, our feet landed at different heights. His foot hit about four inches above the doorknob. Mine was at the same level as the lock. Preferable.

"Let's change places," I said. "Let me hit as near to the dead bolt as possible."

"Works for me." We changed positions. "And I'll aim lower, too," he said.

"You do the count," I said. "You're used to pushing gaggles of sailors around."

"A little inaccurately phrased, but I get your drift. I'll say one, two, three, kick, okay?"

"We kick on the word 'kick,' right?"

"Right. And no more questions, seaman. Let's just do this."

"Aye-aye, sir."

He called it and we kicked. The door trembled, almost wanting to give way but seemed to spring back into place. Even with that slight exertion, I inhaled a deep breath, or tried to. It did me hardly any good at all.

"Once more," he said. "And I'm going to try to get my foot closer to yours. One, two, three, kick!"

This time we heard a splintering sound on the other side of the door. I bent over, holding on to my knees with my hands. I was starting to become dizzy. I put it out of my mind.

"Let's go again," I yelled. "Right now!"

"One, two, three, kick!" we said in unison.

The wood frame shattered into pieces where our feet struck. The door flew open as far as it could, banging against the wall with a whack. Then on shaking hinges, it wobbled toward us. We pushed at it and fell into the wardrobe room, sucking in air that had no right to smell as fresh as it did.

Chapter Twenty-Eight

"Remind me to never step foot backstage of a theater again," Gurn said ten minutes later, as we followed the phone's beam of light to climb the stairs of the empty, dark theater. "Nothing but bad things happen when I do."

He was referring to the last time he'd been backstage after I talked him into going undercover in a small acting role of a client's play. He forgot his one line, panicked, tried to flee the stage, and ultimately landed in horse poop in front of an audience of eight hundred people. It was not his finest hour.

"So noted, but at least we found your wallet where he'd tossed it," I said, grabbing on to the banister and climbing the stairs.

"Looking on the bright side, I'm lucky he only wanted the cash."

"Boy, do I need a shower."

"And food."

"And sleep. And cats to cuddle."

"I'll settle for cuddling with you."

"Sometimes you know the perfect thing to say."

"You've trained me well," he said, laughing. I joined him.

We arrived at the stage door. We paused and looked at one another in the scant lighting of the sat's flashlight. We were free. It was just a case of opening the stage door and stepping out. We smiled at one another.

"Let's get out of here," we said in unison.

He pushed the stage door open. The light of the day in contrast to the dark theater, almost blinded me. I stopped just outside the exit and put one hand over my eyes.

"Wow! It's so bright," I said. "What time is it anyway?"

"Ten of five. We need to get you a new watch."

"One of these days. When I get the time. No pun intended."

I was still looking down from the sun and glanced out to the street. There, two cell phones lying near the curb had been run over several times.

"Oh no! Our phones." I ran over and picked them up. Mine fell apart in my hands. Shards of glass fell to the sidewalk, plus a piece of the cover. I handed Gurn the twisted metal that was once his phone.

"Well, now I'm really mad," I said, looking at my phone. I walked over to the trash can and threw it in. "That cover cost me a hundred dollars."

"Glad to see you've got your priorities straight." Gurn followed me and tossed his phone in as well.

"Hand me the sat phone, darling," I said, reaching out my hand. "We'd better call Richard and alert him as to what's going on. I'd call Inspector Fenner, but I don't know his number off the top of my head." I moved out from under a tree, and punched in his number.

"Hi, Lee," my brother said after several rings. "How are things going?"

"Could be worse, could be better," I said, looking over at Gurn and putting the sat phone on speaker mode. "What are the chances, brother mine, that you can order Gurn and me new cell phones? Or is that something we have to do ourselves?"

"I take it your cellular phones are no longer among the living?"

"Casualties of war."

"You both carried the same phone, and all the info lives in the cloud, so let me see what I can do. You want to upgrade?"

"Not me," Gurn said.

"Me neither," I put in.

"Okay," Richard said. "That's easy. I know a guy who knows a guy who knows a guy, and I might be able to get two delivered to your apartment in a couple of hours. And I'll alert your carrier, so they will be ready to go. Once you get the phones, you'll have to upload all the info from the cloud, though."

"We can do that," Gurn said. "It shouldn't take too long, an hour or two. Thanks, Rich."

"You're a peach, Richard," I added. "By the way, I was right about it being Billie, but she got away from us. Any update on the hit-and-run of Winston?"

"Yes. They found the car, an SUV, abandoned about two blocks away. Registered as stolen by the owner yesterday. They'll have forensics check it out, but it might take a day or two."

"Meanwhile, leaving the heirs vulnerable. But I have one or two ideas."

"I never doubted it for a moment."

"Richard, I need to let Fenner know to put out an APB on Billie and son. Can you find his number for me?"

"No need. It's the second from the bottom of your speed dials. Gurn's first, I'm second, Mom's third. Need I go on?"

"Nope. And thanks for giving this sat phone to me. It helped save our bacon."

"Howzat?"

"I will brag on it later, but I have to hang up now and call Fenner. But Richard, do me a favor."

"Among the other favors?"

"Don't be a grouch. Call Mr. Wong and tell him Gurn and I are coming over within the hour, will you? Thanks."

Gurn's eyebrows shot up. I disconnected and scrolled down in the speed-dial list for Inspector Fenner. After pressing in the number, I turned to Gurn.

"Darling, I will explain everything in a minute. Let me just tell Fenner what's going on first. Meanwhile, why don't you put the theater keys back in their hiding place?"

I handed over the two keys, and Gurn was off to the front of the theater.

Fenner took it well, all in all. He wasn't happy when he learned I had no idea what kind of car Billie and Edgar were in or where they were heading, but what can you do? I was glad he believed me when I told him the middle-aged wardrobe lady and her son were the bad guys.

I hung up and turned to the sweetest man on the face of the earth, walking toward me, who, thanks to me, needed a shower, a shave, and a nap. "All's well?"

"Keys are back where they belong."

"Darling, Fenner promised to check all the airports, bus stations, and keep a lookout for either her car or Edgar's car. Of course, they could be in a rental. All that will be checked out. But that could take hours, and they could be long gone by then. Soooo…"

"Soooo," he said, imitating me, "you think by going to Sea Cliff and looking in Edgar's room, we might find something that would expedite matters?"

"In a nutshell, yes."

He gave me one of his lopsided smiles and drew the keys to his Jeep out of his pocket. "Then let's get going. And I have some gum in the glove compartment we can chew on in case our breath is beyond the pale."

"I wonder what that means, 'beyond the pale'?"

"Outside the limits of acceptable behavior or judgment."

"Hmmm. We'd better fish the hairbrush out of the glove compartment, as well as the gum. Too bad I didn't repack my overnight bag before we started this sojourn."

"You're reminding me," he said, his face lighting up. "I've got *my* overnight kit in the trunk. Fresh shirt, underwear, deodorant, shaving kit, toothbrush, and toothpaste. Two toothbrushes, as a matter of fact. One still in the wrap."

"Say no more," I declared. "Pull into that service station right over there. If I can brush my teeth, wash my face, and do something with my hair, I'll be a happy person. And you'll definitely look better with a clean-shaven face. Not that I don't like it any way I see it."

"After saying that, you can even have my clean shirt."

Chapter Twenty-Nine

Twenty minutes, and two bad cups of coffee later, we were ready to tackle a mansion in Sea Cliff and a from-the-old-school butler. It was a good twenty degrees warmer, so I did take Gurn up on the offer of his pale-blue Egyptian cotton shirt, losing my black wool pullover. I rolled up the shirt sleeves and the bottom of the shirt and tied the tails at my waist for a Caribbean flair. Gurn stripped off his dark pullover, leaving the Khaki military camouflage T-shirt beneath, all the rage with civilians now. We didn't look good, but we did look presentable.

Shortly later we arrived in Sea Cliff. Sea Cliff is a neighborhood in Northwestern San Francisco known for its large, one-of-a-kind houses and astonishing views of the Pacific Ocean and Golden Gate Bridge. This small community sits on a cliff at one side of the Golden Gate strait with the Marin Headlands across the waters. The strait leads into San Francisco Bay and carries every kind of craft afloat, from sailboats to barges to cruise ships. Onward they sail to the city that columnist, Herb Caen, referred to as Baghdad by the Bay.

Sea Cliff is touted to be one of the best places to live in California if not the world. There's even a small, public beach named China Beach. The national park, Land's End, is also located in the neighborhood. Needless to say, but I will say it, the weather's usually stunning. To wrap this up, if you've got the moola — and you'd need tons of it — you'd be living in a California paradise.

We pulled up in front of a palatial home sitting on the edge of the famous cliff. From what Richard told me, the house was built in 1920 and still had the original classic, columned façade. The house and landscaping was separated from the road by a wide sidewalk. Another cobblestone walkway led to the two-story house painted a warm tan and trimmed in bright white. The house was surrounded by emerald-green shrubbery manicured within an inch of their lives. But its well-groomed opulence couldn't compete with nature's backdrop.

Before I got out of the car, I checked to see how I looked in the passenger pull-down mirror. Not too bad if you didn't count the circles under my eyes from lack of sleep. Slamming the doors closed, we headed up the walkway lined on either side by low, box-shaped hedges, and rang the bell at the double-door entrance.

One of the doors was opened by a slender, dark-haired young woman dressed in the same colors as the exterior of the house, a warm-tan uniform with sharp white collar, cuffs, and cap. The bow of her starched white apron was so big, it extended beyond her waist. If we were looking for someone to play the maid in a 1930s' drawing room mystery, here was the gal, down to the teary-eyed, sad look on her face.

"Yes?" she asked in barely more than a whisper, looking down at her feet. Her voice quavered on the one word, sorrow radiating from her. Well, I could see it. The master of the house and his son-in-law were dead, the mistress in the hospital, the daughter kidnapped, and the secretary missing. Quite a scenario. While it must have lightened the workload considerably, it was all pretty disconcerting.

"We're here to see Mr. Wong," I whispered back. "Ms. Alvarez and Mr. Hanson."

"Yes, miss," she mouthed, still not looking up. She stepped back, opening the door wide enough for us to step inside. "I will let Mr. Wong know you are here." Her words were barely audible, but when she finished them, she turned and hurried away.

While we waited, I looked around. The rooms were painted a soft cream color, and rather than being boring, it gave the clean lines of the interior depth and sophistication. We stood in the two-story-high entryway with artwork scattered around on the walls, modern and tasteful. At the back of the room, a curved staircase, simple but with a certain pizzazz, led to the upstairs floor. Next to the staircase was the hallway the young woman scurried down, probably leading to the kitchen and butler's pantry. To the left side of me, a wide-angled archway showed the dining room. To the right, another archway revealed the living room.

I couldn't help myself, but dashed over to the entrance of the living room and craned my neck to look inside. I gasped. The living room was L-shaped, sparsely but elegantly furnished with low, unobtrusive furniture. Nothing to obscure where the focus should be.

The pièce de résistance, of course, was the view through the wall of glass at the end of the room. Centered within the fourth "wall" were sliding glass doors leading out to a small balcony. Even the balcony's safety rails were made of glass. Nothing to block the view.

And what a view it was. The cliffs of the Marin Headlands straight ahead. The Golden Gate Bridge to the right. The Pacific Ocean to the left. Directly in front of me, a grand cruise ship slowly glided toward the San Francisco Bay. All beneath a sparkling, robin's-egg-blue sky. If ever there was a Kodak moment, this was it.

But I saw red, not blue. I had no camera to snap the moment, because my phone had been crushed beneath the wheels of a car. It forced me back to reality. I returned to Gurn's side, anxious to get on with things.

The door at the end of the hallway opened, and Mr. Wong came toward us. He was a tall man and carried himself with regal bearing. The closer he got, the more stress and fatigue lines showed on his face. Were they from the precarious health of his granddaughter or the happenings of the house? Maybe a little of both.

"Good afternoon, Ms. Alvarez, Mr. Hanson," he said nodding to me and then to Gurn. "Forgive my keeping you waiting. I have been on the phone with the mortuary. They have just received the body of

Mr. Del Vecchio, and as Mrs. Del Vecchio is indisposed at the moment; I requested they hold the body until further notice."

"I'm sure you have a great many things to do, Mr. Wong," Gurn said. "We will detain you no longer than necessary. We apologize for any inconvenience."

I knew Gurn spoke Russian, Farci, and Arabic but was surprised to learn he also spoke *To the Manor Born*. I like to feel I speak high tourist, hanging around my mother as much as I do, so went for it.

"And let me add, Mr. Wong, we are grateful for any help." I almost ended with, "you might impart unto us," but stopped myself.

If feathers had been ruffled on Mr. Wong's part, they quickly went back into place.

"Of course, madam, sir. Of course. It is my pleasure to be of service." Having said that, Mr. Wong actually gave a slight bow. "If you will follow me to Mr. Nilsson's bedroom."

Fortunately, he didn't say, "walk this way" or I might have lost it. Fatigue can do strange things to me. We followed him down the hallway from whence he came and through a swinging door. We were in yet another passage with several closed doors. He opened one door leading downstairs.

At the bottom on the stairs, a large room loomed to the left. Your eye was drawn to it because of the glare from natural lighting. I stepped inside the room that looked more like a showroom of a working magician's tricks than anything else. Through this particular set of windows was the top half of the scene with the cruise ship still on its journey to the Bay, the bottom half hidden by a clump of trimmed hedges.

That's right, I thought. We were down in the basement. The panorama, while still pretty danged good, wasn't as glorious as it was from the living room or probably from the bedrooms on the top floor. I tore myself away, determined not to become obsessed by the vista.

I was about to turn and leave when I saw it. The guillotine. In a corner of the room. It was partially covered by a blue tarp, but there was no mistaking it. I froze in place, my mind racing. Were there two of them? Did one live here and one languish at the police station? Couldn't be. Not at eighty-five grand apiece. Mr. Wong must have noticed the expression on my face.

"Is something wrong, miss?"

"That guillotine," I said, walking toward it. "What is it doing here? I thought it was at the police station."

"Yes, miss, but it was returned early this morning. I was informed DNA testing had been completed and it was no longer needed. A Mr. Henry Swan supervised the loading and unloading at the inspector's request so the guillotine would not be damaged in transport."

"Was that Inspector Fenner?"

"Yes, miss. It was decided to put the guillotine back with Mr. Del Vecchio's other effects and apparatus until such time as a sale of the equipment can be made by the executors of the estate."

"How did you get it in here?" Gurn asked, coming into the room. "It looks heavy."

"Through the side door off the driveway, sir." Mr. Wong pointed to a door I'd not previously noticed. "It is not a difficult process, as Mr. Del Vecchio has been transporting his equipment back and forth to events for years. He always used the same company for the process. They are called… " And here he paused before adding the last two words, "Moving Illusions." Mr. Wong actually sniffed as he uttered them, possibly finding the name of the company wanting. He and my mother had a few things in common. Too bad she was determined to stay a widow. Mr. Wong might be right up her alley.

"I take it," I said, "the guillotine still works?"

"I wouldn't know, miss. But Mr. Swan pronounced it 'fit.' I believe that is the word he used. Shall we continue on to Mr. Nilsson's bedroom?" He gestured — in a most gentile way — for me to exit the room.

"Of course," I said. "I'm sure you have things to do."

"Thank you, miss."

Another slight bow from him and we were on our way. We continued through the basement hallway to several closed doors at the front of the house, essentially sans spectacular view.

Mr. Wong unlocked one door, pushed it open, and stepped back to let Gurn and I enter. We stepped over the threshold into a small room that looked like it belonged to a sixteen-year-old boy with very tolerant parents. Dirty clothes were strewn everywhere. Shoes littered the throw rugs. The bed was not only unmade, but the blanket lay to the side with half on the floor. A bed pillow was tossed across the room. Tabletops were covered with dirty dishes, empty beer bottles, used towels, toiletries, and comic books. And it smelled like the inside of a men's locker room on a hot day.

"Tell me, Mr. Wong," I said. "Who made this mess? The police?"

"No, miss. Mr. Nilsson. He kept this door locked and did not allow anyone in his room at any time. He would ask for fresh linen and towels when he felt he needed them. We were instructed this room was off-limits." He sniffed again, long and hard.

"And Mrs. Del Vecchio went along with this?" Gurn asked, looking around him.

"Mrs. Del Vecchio felt Mr. Nilsson's contribution to the household warranted this measure."

"Wow," I said. "He must type one helluva letter."

"Mrs. Del Vecchio explained it was his knowledge of the repair of the automobiles, as well as his secretarial skills. But it did create quite a stir among the staff."

"He also was an auto mechanic?" Gurn asked.

"Yes, sir. I was told his knowledge of the Rolls was extensive, although Mrs. Del Vecchio did find it necessary to take it to the dealership from time to time. If you will permit me, I must return to my duties. Anna will be on the alert to see you to the front door when you are done. She is waiting at the

264

top of the stairs. I would appreciate your finishing this visit as quickly as possible. The household staff is upset enough."

He turned to exit, but my voice stopped him. "How is your granddaughter doing? I understand the operation on her heart takes place either today or tomorrow."

He stood with his back to me for a split second, then turned around with an ingratiating smile on his face. "The operation will take place tomorrow."

"Will you be flying to Portland for it? Are the police allowing you to leave the state?"

It was as if his entire body had sucked on a lemon. "Yes, miss. I leave this evening and return in three to five days. That is why it is imperative I accomplish what needs to be done before then." And with that, he turned on his heel and was gone.

We watched the back of him go down the hall and up the stairs. Gurn closed the door and only then did we speak.

"Well, I certainly got under his skin," I said.

"Did you buy what he said about Madison allowing this room to be in this condition because of all Johan slash Edgar had to offer?"

"Not for a minute. Edgar has something on Madison. Could be an affair. From what Billie said before she locked us up, the third Mrs. Del Vecchio was always on the prowl."

Gurn looked around him and let out a long sigh. "Where do you want to start, sweetheart? This might take us the rest of the afternoon to go through everything. What exactly are we looking for? Remind me."

“Not sure,” I said.

“But we’ll know it when we find it,” we said in unison.

Chapter Thirty

By the superficial looks of the room, it appeared that Edgar planned to return, but when we opened the closet and drawers, it showed a different story.

"He isn't coming back." I turned from a closet with more hangers on the floor than on the pole. "Closet's empty."

"Same with the drawers. Empty," Gurn said, after opening the last one in the bureau. He turned away and looked around him. "But look at the shoes on the floor. Some of them are in good shape. I can understand leaving dirty clothes, but why did he leave good shoes?"

"I'm guessing he thought he was coming into enough money soon to buy a whole new wardrobe. Let's foil his plan, shall we?"

"There's something I can get behind," he said.

I picked up the one wastebasket in the room that was three-quarters full, emptied the contents on the bed, and began to look through the mess. Gurn crossed to the small desk in a corner and opened more drawers.

"Nothing of any value in here," he said. "There's no laptop, but there is a printer. It's a cheap one. He probably decided to leave it."

He opened the printer cover. Inside was a sheet of paper that had been either copied or scanned. He turned the paper over and read it.

"Bingo! Got it."

"That's my man. Not two minutes into the task. What is it?"

"A bill of sale for his car. Sold to Best Deals Car Lot in Sunnyvale. Maybe he needed a copy to send to his insurance company."

"My, my, my, my, my. And that means they didn't use his car to escape in," I said, uncrumpling the last sheet of paper from the pile on the bed. "Let's see what I can find, although I'm sure the police have been through this trash. Phooey. Nothing here but receipts for take-out food. Wait. Here's a bill from a restaurant. Dinner for two. Hmmm."

"Hmmm, what?"

"I know this restaurant. La Maison. Very romantic. I can't see him taking his mother there. That means there's a woman. A woman he is or was involved with."

"I say you call Fenner and tell him what we found. Right now."

"Good idea." I reached for the sat phone, found his number, and pressed speed dial. "Oh, criminy. No signal. I keep forgetting you need an open sky with these sat phones. I'll just run out that side door of the magic storage room. In fact, we could probably leave that way. Save the maid the trouble of letting us out. Or maybe not." I brought myself up short. "They might wonder what happened to us, and it could be thought of as rude. See? My mother's upbringing isn't a total waste."

"Sweetheart, don't overthink this," Gurn said, "and go make the call."

I ran back to the magic room with all Del Vecchio's equipment and opened the door leading out to the driveway. I was about to step out when I heard voices carried by the breeze in my direction. They seemed to be coming from the bottom of the incline where the earth had been dug out in order to accommodate an underground garage, keeping the roof of the building at ground level. People will do a lot of things to keep a view from being obstructed. I didn't recognize the woman's voice, but the man was Wong.

"I'm telling you, Anna, just throw it away. Or give it to me. I will discard it."

"But it was given to me to hold for him." Her voice had a pleading element to it. She went on, as if trying to make her position clearer. "He trusted me with it."

"You were a fool to believe him. And it does not do for you to question my authority, Anna. If you value the security of your position, you will throw the key away and say no more about it. Then after you do, you will go into that wastrel's room and urge that young couple to leave. Remember, Anna, part of our job is to protect the members of this household. It is our duty. Do I make myself clear?"

"Yes, Mr. Wong."

"Do you want to give me the key and I will dispose of it? Or can I rely upon you to honor your word and discard it as soon as possible?"

"I will walk down to the beach and throw the key into the water. I promise."

"Good girl. You will see, ultimately, that it is the right decision."

Mesmerized by the conversation and mind racing, it wasn't until I heard Mr. Wong's approaching footsteps did I realize it really would be better if I hid from view. I dove behind a box hedge just in time to avoid being seen by a butler who, as far as I was concerned, had a few things to answer for.

I managed to get several scratches on my legs from landing in the rough hedge next to a large spider that seemed somewhat surprised to see me. I don't particularly care for spiders, but this one seemed willing to let me invade his turf. I stared at him, he stared at me, and neither of us moved. Meanwhile, Mr. Wong went into the magic storage room, and I heard a click as he closed the door behind him.

Oh, great. He locked the door. Now, how am I going to get back in? I sat up and looked around, brushing a leaf or two out of my hair. *Never mind getting back into the house. You've got to get that key. Lord knows to what, but you've got to get it.*

I stood and jumped over the hedge, about to go down the incline to the garage. Then I saw the back of Anna, the same woman who opened the front door for us, heading away from me and toward the cliff. I followed. The path led to a zigzag stairway built on the side of the cliff ending at a small, private beach below. A couple of facts hit me at the same time. A: If I pursued her all the way down the steep set of stairs to the beach, I would only have to climb back up them again. I was too pooped for that. B: Maybe the element of surprise would have her hand the key over to me, no fuss, no muss. I went with B.

"Anna," I called out to the young woman about to descend the stairs.

She wheeled around, wide-eyed, and frozen in place. "Yes, miss?"

"I'll take that key." I walked closer and extended my hand.

She only hesitated for a brief moment, then placed the key in my hand. "Yes, miss." She bit her lower lip, fighting back tears. "When Mr. Wong finds out I gave you this key, he'll fire me."

"He won't find out from me. As far as I'm concerned, you threw it away."

She looked down at her feet. That seemed to be a habit of hers. "Thank you, miss."

"My name is Lee, Anna. Please call me that. What's this key to?"

"Johan's safety deposit box, miss… er… Lee, at San Francisco Amalgamated. He gave it to me to keep for him," she whispered.

"I see. You were in a relationship with him?"

She nodded and let out a sob. "For four months. He was the most exciting person I'd ever met in my life."

"Really?" I said, trying to keep the shocked look off my face. It was hard to equate the man she was talking about with the mama's boy I'd met earlier. I studied the young woman, younger than I'd originally thought. And certainly, more inexperienced. "Anna, the man you knew of as Johan sold his car recently. Do you know how he got around without it?"

She wiped at her eyes. "He had a rental. A black Ford Explorer. New. He liked it. He said he was going to buy one when he—" She stopped talking.

"When he what? Anna, where did Johan go?" She didn't say anything. "If you know, and don't tell the police, you could be considered an accomplice. That might involve a prison sentence."

She drew in a sharp breath of air and looked up at me. "I… I… Why? I don't understand what's going on. Suddenly, his name isn't Johan. Mr. Wong says he hurt Mrs. Del Vecchio. And now he's gone away for at least six months. I don't understand."

Okay, add a tad simple to the young and inexperienced. "Did he say where he was going, Anna? If so, tell me." I used the no-nonsense voice my mother always used on me when I was twelve and being incorrigible.

"He said he and his mother were driving to Ensenada, Mexico, then flying to Rio de Janeiro. He said he was going to send for me. He said he was coming into some money, and we would get married. I didn't know Johan wasn't his real name. I didn't know."

"But before you join him, you're supposed to go to his safety deposit box, take whatever is in there, and bring the contents to him?" She nodded. "Do you know what's in there?"

She nodded her head again.

"What?"

"Something about Mrs. Del Vecchio she doesn't want known. I don't know what it is, though. Johan didn't tell me."

"How did Mr. Wong learn of this key?"

"When Mrs. Del Vecchio was hurt, the police came looking for Johan. I didn't know where he was. So, I went to Mr. Wong, and told him everything."

"Including that something incriminating about Mrs. Del Vecchio was in the safety deposit box?" She nodded. "And that's when Wong's feudal servitude tendences kicked in."

She looked up at me, her eyes pleading. "I don't know what you just said, but Mr. Wong has been very good to me. He gave me a job when no one else would. He trained me. I don't have anyone to turn to. Just him. I thought I had Johan but..." Her voice drifted off.

"Okay, I can see this has been tough on you, and I think you could use a bit of a break. Let's do this. You're going to become my client."

"Miss?" Her voice conveyed confusion.

"I am a licensed private investigator. If you're my client, I don't have to reveal anything about you, personally, to the police. Unless I consider you to be dangerous. Are you dangerous, Anna?"

"D-d-dangerous?" she stuttered. "No, I don't think so."

"In that case, I can relay information you give me to the police but not tell them the source. But only if you are my client. Do you want to become my client?" She nodded. "Give me your hand so we can shake on it." She placed a limp hand in mine, and I gave it a firm handshake. "So, to be clear, what we've said just now is between investigator and client. Nobody else. Got it?"

"Yes," she said. Anna then looked me directly in the eye and added, "Yes, Lee. Thank you." She started to leave, hesitated, and turned back to me, her voice sad and accepting. "I thought he loved me."

"We've all been there, Anna, at one time or another. It's almost a rite of passage."

Chapter Thirty-One

An hour later found Gurn and me near San Francisco's Union Square trapped behind a demonstration on cleaning up the oceans. They were concentrating in particular on our coral reefs, which are dying from pollution and high water temperatures at an alarming rate all over the world.

I am in favor of our oceans being healthy, even though every time I get on the ocean something unhealthy happens to me. I have been on more than my share of boats that have exploded, sank, or were deliberately driven into a hurricane, where in between riding nauseating, never-ending waves, I was shot.

The sat phone rang as the demonstration was winding down, and it was Mom with good news: Carl was awake. Both Gurn and I cheered loudly. The demonstrators thought it was for them. In a way, it was. Something good happened out of pretty dismal odds. Maybe if Carl could pull through, our planet could, too.

Carl was able to do a little talking before the doctors made Mom and Chief Lel Ti leave the room. They learned Carl had driven to the cabin, looked inside, saw Donna tied up, was about to enter, but was struck on the head by someone from behind. He didn't know who. That was too bad, the chief told Mom on their way out of the room. Donna swore it was Edgar Smith, but it would have been nice to have had Carl's corroboration.

But most importantly, Carl was going to be all right. According to Mom, his mind and reasoning still functioned. His motor skills were there. To make sure, she had him move his arms, legs, fingers, and toes, no matter how loudly the doctors insisted she leave immediately. Do not bandy words about like, "leave immediately," to my mother when she has her own agenda. Better to go shout at the wind.

After the mater and I hung up, I called Richard with the latest update on our favorite employee and longtime friend. More cheering ensued.

Feeling lighter than I had in days, Gurn and I finally arrived at the San Franciso police station. I asked the desk sergeant to tell Detective Inspector Fenner we were there on urgent business. We were escorted to his office less than five minutes later, so I thought things were on the upswing. Sometimes I can be downright delusional.

We arrived at Fenner's office to find a tight-jawed detective inspector standing behind his desk. He leaned forward on taut arms, glaring at us. I didn't know Fenner that well, but even I could tell that if he'd been a volcano, he was about to go one better than Vesuvius. Any greeting I'd prepared to utter froze upon my lips. Needless to say, the officer escorting us beat a hasty retreat.

"This had better be good," Fenner roared. "And you two better have a good reason for going behind my back to the Del Vecchio mansion and snooping around. Unless you're turning yourselves in for obstructing justice."

"It is good," Gurn said in a mild, nonconfrontational tone. "We have information you should know, or we wouldn't be taking up your time. And ours."

"It's our gift to you," I added, adapting Gurn's tone.

"Beware of Greeks bearing gifts," Fenner snarled, "so you'll pardon me if I'm skeptical."

"Well, I'm Mexican American, so that doesn't apply to me." I grinned.

"Well, let's have it," Fenner said, somewhat mollified, but not completely.

"Before we tell you anything," I said, "we did *not* go to the Del Vecchio mansion behind your back. We were there on behalf of my *client*, Donna Del Vecchio. We are *assisting* justice." Once again, I seemed to be enunciating certain words in a sentence just like my mother does. Must be genetic.

"Donna Del Vecchio hired you?"

"Yes."

The volcano went back underground. Sort of. "I see. Then you'd better close the door and sit down. If you have information, be quick about it."

Without saying anything, Gurn unfolded the paper on the sale of Edgar Smith's car and handed it to Fenner. We were both quiet and watched him read.

"Where did you get this?" Fenner demanded after visually scanning the document.

"I lifted the top of the printer in Edgar Smith's room and found it inside. Apparently, he made a copy of it and forgot to remove the original."

Fenner closed his eyes for a beat, then reached for his desk phone. He pressed a button and waited a split second. "Poppy, send out a memo to all departments. Quote: When doing a search and seize, lift the tops of copy printers to make sure nothing has been left inside. Unquote." He hung up and turned back to us with a sheepish grin. "Well, that's embarrassing," he admitted. "Sorry I was a little gruff at the outset. We found Billie Evans' car several blocks away from the theater. That made us think they were traveling in Smith's car. But nothing. No wonder we haven't been able to find them. Now we don't know what type of vehicle they may be in, where they're going, or anything."

"Ah, I have information that might help with that," I said.

Fenner's eyebrows rose but he said nothing.

"I have another client, whose name I am not at liberty to say, who says that Edgar Smith recently rented a late model, black Ford Explorer. I know you'd eventually find it, but I wanted to expedite matters. No thanks necessary."

"Who's the client?"

"Not at liberty to say. As I said."

"Just as I was beginning to cool down," Fenner said. "You go and set me off again."

"Furthermore, my client said—"

"Is this Donna Del Vecchio?"

"No, another client."

"How many do you have?"

"Enough. Continuing, Smith told my client he and his mother were driving to Ensenada."

Fenner reached for the phone again. "Poppy, find me Rudwin and send her in. Pronto."

The door opened almost immediately. This Rudwin had to have been waiting on the other side of the door. Officer Rudwin was a young rookie, possibly in her mid-twenties, with a flawless, pale complexion, dark hair, and dark eyes. She stepped into the room and stood at attention wearing the most starched uniform I'd ever seen. Even her buttons seemed to salute.

"You wanted to see me, sir?"

"Yes," Fenner said. "I have updated information regarding the car and whereabouts of Edgar Smith. Give a call to Best Deals Car Lot in Sunnyvale where Smith sold his car and see what they have."

He extended his hand with the bill of sale. Officer Rudwin took it from him.

"Yes, sir."

"Nothing has been corroborated yet, but as time is of the essence, I want you to also check car rentals in the surrounding areas. Start with San Francisco. We are looking to see if Smith rented a black—" Fenner broke off and looked at me.

"Black Ford Explorer, late model," I put in.

"Possibly heading for Ensenada," Fenner added. "Find that car."

"Yes, sir."

"That's all, Rudwin."

"Yes, sir." And with that, she did a one-eighty and marched out.

Fenner looked at Gurn and then at me. "From the new school. Has a degree in criminal justice. Not too sure how to talk to them, but Rudy's smart enough and thorough. Don't tell her we call her Rudy behind her back. She might take offense."

I fought back a smile and looked at Gurn. He was fighting one back as well. Fenner cleared his throat.

"Do you have more to tell me?"

"Yes," I said. "The key."

"The key?"

I removed the key from my pocket and handed it over to Fenner. He closed his eyes and let out a sigh that seemed to come from as deep down as his shoelaces.

"Where does this come from? Don't tell me. Your nameless client."

"Right. It's to a safety deposit box at San Francisco Amalgamated. Probably near Sea Cliff. Smith gave it to my client for safekeeping."

"Your client is in on this?"

"No, my client—"

"Can we drop the 'my client' routine and at least use a pronoun? This is a woman, right?"

"Yes, but she was totally ignorant of any wrongdoings on his part."

"So she says."

"So she *is*. On my honor."

He stared at me. "Okay. I'll accept that for now. What's in this box?"

"All I know is Edgar told my client it's something the current Mrs. Del Vecchio doesn't want known."

"In other words, Edgar Smith was blackmailing her."

I shrugged. "Mrs. Del Vecchio liked to play around. I don't know if that's what he held over her, though. Anyway, my client was asked to hold the key for Edgar, and when he contacted her, she was to open the box and send the contents to him in Rio de Janeiro."

"Sounds like they were lovers."

"I'm not at liber—"

"Never mind," he interrupted. "That it?"

"For now," I said.

"Okay." Fenner stood. We stood, as well. "I'll have this box checked out right away. If there's nothing else, you can leave now." We turned to leave, but his voice stopped us. "And, thanks. I thought Frank Thompson was exaggerating about you, Lee, but I can see he wasn't. You, too, Lieutenant Commander. But don't let any of it go to your heads. Interfere with police procedure, and I'll come down on you with everything I've got."

"Yes, sir," I said, imitating Rudwin. Then I saluted smartly.

Fenner began to laugh. "Get out of here, the both of you."

Chapter Thirty-Two

"I've been meaning to ask you," Gurn called out from the bedroom. "Do you think Fenner believed you when you said Anna wasn't involved in Smith's activities?"

Brushing my teeth in the bathroom, I waited to answer until I finished. No use spitting toothpaste everywhere. Gurn, meanwhile, was taking the coverlet off the bed and adjusting the pillows just so. He always knows how I like my pillows. I know how he likes his, too. That could be the key to a successful marriage. I'll run it by Dear Abby.

I came out of the bathroom, crawled into bed, all washed and scrubbed, wearing my brand-new lavender silk pajamas as a special treat. "Boy, this mattress never felt so good," I murmured. "In answer to your question, I think Fenner believed me, but maybe not. For now, though, Anna's safe."

"Between the time we left San Francisco and arrived home, they found the license plate number of Edgar's rental and put out an APB on it."

"How do you know that?"

"Rich called on the sat phone while you were in the shower. He has his police radio bands on when he wants to know what's going on."

"I keep forgetting that Mr. Know-It-All tracks everybody and everything. The fact they found Billie's car parked three blocks away from the theater makes it a greater likelihood the two of them are in the Ford Explorer heading for Ensenada. Unless they took a cab. Can you imagine the bill for a trip like that? It would be in the thousands of dollars."

"You're getting punchy from lack of sleep."

"That reminds me. What time is it?"

"Ten minutes after eight. The shank of the evening."

"The shank of the evening," I repeated. "What does that... Oh, never mind. I'm too tired to know." I lay back on the fluffed-up pillows with a sigh. "Lawdy, Lawdy, Lawdy, Miss Clawdy, I am a spent force." Then I added in my best Scarlet O'Hara accent, "But tomorrow is another day."

Gurn let out a big chuckle because he thinks I'm funny. He's great that way.

Tugger jumped up on the bed, followed by Baba. Tugger climbed up on my chest and began to purr. Baba came to my side and snuggled in my armpit.

"I guess we can see who's the favorite cat-parent around here," I bragged.

"You were the one who opened the cans of cat food while I unpacked the car," he said. "So, I'm not threatened. By the way, how many handshake clients do you have now?"

"Just the two. Donna and Anna. It was the quickest way to keep whatever they said legally between the two of us. I didn't want to have to share too much information with the police until I was ready. Besides, it seems to me both need our help, darling."

"Well, I know Donna's story. What's Anna's?"

"When Richard did a quick search on Anna, he found her name is Anna Louise Curry, twenty, in and out of foster homes most of her life. Wong gave her a chance, even helped her get her GED."

"That speaks well of him."

"Then why don't I trust him?"

"Wong is a man of extremes. They can be unpredictable. I remember a vice admiral who got into drug trafficking because his wife had a gambling problem. He's still in the brig. That doesn't mean Wong has done anything wrong. Besides, Billie already admitted to killing Marvin the Magnificent."

"Only to us, when she thought we were going to suffocate in that tunnel. I don't know how much that counts in a court of law. It might come down to 'he said, she said.' But the real question of the day is, how did she do it?" I lay back on the pillows stroking a purring Tugger, and thinking, thinking, thinking. Or trying, trying, trying. Gurn interrupted my lagging thought processes.

"Table it, sweetheart. We've been up for nearly thirty-six hours except for a catnap here and there."

"But catnaps do us so much good, don't they, Tugger?" I asked of my orange-and-white feline love muffin. Tugger chirped his approval.

Gurn continued as if the cat and I hadn't spoken. "I've turned the sat phone and landline off,

and the new cell phones haven't been programmed
yet—"

"Wasn't that nice of Richard to order those and
send them to us? He can be such a sweet brother.
Such a sweetsie-poo-poo."

"And now you've become maudlin. I also put a
Do Not Disturb sign on the door. All that's left is
for you to turn the light out, sweetheart. Let's get
some sleep."

"I may have to have some more of Tío's chiles
en nogada. It was so sweet of him to have it
warming in the oven."

"I know. Everybody's sweet. Put the light out."

I yawned and stretched, knocking Tugger off-
balance. He ambled over to the middle of the bed,
in between Gurn and me, curled up, and went to
sleep.

"Maybe a snack later," I said, reaching for the
light. "Good night, darling." But all I got in
response was a snore.

Chapter Thirty-Three
Wednesday

A sandpapery lick of my nose woke me up at what had to be 8:00 a.m. A hungry cat is the most reliable alarm clock I know, and Tugger likes his breakfast at eight. Stretching, I looked over at Gurn's side of the bed. Instead of his head on the pillow, there was Baba curled up, with her face half buried in her fluffy tail. I sniffed the air. Freshly brewed coffee.

I threw back the covers, picked up Tugger and carried him to the door of our Mexican-tiled kitchen. With its large skylight, a beam of sunlight shined down on my husband's back at the stove. I set Tugger down on the floor, tiptoed over, and embraced Gurn from behind while he was scrambling eggs in a pan.

"Aha!" I said, hoping to surprise him.

"Aha, yourself," he said, turning around and kissing me full on the lips.

"Well, this is nice," I said when we broke free. "Finally, a decent cup of coffee and a kiss to die for. What could be better?"

"Scrambled eggs?"

"Lovely." Tugger's yowl broke into our moment. Without turning around, I said, "Aha! Maybe I should feed the cats first."

"Maybe you should," Gurn agreed. "I'll pour your coffee."

"Thank you, darling." I reached into the cabinet and looked over the array of deluxe canned cat food. "Aha!" I said, choosing a can of sardines in EVOO.

"Is everything an 'Aha' to you this morning?"

"Why not? And putting a murder charge aside, it's a lovely day and we're alive to live it."

"I can't argue with that philosophy. We've had a few hairy moments lately."

I reached for the electric can opener, and the ritual of opening cat food began. Baba, even while in a deep sleep in the bedroom, heard the can opener and came running. With two cats dancing around my feet, I still managed to put the contents of the cans into their bowls without spilling anything. I set the bowls down on the floor, and Gurn and I watched them eat for a moment.

"You know, the way they act," I said, "you'd think they hadn't eaten in days."

"Just like sailors on liberty. Come drink your coffee before it gets cold."

I crossed to our small kitchen table and sat down, reaching for the creamer and sugar bowl. "Do you miss it?" I sipped my coffee and closed my eyes at the sheer heaven of it.

"Miss what?"

"Being in the Navy. A SEAL."

"Everything has its season. At thirty-six, I'm a little too old for the SEALs. And I still am in the navy, sweetheart. But after fifteen years, no longer on active duty. Ready Reserve. Plus, I have my fracas with the Pentagon from time to time to look forward to."

"What are you talking about? They love you there. They hang on to every word you say."

"But we all like our rough-and-tumble coexistence with one another. Makes each side feel more justified."

"So, you're happy?"

"Couldn't be happier. I have everything a man could want or need. And then I have the pièce de résistance. You."

"I love it when you speak French."

"What brought this on?"

"Just trying to keep the lines of communication open, darling."

"And are you happy, mi cielo?"

"Delirious. Or is it deliriously?"

"As my mother would say, 'We are blessed.'" He raised his cup of coffee in a toast.

"And as my mother would say, '*indubitably*.'" I raised my cup in a toast, as well, but was interrupted by what sounded like the ringing of a phone. "Is that a phone I hear?"

"Yes, I downloaded all our info on our new phones this morning. They're on the dining room table ready to go. That's your ring."

"How long have you been up?"

"Since six." The ringing continued. "That's probably Rich telling you the latest on something. Maybe it's an update on Carl."

"Then I'd better get it." I stood up, groaned, stretched my back a little, and went to the phone, saying, "I need to do a barre."

It was, indeed, Richard. "Hey there, you. How are you?"

Just then the doorbell rang with a simultaneous banging on the door. Richard said something I couldn't hear due to the ruckus.

"What? Richard, I can't hear you." The banging on the door continued. "Just a minute," I said into the phone. I carried it with me to the door. Peeping through the peephole, I saw it was Frank Thompson, his expression looking like he'd eaten sauerkraut topped with a dill pickle and several lemons.

I swung open the door, feeling slightly sour myself. "What's wrong, Frank? For heaven's sake, it's eight o'clock in the morning. It's Frank," I said to my brother on the other end of the line.

"That's what I've been trying to tell you. He's there to give you some good news and some bad news," Richard said in my ear. "Now I'm hanging up." And he did.

"I'm here to give you some good news and some bad news, Lee," Frank repeated unknowingly. He stood in the doorway. "Oh, here's your Do Not Disturb sign." He thrust it at me. "What do you want to hear first, the good or the bad?"

"Let's have the good news first. Bouy me up."

"Hey, Frank," Gurn called out before Frank could answer me. "How about some coffee?"

"I could use some," he said, stepping past me and heading for the kitchen. I trailed along.

Now standing, Gurn handed Frank a steaming cup of coffee, then gestured for him to take a chair. Gurn sat down as well. I remained standing in front of the kitchen table.

"Well? What's up?" I balled up the paper sign, threw it on the table, and crossed my arms over my chest. "I'm desperately seeking sanction."

Frank took a sip and then said, "The good news: they picked up Billie Evans and Edgar Smith on I-5 just past LA at ten thirty last night. They've been interrogated ever since. I called both of you, but it went directly to voice mail."

"That's fabulous," I said dropping my arms as the pitch of my voice rose. "Did they confess? Are they arrested? Am I cleared of all charges?"

"And that brings me to the bad news," Frank said over my questions. "While we can charge Smith with kidnapping, he says he only *told* Donna he'd killed her husband and father to scare her into giving him the bank account number in the Cayman Islands. He said he didn't kill them. And we have no physical evidence to link him to the murders other than Donna Del Vecchio's account of what he said to her. And as for Billie Evans, she denies everything. She says she and Edgar Smith were never in the theater yesterday. That you and your husband are trying to shift the blame for Del Vecchio's death onto her."

"What?" Gurn said.

"Liar, liar, pants on fire," I said, hardly able to contain myself.

"Let me finish," Frank said, holding out his hands to stave off any further protests from either of us. "She did admit she is Elizabeth Hofsted, but said it was a coincidence Marvin came to the theater where she works. That she hadn't been in contact with him for nearly thirty years. And there's more. At the time you say you were locked in the tunnel, Billie maintains she was driving with Smith to the Mexican border, and of course, he backs her up. It becomes a case of 'he said, she said.' Furthermore, she maintains there is no way she could have killed Marvin Del Vecchio, as she was nowhere near the stage when it happened, has dozens of witnesses who can testify to that, and that we can't prove otherwise. Which we can't," he added.

"You mean she just walks?" Gurn's incredulous tone mirrored my feelings.

"No. We can get her on other charges," Frank said, "such as being Smith's accomplice, aiding and abetting in kidnapping, and fleeing with a felon – but murder? No. At least, not yet. And nothing so far that keeps her from claiming her share of the inheritance, as her actions were not driven by the inheritance."

"Of course they were," Gurn sputtered.

"According to their lawyer—and she has lawyered up—she was merely trying to help the child she gave away at birth make a fresh start. Everything she did was driven by her need to make it up to him for having given him up for adoption."

"She's pulling the loving-mother card?" I asked.

"And what about Edgar?" Gurn asked. "Kidnapping Donna, holding Carl captive, nearly killing him? What happens with that?"

"Smith maintains he was mentally and emotionally disturbed by being taken in by several families who did not love him, and ultimately returned him to the orphanage. Or rather, their lawyer maintains this. The fact that at age nine he broke into other people's homes, stole cars, and attacked two foster parents with knives never came into it. His juvenile record is off-limits, so that doesn't help."

"He's pulling the traumatized-orphan card?" I asked.

"Well, then, who killed Steven Kutner if it wasn't Edgar Smith?" Gurn demanded to know.

"Nobody's gotten there yet. And believe me, Dabuda Lel Ti is disgusted, right along with the rest of us. She was counting on having Smith returned to Tahoe to be arraigned and stand trial."

"Sounds like Ma Barker and her son know how to play the system," I muttered.

"So," Frank said quietly, "until we can figure out how Billie beheaded a man onstage from her wardrobe room in the basement, she cannot be charged with his death. If all goes as it's going, I have to bring you to Judge Plenca on Monday to face possible charges."

"I understand." My voice sounded smaller than I'd meant. "And even if I don't go to prison, unless I find out how she did it, there will be the thought in everyone's mind that I beheaded this man, whether on purpose or accidentally. This could follow me around for the rest of my life."

"I'm afraid so," Frank said softly. He stood, reached out, and took my hands in his. "And I am sorrier about this than I can say."

"We'll fight it, sweetheart," Gurn said. "And don't worry. We'll win. It's time for *us* to lawyer up. At eighty-three, Jim Talbot may be the one of world's oldest practicing attorneys, but he certainly is one of the smartest. I'll give him a call." Gurn rose, heading for his phone in the dining room.

"I have to go," Frank said, looking at his watch. "I've got a meeting with the mayor on next year's budget." He looked at me. "You okay?" I nodded. He looked at his watch again and was gone.

Alone in the room, I sat down in a chair. Or more like fell into it. Tugger jumped into my lap, stood on his hind legs, wrapped his front legs around my neck. Purring, he nuzzled the side of my neck. I buried what I could of my face in his soft fur and whispered, "Tugger, Mommy is so screwed."

Chapter Thirty-Four

"We need to be at Jim Talbot's office at ten. It's nearly nine now so we'd better get a move on," Gurn said, eating the last of his scrambled eggs. "Finish your eggs and don't give up hope."

I tried to smile, but I felt like Susan Hayward in *I'll Cry Tomorrow*. Death row, here I come. "If only I knew how she did it," I lamented. "How did it get done from the wardrobe room in the basement to onstage in front of hundreds of people?"

I was aware of Tugger doing a figure eight around my legs. "Tugger," I said, looking down at him. "What's the matter? I fed you not an hour ago."

Never make eye contact with a cat unless you want their heart and soul uttered to you in one single meow. He uttered it now, plaintive and loud.

"What do you mean, you're starving? You can't be. I just fed you." Another wail, long and pitiful.

"Honey," Gurn said, "I'm going to take a shower. Don't be too long."

"Of course not," I murmured, directing my attention to my weird-acting cat.

Not to be left out, Baba joined in with her own meow, soft though it was. I stood, indecisive.

Should I take a shower or feed the cats a second breakfast? Caterwauling won out.

I turned for the counter under the cabinet with their cat food. Anticipating me, Tugger made a dash across the kitchen and jumped the three and a half feet to the countertop, landing with the grace of Nijinsky.

"Tugger," I said, leaning into him. "You know you're not allowed on the countertops when daddy's home. Get down," I ordered.

He ignored me, as usual, my well-trained, obedient little feline boy. He was well-trained, thanks to Tío, not me. I took a deep breath, picked him up, and set him on the floor. He immediately jumped up again.

I gave up, which is my wont. This is why I am not a good trainer of cats, husbands, or hair. It's all beyond me.

"Okay," I said, giving in. "But if we-know-who comes into the kitchen, I don't even know who you are."

I opened the cabinet door, swatting at his long, up-reaching and perfectly groomed tail to keep it out of the way. I grabbed a can of tuna-belly fillets, another of their favorites, and pulled the electric can opener forward from the back of the counter.

Suddenly, Tugger became very well-behaved. He sat with legs together, wrapped his tail around the whole of him, and stared at me. I put the can in, lowered the top of the opener onto the lid of the can, and pressed the button. There was the *whir, whir* sound. Done, I pulled the can away, the lid staying where it was.

Tugger continued to stare at me. I stared at the can opener. Then I let out a shriek.

"Oh my gawd," I yelped. "That's it! That's it! And you did it, Tugs! You!"

I grabbed Tugger, crushed him to me, and kissed him soundly on the top of the head, not once, not twice, but three times. He is good for maybe one smackeroo. After that, all bets are off. He struggled, broke free from my embrace, and dropped to the floor. Giving me his "yuck" look, he stalked out of the room.

Baba glanced from Tugger to me and then back again, torn. Should she follow him from the room? Or should she stay, hoping to get a second breakfast?

"Baba, come to Mommy. I want to give you a few of those kisses your big brother wouldn't let me give him."

You never saw a cat leave a room so fast.

Seconds later found me racing to the bathroom. Gurn was still taking a shower, steam rising from the top of the shower door, as was his voice, singing, "This Nearly Was Mine" from *South Pacific*.

"Darling, darling, darling," I shrieked, banging on the shower door. "I know how she did it. Tugger showed me. I'm saved." I turned away and went to the corner of the room where the wastebasket was.

"What?" The water went off and the shower door opened.

I looked inside the wastebasket. Empty. "No, no, no, no, no!"

"You know how who did what?" Gurn asked, wrapping a towel around him.

"Billie. Where's the trash? Where is it?"

"The trash?"

If ever there was a time to panic. This was it. So, I did. "Yes, yes, yes, yes, yes. Trash, trash, trash, trash," I screamed, looking at him.

"I-I took it out. Earlier," he stammered. "It's Wednesday, trash day. In fact, it should be picked up any minute."

"No, no, no, no, no," I said, tearing out of the bathroom and running for the front door. Barefoot and still in my pajamas, I took the stairs down to ground level two at a time.

"Trash, trash, trash, trash, trash," I yelled, running past a gardening Tío and heading for the large trash cans at the end of the drive.

"*Que?*" I heard Tío ask, as I flew by.

At that moment, Mom's beige Jaguar turned into the drive, almost hitting me. Or rather, I almost hit her. I bounced off the hood as Mom jammed on the brakes.

"Liana? What on *earth*?" she said, opening the car door.

I dashed around the Jag and arrived at the four trash cans. They were empty. One even lay on its side. I looked down the street to see the back end of one of Budilov's Refuse Pickup trucks.

"No, no, no, no, no," I shrieked again.

By this time, a terrycloth-robed Gurn, an uncle still holding a trowel, and a perplexed mother joined me at the end of the driveway.

"What is going *on*?" Mom demanded to know.

"That truck holds the key to Lee's freedom," Gurn said, with a clenched jaw.

"¡No me digas!" Tío exclaimed.

I never felt so defeated. "By the time we get to them, it'll have been ground up into a pulp," I wailed.

Mom said nothing, but ran to her car and hopped in. She pulled out of the driveway so fast, gravel flew in every direction. Then she careened down the street at what seemed like a hundred miles an hour.

By the time the truck got to the end of the street, so had Mom's Jaguar. She pulled in front of the truck, cutting the driver off.

Gurn, Tío, and I started running. Thirty seconds later and panting, Gurn arrived with me right behind—he's got longer legs—to find Mom smiling and chatting with Mr. Budilov.

"Anything for you, Mrs. Alvarez," the short, overweight man said. Like most of the men in my mother's life, he worshiped her from afar. She was the unobtainable goddess. Lancelot's Guinevere, if you will.

"Here is my *daughter* and her *husband* now," Mom said, not saying a word about me being shoeless and in my pajamas or Gurn being in his bathrobe.

Mr. Budilov looked at us both from top to bottom. But because Mom hadn't mentioned anything about our attire, neither did he. Neither did his son, Jerry, standing at the back of the truck, taking all this in. We were the unmentionables.

"Liana, *dear*," Mom said. "I was *explaining* to Mr. Budilov, that something of *extreme* value was *accidentally* thrown away and that we *must* retrieve it. He has *offered* his son, Jerry's, *services*. He'll go into the truck and *search* through… *things*… for whatever it is."

"Yes," said Mr. Budilov. "You're lucky we hadn't started compacting our trash yet. It uses a lot of power, so I don't begin the process until the hopper is half-full." He went on in that slightly formal tone that Mom seems to bring out in people. "I do have to say, this is highly unorthodox, and we do have insurance to consider, but we'll do our best. Anything for Mrs. Alvarez," he said again. If he'd been wearing a hat, he probably would have doffed it and taken a low bow.

Mom smiled at him benevolently, then turned to me. "You have but to *tell* us what it is, Liana. *Dear*."

"Yes, yes, yes, yes. So, what it probably looks like right now is a crushed disco ball. But what it is really, is sort of a bathing suit with spangles all over it."

"Do you have that, Son?" Mr. Budilov turned to the silent Jerry, no more than twenty, who merely nodded. Jerry began to climb up the ladder attached to right side and rear of the truck. He was wearing knee-high rubber boots with the bottoms of his gray coveralls tucked inside. Fearlessly, he jumped right into the open top and down among all the refuse they'd collected so far. Better him than me.

However, suspense overtook me and before anyone could say anything, I jumped onto the ladder and climbed up. Jerry was moving through a mélange of old newspapers and magazines, moldy bread, broken egg shells, gnawed-on chicken wings, used paper towels, doggy doo, rancid cheese, peanut butter, empty potato chip bags, used food containers, an odd shoe or two, not to mention spoiled fruit of every variety. A cornucopia of disgustingness.

"Here, here, Ms. Alvarez," I heard an alarmed Mr. Budilov say from below. "You can't be up there. You have to come down. It's dangerous, and the insurance doesn't cover this."

I went up another rung. A mighty stench came blasting up. It was so foul that I felt I should let go of the railings and applaud Jerry's guts for going in. I had no idea garbage looked and smelled like that in the latter stages of decay.

"Jerry! Jerry," I called out, noticing something. "Over in the corner. That sparkly thing. I think that's it. No, no, over there!" I yelled again, letting go and gesturing with both hands.

That's when I lost my balance and fell in.

Chapter Thirty-Five

I landed in I know not what, but it was yucko, wet, and stinking. Jerry sloshed over and yanked me up.

"You okay?" Jerry asked, finally speaking.

"Yes, yes," I said. "Did you get it?"

The lad of few words handed over a balled-up, garbage-covered garment with a sparkle or two still showing through all the debris. I opened it up and shook out an empty sardine can, dried beans, and sour yogurt.

"Eureka! This is it." I tried to keep from slipping and falling down again and grabbed on to a hook attached to the wall of the hopper. I turned to Jerry. "Isn't this wonderful?"

Before Jerry could answer, if he was going to, I heard Gurn's anxious voice calling down from where I'd been only moments before.

"Honey, are you all right?"

"Yes, I'm perfect. Jerry found it." I waved the costume like a flag and got smacked in the face with a freed slice of lemon. I turned to Jerry.

"Okay, we need to get serious now. How do we get out of here?"

"Lee, throw up the costume," Gurn said. "You should have both hands free."

"Guard it with your life, darling. Your life." I tossed it up reluctantly, then turned to Jerry. "Okay, now what?"

"See those rungs there?" Jerry pointed to a series of rungs running along the side of the wall of the hopper and leading up to the ladder I'd fallen from. "Put your right foot there and your left foot there. I'll push from below."

It was a lot of conversation from the youth, but I wondered about the "push from below" part. I was about to learn. Bare, slippery feet don't have much staying power on slick, gunk-covered rungs. I gave it my best shot, but struggled and failed to keep hold of anything with my slimy hands and feet.

I wound up sitting on Jerry's shoulders while Gurn grabbed my wrists from above. Jerry pushed, Gurn pulled, I grunted. Finally at the top, I lay for a moment bent over at the waist, bottom half inside the hopper, top half facing the pavement below, duff in the air. No photo op here.

"Sweetheart," Gurn said, breathing hard and standing below on the ladder. "What has to happen now is you turn around so you can descend the ladder with your feet. Think you can do that?"

"Listen," I gasped, "Why don't you leave me here, say, for an hour or two, maybe three, and come back later? I'll be fine. I'll just hang out."

I heard my mother's voice from below. "Liana, you are behaving *outrageously*. Mr. *Budilov* has spent *enough* of his day *helping* you and is *already* behind schedule, are you *not*, Mr. Budilov?"

"Well, yes, but I don't want to—"

"Come down from there this *instant*, young lady," Mom said in the same tone she used when I was ten and had climbed in a tree to watch the new next-door neighbors swim nude in their pool.

"Yes, ma'am." I threw my legs up and lay prone on the three-inch width of the hopper's side. If this was what tightrope walkers did for a living, they could have it. It was all I could do to keep my balance and not roll off.

Gurn's hands were on my feet, giving them a gentle tug. "I've got you sweetheart. Just lower your legs, and I'll guide your feet down to the rungs of the ladder."

I closed my eyes, commended my soul to God, and swung my legs around. I stood, took a deep breath, and felt a cloth smack me in the face.

"Dry your hands on that," Mr. Budilov said from below. "It will make them less slick."

Now he tells me. I did as ordered, though. Throwing the used towel down, I grabbed the rails at the side of the ladder with renewed strength. But I still kept my eyes closed.

"Remember, sweetheart," Gurn said. "I'm right beneath you. You can't fall."

And down I went, guided by Gurn. When I felt the ground and Gurn's arm around my waist, I opened my eyes to see Mom, Tío, Mr. Budilov, and Jerry staring at me. How Jerry got down ahead of me I had no idea, but decided not to delve. Instead, I focused on the condition of my brand-new silk pajamas. A total loss. One sleeve was ripped at the elbow, and they looked as if I'd been in a paintball war of the odiferous variety. With a sigh, I tugged at the apple core entangled in my hair, threw it to the ground, and scanned the surroundings for Gurn holding my passport to freedom.

"Now, you're not going to sue, are you, Ms. Alvarez? I told you not to go up that ladder. I told you." Mr. Budilov gave me an anxious eye.

About one hundred times more anxious than Mr. Budilov, I turned franticly to Gurn. "Where is it? Where is it? Where is it?" Then I realized everyone was staring at me. "Oh, I'm sorry, Mr. Budilov. Did you say something to me?"

"Sue me! Sue!" He looked as if he might have a stroke on the spot. "Are you going to sue me for falling in? My insurance would double if not triple. I can barely pay it now."

Mr. Budilov looked so frightened by the prospect, I lost all thoughts about the costume and tried to reassure him. We all did. There were four simultaneous denials of any chance of that happening. It was a cacophony of don't-be-ridiculous, but they seemed to have little effect on the king of trash, until Mom reached out her hand and touched his arm. A silent calm descended.

"Here," Gurn whispered in the quiet, handing me the wadded-up bundle.

I searched for the evidence that would save me. There it was! I took a deep breath, inhaling deeply of the most welcomed stink of my life. Then I clutched it unto me like a newborn babe.

Meanwhile the drama between the trash man and my mother continued.

"*Heaven* forfend, Mr. Budilov," Mom said regally. "*You* have done us a service, *above* and *beyond*. We are in your *debt*. We simply *cannot* thank you enough."

"It was nothing, Mrs. Alvarez. Anything for you, Mrs. Alvarez," he repeated. This time he did bow.

Her royal position established, Mom went on. "And you *must* take a pledge in the sum of one *thousand* dollars from Discretionary Inquiries for Mrs. Budilov's *ongoing* Breast Cancer Research fundraising. It is *such* a worthwhile endeavor. She is doing *well*, Mrs. Budilov?"

"She has recovered completely, Mrs. Alvarez. She will be pleased you asked about her and to learn of your donation."

"*Nonsense*. It is *we* who are *thrilled* to learn of her regained *health* and her *fight* for a cause *most* worthy." Mom turned to me with her brightest smile. "Before you *leave*, Liana, to take a *long* shower, possibly you have something to *say* to Mr. Budilov?"

"Yes, of course. Thank you so much." I reached out a hand to shake. He looked at it, took a sniff, and backed up. Being downwind of me, I understood. I decided to give him a small salute. "Thank you for your help, Mr. Budilov — and you, too, Jerry." I turned to my mother. "I would ask you for a ride back home — "

"*Surely*, you jest."

"But, of course, we will walk," I finished with as much dignity as I could muster.

I looked down at me, covered in pretty much everything disgusting, then at Gurn who was not nearly as foul-smelling. Nonetheless, he wrapped his arm around me. Greater love hath no man.

* * *

"That's great, Inspector Fenner." I listened and nodded. "I understand. It's going to take a while to pull it together, but Friday sounds perfect. And thanks for forcing everyone in the game to be there."

I hung up and turned my towel-wrapped head to Gurn, whose own slicked back, wet hair reminded me of the shower we'd shared a short time before. He looked at me questioningly.

"It's done," I said. "And Fenner is being very cooperative, especially as I now have the means of showing how Billie accomplished it."

"You're not going to tell them?"

"It will have far more impact if I demonstrate, costume and all. According to Fenner, Henry Swan has already agreed to check out the guillotine before we use it and afterward to make sure everything's kosher. All the heirs will be there, including Billie and her son. Probably even Madison. She's being released from the hospital tomorrow morning. Oh, yes! Henry is bringing two cabbage heads."

"Don't tell me we're making coleslaw."

"Part of the demonstration, darling."

"And this demonstration is being done before the official reading of the will?"

"Yes. Ten a.m. The reading is at three thirty."

"So, day after tomorrow is all set? We get a bit of a respite? A day to ourselves?"

I nodded.

"Then why don't we retire to the bedroom and pick up where we left off in the shower?"

He grinned at me. I grinned back.

"Two minds with but a single thought."

Chapter Thirty-Six
Friday

On Thursday I'd binged-watched *Matlock* reruns most of the day in preparation for Friday's defense. I wanted to learn a few tips from a lawyer who never lost a case. True, it was a television lawyer, but the character had a lot going for him. Presence, confidence, and the ability to make things crystal clear to a jury, step-by-step. "Learn from the best," that's my motto. Even if they are make-believe.

Then as a reward, I'd also watched Barbara Stanwyck in *Meet John Doe*, a 1941 American comedy-drama film starring her and Gary Cooper. The film is about good winning over evil no matter what the odds. By the time I went to bed, I was stoked.

* * * *

We arrived at the Del Vecchio mansion early the next morning. Parked next to the curb were two San Francisco police cars, a North Lake Tahoe police car, and two nondescript dark, late-model sedans. One I recognized as Frank's. In the driveway sat a silver-gray station wagon beside a blue Mercedes-Benz looking right off the showroom. Mom's beige Jaguar was across the street. Everyone seemed to be there even though it was barely 9:30 a.m.

I was glad I was wearing my raincoat when I got out of the car. It was an overcast day and on the cool side. A slight breeze blew off the water, chilly and damp. The feel of the rawness on my face only helped to sharpen my resolve. Weather can do that sometimes.

Gurn looked as handsome as ever. He was wearing one of my favorite outfits, a V-neck cashmere sweater in slate-green, with slacks a slightly darker hue. While the colors were cheerful, the look on his face was not. He was the most somber I'd seen him in months. But then, his wife's freedom depended on the outcome of how the day went, something neither of us might be able to control.

Anna opened the front door before we even knocked. Apparently, she'd been watching for us. She stared at me and then mouthed, "He's here." I could only assume she meant her errant lover, Edgar Smith, the ex-Johan Nilsson.

We followed her down the stairs and into the magic room. The first thing I noticed was the guillotine had been pulled from the corner of the room to dead center. The second thing was the row of chairs against the far wall with some people sitting in them and others standing behind the chairs, mostly uniformed police officers.

Scanning from left to right was Madison Del Vecchio, blue nail polish in place. Then David Del

Vecchio, Donna Del Vecchio, their mother, Claudia Del Vecchio, her significant other, Paul Rinken, looking fresh from one of his health clubs, and the three Del Vecchio estate attorneys, whose names I didn't even bother to learn as I had enough on my plate. What looked like a junior attorney was nervously plucking at the latch on his briefcase.

Next to Plucking Junior was Wyman Del Vecchio, the remaining half of the twins, looking so angry and malevolent, you'd think he ran over his brother himself. Maybe he did.

To his left, Henry Swan sat reading something amusing on his phone. Next to Henry was Tío, then Mom. Tío sat with his eyes closed. Mom was writing in her journal. And at the end of the row, brother mine sat next to Vicki, both holding hands and leaning into one another.

Off to the side, Billie and Edgar were seated and handcuffed to their chairs with armed officers standing on both sides of them. Fenner was taking no chances. Behind this separated party was a man in a pin-striped suit, leaning against the wall, also with a briefcase in his hand. I surmised it to be their new attorney. It was all I could do not to boo. Mother Love, Traumatized Orphan, indeed. Gimmeeabreak.

On the opposite side of the room, Police Chiefs Frank Thompson and Dabuda Lel Ti were in a deep conversation with Detective Inspector Bill Fenner. A lot of titles here. The only one missing was Mr. Wong, butler-at-large, off in Washington State and dealing with his granddaughter's heart operation. From what I'd been told, he was under a twenty-four-seven watch until it was established who did what to whom.

Frank saw us standing in the doorway and gestured for us to come to him. We hurried over, and when I turned around to face the guillotine, I saw the group had more or less formed an "audience" with a clear view of the front of the guillotine, the same as the audience had in the theater on that awful night.

Before I could comment on it, Frank said to me, "We have some good news. Last night Chief Lel Ti found the tire iron that she believes was used to attack Carl and possibly Steven Kutner."

"A half a mile away from the cabin, in a gulley," Chief Lel Ti explained. "The tire iron has gray and dark-brown hairs on it. I'm betting this was the weapon used on both men. Forensics is checking for hair and blood samples now for a match to the victims, but the fingerprints are definitely Smith's. We should know more soon."

"Smith continues to deny having anything to do with Kutner's death," Fenner jumped in with, "but we may soon be able to prove otherwise." He turned to me. "And if you can wrap up how Billie Evans, aka Elizabeth Hofsted, managed to pull off a beheading while never leaving the basement wardrobe room, we've got the two of them."

"It's your show, Lee," Frank said. "Take it."

I nodded and looked at the row of people. Not just my audience but also my jury. I turned back to Frank. "Who has the cabbage?"

"Henry Swan," Frank said. "He says he'll do whatever you say."

I nodded again and crossed the line of chairs toward Henry. Gurn stayed with Frank. As I walked by David and Donna, both looked up and smiled at me. I returned their smiles not showing the nervousness mounting up inside me.

Then I passed my family. Tío's eyes sent love beams strong enough to quell any of my nervousness. Mom gave me a radiant smile, also filled with love, but mostly pride. Then Richard winked, and gave me a thumbs-up, while Vicki blew me a kiss. I looked back in Gurn's direction, and he put his two hands together in a heart shape in front of own heart. At that moment, I felt as if I could slay a dragon.

I paused in front of Henry Swan, whose large frame was crammed into the smallish chair. He looked up and smiled.

"Do you have the two cabbage heads?" I asked, stepping back to allow him to rise. He reached for a paper bag under his chair.

"I brought three. You never know," he said, gray eyes twinkling. He stood, his six foot four looking down at me. "I don't know what you're going to do," he whispered, "but I'm pulling for you. By the way, Sailor sends a friendly meow."

"Kiss him on the noggin for me, Henry," I said in a like tone. "If you would please go stand by the guillotine."

I waited until he was at the head of the killing machine. Then I stepped back and addressed the group as a whole. Don't fail me now, Ben Matlock.

"Good morning, everyone. For those of you who don't know me, my name is Lee Alvarez. I am a private detective and the person who was onstage with Marvin Del Vecchio when he died." I took a deep breath before adding, "And I am about to prove that not only did I *not* have anything to do with Marvin's murder, but how the person who killed him accomplished it."

I gestured to Henry. "This is Henry Swan. He created the guillotine illusion, and he and he alone is going to work it. I will only go near the guillotine when it's time to prove how the murder was done." I saw Billie squirm in her chair but ignored her and turned to Henry.

"Very basically, with this illusion there are two positions for the blade: safe and danger. I don't think the intricacies of the illusion need to be explained. All you need to know is we will first do the 'safe' part of this trick. I am going to ask Henry to put the guillotine into the safe mode, which means it will *not* cut a cabbage head in two. Henry, if you please."

Henry came to the side of the guillotine with the levers, did his thing, and turned back to me.

"It's now in the safe mode?" He nodded. "Good. Henry, will you take one of the cabbages, put it in the pillory, and release the blade? Remember everyone, this is where the cabbage will *not* be cut in two, no matter how it looks. Ready, Henry?"

Again, he nodded. He put his hand inside the paper bag, took out one of the three cabbages, placed it in the proper position in the pillory, and then went to the side of the guillotine where the rope attached to the blade was tied off.

True to the majority of larger guillotines made, there was an upper crossbar with a hole in the top for the rope and a groove along the top and side to guide the rope. Henry unwound the rope at the tie-off with one hand, stepped back, and released it. With a loud whooshing noise, the blade dropped. Nearly everyone in the room flinched or gasped out loud.

"Thank you," I said. "Henry, please raise the blade and show everyone here the cabbage head."

He pulled the blade to the top of the mechanism, tied the rope off, removed the top of the pillory, and picked up the whole cabbage, showing it to the audience. A few "Oohs" and "Aahs" could be heard.

"Now, Henry, please put the lever into the 'danger' mode."

He returned to the same spot by the side of the guillotine and pulled the lever out.

"Now repeat the process with the cabbage head and drop the blade."

Henry obliged, and the same loud, frightening sound of the blade coming down happened again. Within a split second, half the cabbage head wobbled and rolled off the base and onto the floor. This caused huge gasps from everyone, including the lawyers and police.

My new assistant picked up the half head of cabbage, held it over his head, and did a half circle so everyone in the room could see it. More oohs and aahs. I looked over at Billie. She stared back, long and hard. There would be no breaking her. Not until my demonstration was over.

Still standing to the side, I said, "Henry, will you please put the guillotine back in the safe mode, and place another cabbage in the pillory?"

He nodded, went to the side of the guillotine and pushed the lever in. He removed another cabbage head from the brown bag and placed it in the pillory. I gave him a wait signal and turned back to the audience, pausing a half beat.

"Drop the blade, Henry." He did. Same whooshing noise, same everything, but no sound from the audience, who stared intently at the cabbage head. "Henry, show the condition of the cabbage."

He pulled the blade back to the top, went over, picked up the whole cabbage, threw it up in the air catching it several times to make the point of it being in one piece. Great assistant.

"Henry," I asked, "would you please check once again to see if the lever is still in the safe mode?"

Henry walked around the guillotine to the levers. He looked and said in a firm voice, "Yes, it is in the safe mode."

"Thank you. Will you put the cabbage back in the pillory as before?"

"Of course," he said, and did.

"Inspector Fenner," I said, directing myself to him. He looked at me somewhat surprised. "You're familiar enough with this guillotine, at least enough to know where the safe and danger levers are." He nodded, perplexed. "Will you please step over to the guillotine and verify that the lever is in the safe mode? But please don't touch anything."

With a shrug, he did as I asked. After bending down and looking but not touching anything, he said, "The button is green and says safe. Furthermore, it is pushed in and in line with the framework. I would say from what I've learned about this thing, it's safe."

"Thank you. Go stand next to Henry, if you please."

"Sure." He shrugged again but did as bidden.

It was time. I undid the ties of my raincoat and opened it to reveal a high-neck, long-sleeve black leotard and black tights, used mostly for my barre exercises. Over the leotard I wore the ragged assistant magician's costume pinned together in several strategic places. The condition of it caused a few titters to rise from the audience. But the essential piece to the costume, my passport to freedom, had remained intact, a credit to the wardrobe supervisor's sewing talents and a lot of luck on my part. I glanced in Billie's direction. She shrank as far back in her chair as possible. I turned back to the audience.

"How many of you recognize this costume from Saturday's performance? Yes, it is a little the worse for wear, but I think still recognizable." I turned to the stage manager in the back row. "Zack, please stand. Does this look like the costume you brought to me from Billie Evans in the wardrobe room five minutes before I was scheduled to go on in the Marvin the Magnificent act?"

He studied it for a moment, then said, "Turn around."

I did.

"Yes, I recognize that small pink bow centered in the back. I thought it was silly looking but didn't say anything to Billie when she handed it to me."

"What time was that?"

"Eight fifty. I remember going myself to the wardrobe room because the ASM ran up to me and said it hadn't been delivered to you yet. I needed to know in order to possibly change acts around — put on the juggler — until it was ready. You couldn't go on without it."

"The ASM is the assistant stage manager," I clarified.

"Yes."

"And then you left the dressing room while I put it on, correct? How long a time was that?"

"Two or three minutes. You were ready otherwise."

"And then we walked upstairs, you went to your podium to call the show, and I waited in the wings. You saw me that entire time. Is that correct?"

"Yes."

"Then I went onstage and started the act with Mr. Del Vecchio. True?"

"True."

"And at no time did I have time to alter, add to, or change the costume given to me by you from the wardrobe supervisor?"

"I don't see how," Zack said simply.

"Thank you." I turned from him, back to Henry and Fenner. "And you both have seen that the lever is at the safe mark, correct?" Both men nodded. I crossed my arms in front of my chest and walked to the same place on the guillotine where I needed to stand in order to see the safe sign. I began my announcement.

"You will notice I am wearing four-inch stilettos, not the same shoes I wore that night, but identical in height. And I am wearing the costume the same way even though much of it is pinned together. It is important for all of that to be the same in order for this to work.

"While not touching the guillotine, I am going to walk past it and join the two gentlemen. When I cross over to you, Henry, I want you to drop the blade, but not before. Understood?"

"Understood," he repeated.

I turned to the left and walked to the head of the guillotine, arms still folded, and stood beside Fenner.

"Now?" Henry asked.

"Now."

The blade whooshed down, cutting the cabbage in half. The only thing that could be heard in the room was a small thunk as the half cabbage rolled off the base and onto the floor.

"What the—" Henry said.

Fenner looked stunned. "What's going on?"

I turned to both men. "Please go check and see that now the lever has been moved to danger."

Both men crossed to the lever. Henry was the first to speak.

"But how?" He had an astonished look on his face.

"A strong magnet and the use of skilled sewing, courtesy of Billie Evans, aka Elizabeth Hofsted," I said.

I released a pin or two, and the costume dropped to the floor. I stepped out of the costume, picked it up, and turned it inside out. I found the spot right below the waistline holding the sewn-in magnet with neat little stitches and thrust the material under Fenner's nose. His nose wrinkled a little from the smell, but he didn't pull away. Evidence can do that to a policeman.

"Billie knew how tall I was and the height of the heels I would be wearing. That made it possible for her to place the magnet in just the right spot of the costume, so when I walked by it would be at its strongest." I turned to Henry. "Henry, remember when you said the only thing different with the guillotine was the safe-danger lever felt smoother?"

He nodded, the bafflement leaving his eyes. "The circumference had been filed down, making it imperceptibly narrower."

"Not enough to notice, but enough to make it easier to be pulled out of the safe mode and into danger when the magnet passed by. And did you know, that hand stitchwork is as individual as handwriting? Every person's is different. I'm sure if you examined the hand stitching in the wardrobe room, you'll find this costume was sewn by the same person."

There was a commotion in the corner of the room where Billie and Edgar sat. Only Billie was no longer sitting. She'd leapt up and yanked at the handcuffs that held her to the chair. The surrounding officers tried to restrain her, and even her lawyer put a hand on her shoulder but pulled back when he saw her wild behavior. Edgar yelled, calling out her name repeatedly. Billie was finally pushed back into her chair, but she never took her eyes off me.

"So, you finally figured it out," Billie screamed at me. "Well, good for you. You're smart. Unlike Marv."

In a room that was deathly quiet, she gave off a bitter laugh. It seemed to echo off the walls. Then she spoke again, breaking the silence.

"I was worried he'd recognize me, spoil the plan. So, I stayed out of the way as much as possible. I could have saved myself the trouble. He never paid any attention to me. I was just somebody to make tea for him or fix a tear in his costume."

"That must have hurt," Gurn said from where he was standing, using his skills as a trained hostage negotiator.

"Hurt?" she spat. "You have no idea. You know what I meant to him? Nothing. That's what anybody means to him. I should have known that when he threw me aside for that Italian bimbo."

"Excuse me," said an indignant Claudia from the other side of the room.

"Oh, shut up, you bitch," Billie screamed at her. "What would you know about really loving a man or anything? You just wanted to marry him so you could stay in America. And don't get me started on the sex-starved Madison who threw herself at anything in pants. You don't think I know about your sort?"

Billie's tirade made both women's jaws drop in shock. Edgar sat in his chair, head lowered, sobbing. Ignoring him, Billie turned back to me.

"Marvin's lawyer offered me a settlement that lasted maybe five years if I was frugal, and I was stupid enough to take it. That was me then. Stupid. Loving the man. Hoping I could win him back. But here I am now. Old. No future. Working paycheck to paycheck. Living in a rented studio apartment, with nothing to look forward to but loneliness and death.

"At first I was worried about meeting him again. What would I say if he recognized me? But I came to realize he was too self-absorbed to notice anyone but himself. Can you imagine? When he showed up at the theater—the first time I'm seeing him in nearly thirty years—he didn't recognize me. A week of being in the same theater with me and he didn't even know who I was. Married to the man for ten years. Sure, I've changed, but nobody changes that much. No matter what I looked like on the outside, he should have known me. But that was Marvin. He never had much going on upstairs, if you know what I mean." She tapped the side of her forehead. "But there was his father's money. And I didn't want my son or I to wait any longer for it."

"When did you rig the guillotine, if I may ask?" Gurn said, his voice loud but charming.

"After I met his mouse of a daughter, I knew it would be easy. A little attention, a little flattery, and she'd show me anything I wanted to know about the guillotine in between rehearsals. Like Marvin, she didn't have too much in the brain department."

I looked over at Donna. Her face was flushed, with a look of betrayal in her eyes.

I turned to Billie. "No, let's tell it like it really was. Donna trusted you, was nice to you, and answered a few questions. And you used that information to kill her father."

"Yes, I did. I admit it. I killed him. He was a gutless, selfish weasel. I hated him. Hated him. I waited until the night before the performance and did what needed to be done to the guillotine's lever. I wanted his death to be in front of hundreds of people. And I waited until the last moment to fix the costume you would be wearing with the magnet. You were my flunky."

She sneered at me. I smiled at her.

"Not anymore."

Chapter Thirty-Seven

"What's troubling you, sweetheart?" Gurn stood in the doorway of the kitchen while I lay in one of the lounge chairs on our back deck.

"What makes you think there's anything troubling me? It's a beautiful evening; all the charges against me are going to be dropped; I weighed myself a few minutes ago, and with all this running around, I lost two pounds, which means carrot cake tonight, and… " My voice dropped off. "Oh, rats. Who am I kidding? Something is bothering me."

"That's what I thought. You're about as tense as I've ever seen you, even though you're trying to pretend you're lounging. And you certainly don't sound happy. What is it?"

I shook my head. "I just don't buy it."

"Buy what?"

"I don't think either Billie or Edgar killed Winston, tried to run David down, or tried to kill Madison with carbon monoxide. I mean, why? It doesn't make any sense. I understand Billie killing Marvin. Vengeance. I understand Edgar murdering Steven Kutner. Blackmail. I understand Edgar hitting Carl over the head. Self-preservation."

"And kidnapping Donna?"

"Steven's money from the Cayman Islands. But I don't get David and Madison. Or Winston. Why?"

"The tontine. The less heirs left alive, the more money they inherited."

"Maybe." I shook my head again. "No, something's off. Edgar would have had to spend too much time in the Bay Area to do any of those acts. Sitting in a car, waiting for David or Winston to be crossing a street? Waiting for Madison to be alone in the house and then striking? That suggests surveillance. I don't think Edgar has the brains or patience for that sort of thing."

"Maybe it was Billie. You said she had a lot of leeway in her work hours and she's a lot closer."

"No, I don't think so. All she wanted was vengeance against Marvin and her fair share of the inheritance. She never said anything about wanting more. Neither of them did. Not only were they pretty verbal about what they wanted, the timing of Winston's murder and Madison's and David's attempted murders would have meant being in too many places at the same time."

"So, what are you thinking? There's a third party out there wreaking havoc and trying to murder the Del Vecchio inheritors, one by one?" He let out a laugh and then choked on it. "Tell me no. Please."

"That's exactly what I think. Marvin's decapitation started this person thinking and then the demise of Steven clinched it."

"That's certainly when things started to happen."

"Someone out there is trying to eliminate the Del Vecchio heirs and saw the opportunity for Billie and Edgar to take the blame. You have to admit, it's kinda perfect."

"Just for the record, sometimes the inner machinations of your mind scare me."

"Thank you, darling."

I picked up my phone from under the lounge chair and hit the speed dial. "Richard, I'm glad I caught you. Did you check all the files on Kutner's flash drive? You did. Nothing else on there that might suggest another blackmail victim? No? Hmmm. No, nothing I can put my finger on. Thanks, Richard. And get some rest. You deserve it." I hung up.

Gurn stared at me for a minute or two. "Are you going to sit out here most of the evening and ruminate on this?"

"I believe I am."

"In that case, why don't I bring you a glass of wine?"

"Thank you, darling. And could you bring me Tugger? He helps me think."

"A chard and a cat coming up."

Chapter Thirty-Eight

"You're sure about this?" Frank said.

"Almost."

It was nine o'clock, and I'd reached him at home. He wasn't happy to hear from me at that late hour, something about *Blue Bloods* being on, but at least he listened while I droned on, ending with,

"'Follow the money', that's my personal motto."

"You and your mottos. And since when is that your personal motto?"

"Since today. I've adopted it."

"Lee, there's a lot of money and a lot of people to follow."

"Not really. Suspects have dwindled off."

"Listen, as far as Madison's attack, in looking at her past more carefully, Fenner discovered she has a string of discarded lovers as well as their angry wives. And as for Winston Del Vecchio, who's to say it wasn't a lunatic driver and the man was in the wrong place at the wrong time?"

"What about David?"

"A coincidence. The world is filled with bad drivers."

"Two different stolen cars, right? Both taken from San Francisco. One from Jackson Street near

Gold, the other from a parking lot off the Embarcadero."

"Well, you've done your research," Frank admitted.

"I don't believe in this type of coincidence, and it's too convenient. If my plan works, we'll know."

"And if it doesn't work?"

"Then I'll be known for the idiot I am."

"You're not an idiot. Far from it."

"Then help me out, Frank. It will be much harder to do this without you."

"You're going to do it regardless of what I say?"

"Yes. And think about it, Frank. You don't want someone getting away with murder, do you?"

He let out a deep sigh. "It's not exactly part of my job description."

"Exactamundo."

"All right, all right, all right. What is it you want me to do?"

"Before we get into that, I have another thought. Did anyone check the traffic cameras near Bo's Ale House in Milpitas for the car that nearly hit David?"

"It never got reported. We didn't know anything about what happened until earlier today until you mentioned it. It's still not official."

"Regardless, you might want to do that."

"Sometimes I wonder who's running this investigation, anyway."

"'Many hands make light work.'"

"If you say that's another one of your mottos, I'm going to reach through this phone and strangle you."

"Now, now. Remember your blood pressure. Here's the plan," I told him.

"And this is for Sunday?"

"Yes, I need time to get all my ducks in a row. But I'll make the call Saturday night. State my case. Overnight stewing is always good for bringing on the jitters. Now, you know your part, right?"

"Yes. But good God, Lee. Are you sure you don't want to be a doctor?"

"Not a chance. The thrill of the chase, Frank. The thrill of the chase."

* * *

The doorbell rang at exactly 10:30 a.m. Sunday morning, eight days after this nightmare began. I went to the door deliberately wearing something feminine and flowing. I even had on makeup. I opened the door and faced Paul Rinken.

"Right on time, Mr. Rinken. Or may I call you Paul?"

"Mr. Rinken will do." He pushed past me and into the apartment. Turning around to stare me down, he said. "Who else knows about your phone call to me, Ms. Alvarez? Your husband?"

"No. Sometimes it's better to play things close to the vest. Besides, Gurn's off golfing. It's just me." I almost said it's just little ol' me, but thought that might be a bit over the top.

"Well, I'm here as ordered, Ms. Alvarez. Why don't you tell me about this incriminating evidence you think you have linking me to the attack on three people? As I told the police, all three times I

328

was at my gym in Jackson Square. My assistant even backed me up."

"Not quite. Your assistant, Nancy, is a very sweet girl. Quite taken with you. But when I explained to her the penalty for perjury, she suddenly wasn't so sure you were around when you said you were. And there is a back door to the gym, one which only employees and you have access to. The SUV stolen from Jackson and Gold was only two blocks from there. The car used the following day came from about six blocks away. But most compelling is the Milpitas traffic-camera video footage, which the police haven't looked at. Yet. But I already have copies of it, thanks to friends of friends, and you take a very good picture." That was a complete lie, but nonetheless, I delivered it with a bang. Then I smiled sweetly. "Once the police are alerted, I'm sure they'll find even more evidence."

"What is it you want? Money? I won't have any for couple of months."

"Or at least, Claudia won't."

"Same thing. Now that the will has been read, we're getting married next week. What's hers is mine."

"But you want more. The less heirs, the bigger the reward. And the sooner it comes."

"The way the will is set up now it comes in in dribs and drabs. I'm not going to see the ten or twelve million dollars, not for years. So, you're right. I want more. But let's get back to you. How much do *you* want?"

"Fifty thousand to start with."

"To start with?" He was visibly amused.

"We're not talking about dipping your hand into petty cash. We're talking murder, Mr. Rinken. The murder of Winston Del Vecchio. Plus, the attempted murder of Madison. And then there's the attempted hit-and-run of David, Claudia's son. Takes a lot of nerve to try to run down your future wife's son."

"You'll find, Ms. Alvarez, nerve is something I have an abundance of." He withdrew a gun from his pocket and aimed it in my direction.

"I hope you have a license for that. One more thing to add to prison time." I stepped forward. Confused, he backed up.

"Anybody ever tell you you're a smart aleck?"

"All the time. So, you're admitting you did those things?"

I stepped forward again. He backed up again.

"I admit nothing."

"Then why are you holding a gun on me?"

"Because you've been nothing but a pest from the very beginning."

"Well, now you've hurt my feelings."

"I only did what Marvin's first wife would have done, eventually. Her and that crazy son of hers."

"But it wasn't her and her crazy son. It was you. Little ol' you," I drawled. If I could have been more annoying, I don't know how.

"Yes, it was me!" he shouted. "You damn well know it was me!"

He took aim at my chest just as the bedroom door burst open and Gurn rushed in. Before Rinken knew what was happening, Gurn seized him from behind in a neck lock, a wrestling move in which Rinken's neck was held immobile. Then he grabbed the man's hand with the gun and pointed it up to the ceiling. They danced around a bit, both being strong men and in good condition. But try as he would, Gurn could not wrestle the gun out of the man's hand from the awkward position he was in.

When they knocked over one of my favorite lamps, I knew it was time to intervene. I ran forward, and gathering the skirt of the kaftan out of my way, kicked the man soundly in the gonads. Gurn yanked the gun out of the Rinken's hand as he dropped to the floor, doubled over and moaning.

"Thanks," Gurn said. "He was a tough one."

"My pleasure. Did you get all that, Frank?" I said into the mic tucked inside the kaftan. I listened but had to pull the earpiece out from the sheer volume of his yelling. I held it away from my ear and still could hear every word. "Frank, Frank, calm down. I had to goad him. He would have never confessed otherwise. Don't worry, we had this choreographed. I backed him up to the bedroom door, and Gurn was on the other side, waiting. And don't forget my bulletproof vest. You know, nobody told me how hot they are. I can't wait to get out of this thing."

I yanked the kaftan off over my head and stood in shorts, a tank top, and Gurn's bulletproof vest. Yes, it was too big for me, but one must adapt. While untying the vest, the doorbell rang again. Gurn was sitting on the sofa with the gun pointed at a moaning, still prostrate man.

"Would you get that, sweetheart?" he asked.

"Must be Palo Alto's finest. Cats locked up in the bathroom?"

"Of course. Tugger would have bit this man's hand off if I'd let him."

I went to the door, opened it, and the process of arresting a murderer ensued.

Chapter Thirty-Nine

"Are you nervous, Mom?" I looked at my mother, seated in front of the makeup mirror, dressed in her white silk robe, and carefully applying lipstick.

Two weeks had gone by, and a lot of things had happened. Most important for me, was being officially cleared of all criminal charges.

And I finally met Judge Plenca in the flesh. Stoic, no-nonsense, and eyes that could bore a hole in a brick. I cannot imagine facing her on any charges, even dropping a piece of gum on the sidewalk. Just being in the same room with the judge made me want to leap up from my chair and shout, "I did it, I did it! Take me away!"

Mom's voice brought me back from Plenca's chambers. "*Nervous?* Why should I be *nervous?*" She looked at me as if I was stark raving mad. She does that often.

"What?"

"Pay *attention,* Liana. You just *asked* me if I was *nervous.* I am *responding.* Of *course* not. I know *all* my *lines* and *lyrics.* And I am in *fine* voice."

And to prove the point, she belted out a scale for me. Well, not belted. Mom doesn't belt like Ethel Merman. More like Maria Callas.

"Sounds great, Mom. Well, I just meant you being nervous with a full house out there. Nearly all the audience is back, and when David offered to perform the act he's taking to Vegas, the place sold out in a matter of hours. The Sons and Daughters of Fallen American Heroes is a sellout and then some. They're hanging from the rafters."

She turned and looked at me. "The theater *has* no rafters."

"It's just an expression, Mom. Like Bob's your uncle."

"I don't *have* an Uncle Bob."

"It's just an—"

"*No* one in the family does. Even your father, *Roberto*, was never called *Bob*. By anyone. I would have *never* allowed it."

Saved by a knock on the door.

"Half hour, Mrs. Alvarez." I recognized Zack's voice, crossed to the door, and flung it open.

"Hi, Zack."

"Why, Lee," he said in surprise. "How are you?"

"I'm well. And thanks again for helping me prove my innocence."

"I only told the truth. What a shock! I've known Billie for years. I had no idea. You know, Lee, you could have been a lawyer."

"Matlock?"

"Perry Mason."

"But definitely a television lawyer. Just less Southern."

"You made quite a case for yourself that morning. But I guess 'Desperate times call for desperate measures.'"

"Shakespeare?"

"Hippocrates."

"Ah! The famous Greek physician."

The smile left Zack's face. "What are you doing backstage?"

"Don't panic. My career as an assistant magician is behind me. I'm not here to perform. Just wishing Mom good luck."

"You mean, break a leg," he corrected. "It's bad luck to wish someone good luck in a performance."

"Right. I forgot. Although, before I got here, I broke a mirror and I'm none the worse for it."

"Seven years of bad luck awaits you in the future," Zack said matter-of-factly, then turned away and walked down the hall.

"What if I glue it back together?" I called after him, with a laugh. "But, anyway, I don't believe in such things. I don't think," I added to myself, as I closed the door.

I turned back to my mother, still applying lipstick. "I'm going out front, Mom. We'll see you after the show."

"Is *Gurn* in the lobby?" she asked, admiring her application of Red Spice in the mirror.

"Yes, with Tío, Richard, Vicki, Frank, Abby, and the rest of Palo Alto."

"My *friends* are so loyal," Mom replied in her own queenly fashion. She rose and went to the closet. "Before you go, help *zip* me into my *gown*, will you, Liana?"

"Of course." I crossed to where she stood at the closet.

Searching through the costumes hanging there, I saw her begin to fluster.

"What is it, Mom?"

"My *gloves*. The long white *gloves* I wear for the *first* number."

"They're on the makeup table." I pointed to them. "Let's make sure you have everything else."

We searched the room for the various costumes and props she'd need. My mother was becoming increasingly on edge.

"Mom, you've got this. You'll be fine."

"It is *difficult* without anyone to *assist* you. And I have that *quick* change in the *wings* into the peignoir for the 'Bewitched, Bothered, and Bewildered' number." She looked at me.

"Don't give me that pleading look, Mom. My days as an assistant anything are over. Especially in a backstage setting. Tell you what, I'll find Zack and tell him you could use a little help with your costume change." I opened the dressing room door to leave, looked down the hall, and spied Bo leaning against the wall by David's dressing room.

"Bo," I called out. "How are you?"

"Lee! Fancy seeing you here," she said, walking the length of the hall in my direction.

"You helping out David tonight?"

"No, he doesn't need my help. I like being backstage. You have to dress up to be in the audience."

I checked her out. Sure enough, she was wearing her "Bo's Ale House" T-shirt and jeans. By the time she reached me, I had an idea. I grabbed her by the arm and dragged her into Mom's dressing room.

"Mom, this is Bo. Longtime friend of David Del Vecchio."

Ever the lady, if my mother was surprised by Bo's outward appearance—lady sumo wrestler in a T-shirt—she didn't show it at all, but gave her a radiant smile.

"Bo—and I can't seem to remember your last name—this is my mom, Lila Alvarez."

"Bo Thacker. Nice to meet you, Mrs. Alvarez." Then Bo smiled her own radiant smile, and I could see my mother took to her instantly.

"Bo, I have a favor to ask of you," I said.

"Anything. You saved Dave's life and fortune."

"Well, I don't know that I saved his… but never mind. Bo, if you're going to be backstage anyway, would you mind helping Mom in and out of her costumes? She has a quick change—"

"Say no more. There's nothing backstage needs doing that I haven't done." She turned and looked at Mom. "I will be your own personal dresser tonight. Why don't you and I go in the wings where your quick change takes place and do a little run-through? I like to work everything out beforehand."

Those were the golden words to use with Lila Alvarez. I left the two of them making lists and gathering up costumes and props for the performance.

Chapter Forty

I entered the lobby relieved I hadn't gotten roped into helping Mom in and out of her costumes. A well-dressed crowd was roaming around, although now and then you would see someone in a T-shirt and jeans. That's all some people want to wear, no matter what, where, or when. As for me, dressing up for an occasion is all part of the experience. Gurn, too. One of the like-minded things we share.

That evening I was wearing my off-the-shoulder, royal-blue satin sheath, circa 1964. I like to cruise consignment stores — much to my mother's dismay — for one-of-a-kind things from way back when. I'd found this treasure several months ago and hadn't had a chance to wear it yet. My hair was done in a tight French twist, all the rage in the '60s. As far as I'm concerned, it never went out of style. I finished the look off with the sapphire earrings and necklace Dad gave me one Christmas.

I saw Gurn across the lobby chatting with Frank and Abby. Gurn was wearing a navy-blue double-breasted suit, light-blue shirt, and cream-colored tie. Frank looked very dapper in a charcoal-gray suit, crisp white shirt, and diamond-patterned, dark-gray tie. Abby had on a stunning linen pantsuit, coral in color, that set off her caramel complexion. Dark-brown hair was stylishly done in intricate cornrows gathered at the top of her head and ending in a high, long ponytail. She had the kind of fashion sense Lila Hamilton-Alvarez approves of. Or of which Lila Hamilton-Alvarez approves, whichever. I was about to call out to them when I found Donna Kutner by my side.

"Donna, I haven't seen you in weeks." I drew her into a quick embrace. She hugged me back, then gave me a warm smile.

Gone were the fatigue lines and circles under her eyes. Donna wore little makeup, but her natural coloring was enhanced by the pale-green-and-pink-floral A-line dress she had on. A gold heart-shaped locket hung on a chain around her neck, her only jewelry. Dark hair fell in ringlets around her face and cascaded over shoulders down to her waist. If you didn't know her real story, you'd think she was a fairy-tale princess.

"How are you?"

"I'm doing okay, Lee. I'm sorry I didn't get in touch with you sooner, but I think you know the house has to be sold as part of the terms of the will, so I've been busy sorting through things and packing. Mr. Wong has been a big help. You know"—and here she paused—"in some ways, he was more of a father to me than my own. I'll miss him, but I know he'll be happy in Seattle."

"I understand his granddaughter is doing even better than expected."

"Yes. He sends me pictures of her every day. He is so proud."

"And what's in store for you?"

"As soon as the house is closed and on the market, I'm going to Las Vegas to be near David."

"To be his new assistant?"

"No, just a break from all of this. Temporarily into another world."

"That's for sure."

"It's a chance for David and I to spend some time together. Then in a few months, I'm returning to nursing school. I talked it over with my advisor, and after some brush-up courses, which I can take in Vegas, I can pick up where I left off getting my RN degree."

"Way to go! Congratulations," I said. "I've been thinking about your mother. How is Claudia doing?"

"Oh, about as well as can be expected after she found out the man she loved and devoted years of her life to, wasn't who she thought he was. But I can relate to that. I never suspected in a million years Steven would go to the degree he did to get what he wanted." She let out a sigh. "Like mother, like daughter, I expect."

"Jeesh, I hope not. I mean, let's hope we can learn from our mistakes."

"Mom's going to devote herself to taking care of her parents." Donna's blue eyes twinkled. "She says."

"I'm sure the inheritance will go a long way to helping with that."

"Oh, yes, it will help with her parents' care. But with men? I don't think so. My mother is the type of woman who can't be without a man in her life. Personally, I'm looking forward to being on my own with no one telling me what to do or think. I'd like to know who I am before I get involved with anyone again."

"I'm impressed. I was a few years older than you when I discovered that."

"I can't take total credit. I've been seeing a therapist three times a week, thanks to David's suggestion." She changed subjects. "You know, he's not taking the inheritance. David doesn't want anything to do with it. He calls it 'blood money.' He signed the money over to the ASPCA."

"David mentioned that to my uncle last week, and Tío passed the news on to us. Tío has something like that set up in his will, but needless to say, not for the same amount." We both laughed. "In the past couple of weeks, your brother and my uncle have developed quite a friendship over their shared love of animals. In fact, Tío is taking two of the puppies David's been fostering, and will find them homes here in the Bay Area. David's keeping Buddy."

"And I'm so glad. Buddy is such a sweet little dog. Honey Boy just adores him."

She laughed, then sobered, looking directly at me. Not exactly in a challenging way, but in a this-is-how-it's-going-to-be way.

"You've heard the saying, 'The love of money is the root of all evil?'" I nodded. "But it doesn't have to be like that."

"No, it doesn't," I agreed.

"So, I'm taking the money. My brother understands I don't see it the way he does. And I can certainly use it while I'm at school. Maybe even start a fund for other students in need. And along those lines, here's a check for your fee."

She pushed a sealed envelope on me. I took it with surprise.

"A check? You don't owe me anything. I thought we agreed—"

"If it hadn't been for you," she interrupted, "David and I might have been killed by Paul before anyone knew anything. And probably Mom, too. It's from the three of us. For services rendered," she added with a huge smile.

Before I could make further protest, she again abruptly changed the subject. "I saw on the news Billie's trial starts next month. That's another reason I'm going away. I don't want to be here for it."

"If it means anything, it'll be pretty cut and dried. The DA has a solid case for first-degree murder charges, and he's asking for life imprisonment without parole. Billie will live out her days in prison."

"And then there's the trial for my cousin's murder, but that's a long way off."

"But not nearly so cut and dry. Paul Rinken is pleading temporary insanity for Winston's death and the attempted murders of Madison and David."

"How do you know all this?"

"I made it my business to know. I want to make sure these people pay for their crimes. And they will."

"It won't make it right," Donna said, shaking her head.

"No, but it's a start."

"Do you know what's happening with Edgar Smith?"

"He's been returned to North Tahoe and faces charges of unpremeditated, third-degree murder. His lawyer is claiming self-defense. But there are several facts working against that plea: he covered it up, and Steven was blackmailing Billie and him. Your kidnapping and Carl's aggravated assault charges are being added somewhere along the line."

"It's all so sordid." Her voice was soft yet filled with emotion. "And evil. I never believed in that word before, but I do now."

I had no answer for her. Or wise mottos. It *was* sordid. And evil. An old-fashioned word, but when it applies, it applies.

"You know," Donna continued, "I haven't told anyone this, not even David, but I'd asked Steven for a divorce the day before he disappeared. I couldn't take it anymore. All the lies and deceit. But I'm going to try to learn from this, especially my part in it."

"Don't go too wild with that, is my advice," I said. "You're an innocent victim. You married a man and believed in him. There's nothing intrinsically wrong with that. You just chose the wrong guy. As my mother once told me, there're a

343

lot of lowlifes in the world but a lot of good people, too. The trick is to be able to tell the difference. Actually, Lila Hamilton Alvarez didn't phrase it quite that way. More along the lines of, 'We must endeavor to become discerning' but it's the same idea." It was my turn to change the subject. We were into heavy stuff for a night at the theater. "Are you here with anyone?"

Donna immediately brightened and smiled. "Yes, Madison. No matter what anyone says about her love life, she's been a good friend to me. She tried to keep my secret and protect me when I ran away to the cabin. Maddie was as shocked as I was when she learned the real identity of Johan."

"Edgar seems to have fooled everyone," I remarked.

"Well, you just don't expect people not to be who they say they are. Maddie's moving on and says I should do the same thing. She's bought an apartment on Nob Hill. Oh, look, she's over there talking to your husband."

I glanced in the direction she was pointing in. "Is she now?"

"Look out. Shark in the water," Donna said, the expression on her face changing from sweet and innocent to worldly. "Maddie's wearing her new, slinky red gown. That means she's shopping for a new husband." Donna gave me a meaningful, sly look. "And that means she won't be chatting with Gurn long. She knows he's not interested and is much too young for her. She likes them fifty-plus and very rich."

"Why, Donna Del Vecchio Kutner. There's more to you than meets the eye. I do believe you're going to be all right."

Chapter Forty-One

To celebrate Mom's victory and the success of the fundraiser, Gurn and I took the family, including Frank and Abby, to the Top of the Mark cocktail bar at the Mark Hopkins Hotel. With its 360-degree views of the city of San Francisco and live music, the Top of the Mark can be very romantic. Or not. At the moment I was dancing with my brother, Richard. He was counting out loud in my ear.

The last time Richard and I danced together, he was five and I was eight. It was to the opening number of *All That*, a "Saturday Night Live" for the Nickelodeon crowd. Richard was trying to dance hip-hop and I was trying to stand on my toes like a ballerina. The parents videoed the event, and for decades it got hauled out on Thanksgiving and shown for laughs. On us. I still cringe at it.

But this night, Richard and I were pretending to be adults and swayed to the four-piece band, playing "I've Got you Under My Skin."

I smiled at Richard. "Well, look at you, little brother. You actually have some rhythm."

"Don't look so surprised, big sister. Vicki's been teaching me how to dance. I can even do the cha-cha, kind of."

"A small tip, Richard. Don't count out loud."

"Was I doing that?"

"A little. But look at you," I said, moving on to the positive. "You look terrific. I didn't even think you owned a suit. Don't tell me. Vicki?"

"We're going to her friend's wedding next week at the Ritz Carlton in Half Moon Bay. It's very formal. It was either this or a tux."

"I can just see you in a tux."

"No, you can't. This is bad enough. But I bought the suit online. One hundred percent wool."

"You can buy suits online now?"

"Yeah, just send them your measurements and one, two, three, you've got a suit. I don't like the tie, though. And I wanted to wear cuff links, but that didn't work out. So, I pinned the cuffs together for tonight. See?"

He removed his hand from mine, raised his arm, pulled back the sleeve of his light-gray jacket, and exposed his cuff. Sure enough, a small, gold safety pin held the cuff together.

"Didn't the shirt come with its own buttons? Not everybody uses cuff links."

"Sure, but at the last minute I thought I had a pair of Dad's cuff links somewhere, and I cut the buttons off. I couldn't find the cuff links, but it was too late to ask Vicki to sew the buttons back on before we left."

I continued smiling because there was no point in saying, *you don't need to cut the buttons off when you use cuff links. Honest. And you don't know how to sew on a button, you knothead, you?* There was no point in saying any of that, because here was a one-of-a-kind brother who, whether he wore a stretched-out T-shirt or a tux, was simply the best.

So, I merely said, "Just keep the sleeves of your jacket down over the cuffs. And for heaven's sake, don't mention this to Mom. She's stressed enough."

"Are you kidding? Do you know how much praise she gave me when I showed up tonight in a suit and tie? What is she stressed about?"

"She's fuming because the orchestra cut six measures of her opening song, "Zip." Not enough zip-zips, and it threw her blocking off."

"She sounded great, though, Lee. And she got a standing ovation for "Bewitched, Bothered, and Bewildered.""

"Yup, with nobody the wiser. It was a good night, regardless. The fundraiser collected over fifty thousand dollars for the Sons and Daughters of Fallen American Heroes, Carl is being released from the hospital tomorrow, the city filled in the remainder of the tunnel, and it winds up that nobody is suing the theater for anything, much to the relief of the Babonas family."

"All's well that ends well."

"Richard, if that's not Shakespeare, I'm going to go outside and throw myself off a cliff."

"There aren't any cliffs around here, and of course it's Shakespeare. What made you doubt yourself?"

"I've been batting zero to naught lately, on quotes, sayings, and mottos."

"You know my favorite motto?"

"I've had a martini, so hit me."

"'Be Like the cubist. Roll along.'"

"That's a motto?"

"My favorite one."

"I don't even know what it means, Richard. What happened to 'M&Ms melt in your mouth, not in your hands'?"

"There are several little-known facts about how Cubism ties in with the history of the computer," Richard said, revving up to the subject. "Even though Cubism was one of abstract art's most important movements, its name actually began as an insult. Art critic Louis Vauxcelles—"

"Wait, wait," I interrupted, "I see Gurn signaling to me. I should go see what he wants. Might be important. Excuse me, Richard. We can pick this up later. Maybe tomorrow? I promise. And thanks for the dance."

"Oh, sure," he said, leading me off the dance floor. "It can wait. Although, I should explain it to Vicki, anyway. She's probably wondering about this herself."

"Maybe she'd like to have a nice romantic evening with her husband. Why don't you ask her to dance instead?"

"Dance?" He thought for a moment. "I suppose I could do that."

"Good boy." I left my brother and veritably flew into Gurn's arms. "Hello, darling. How are you? I haven't seen you in far too long."

"It's only been about fifteen minutes, but I was missing you, too." He gave me his gorgeous lopsided smile. "Have I told you how beautiful you look tonight?"

"Yes, but not recently enough."

"Well, we have two glorious weeks in Bali coming up in a few days. I'll tell you every fifteen minutes or so once we get there."

"Bali." I sighed at just the name. "A tropical paradise. Stunning beaches, lush landscapes, and mesmerizing sunsets that have captured the imagination of travelers worldwide."

"That sounds like a travel brochure."

"It is. I memorized it." I laughed. I leaned my head against his shoulder and fell into the rhythm of the music. After a moment or two, I said, "Gurn, darling..."

"Yes, beloved?"

"I've realized once again I am a lucky woman. I don't think I could have ever proven I was innocent if it hadn't been for all the people who helped and fought for me. Thank you for seeing me through that terrible time. I can't even believe it was only three weeks ago."

"My pleasure, sweetheart. But if you could refrain from getting involved in the future with magic of any sort, it would be greatly appreciated."

"Done."

"Although, I have to say, David Del Vecchio has quite an act. I still can't figure out how he did it. Remember when he came into the audience and that woman volunteered to help him with a trick?" I nodded. "How he made the playing cards come up with her birthday, date, and year, I'll never know. Very snazzy."

"Darling, I've been thinking."

"Uh-oh."

"Why do you say, uh-oh?"

"Because when you say 'Darling, I've been thinking,' that usually means I have to break down a door, or we're going to get trapped in a tunnel with no air."

"That was just the one time we were trapped in a tunnel with no air. One time. Of course, if we played it wrong, one time would have been enough," I muttered.

He threw back his head with laughter. "I'm only teasing you, sweetheart. What have you been thinking about?"

"I don't want to accept the Civilian Medal of Appreciation Award." I rattled on, "I mean, it's very sweet of Fenner to nominate me for it—and unexpected—but I don't want to draw the attention to myself. I'd rather just put this whole episode behind me."

"Your mother thinks it will be good for the reputation of the agency."

"Oh, no. She's going to try to talk me into it, isn't she?"

"If everything goes true to form, yes."

"That was the most horrendous week of my life," I whined. "My favorite slingbacks were ruined, not to mention my brand-new silk pajamas, and everybody thought I decapitated a man. Pretty dismal stuff. Did I show you the check from Donna for services rendered?"

"No, you didn't. How much is it for?"

I looked around me, then pulled the folded check out of my bag and handed it over. He unfolded it, looked at the amount, and his jaw literally dropped.

"That's a lot of zeros."

"I know, right? So, here's my plan. If Mom doesn't back off on this award thing, I'm going to threaten to rip up the check. And as it's been made out to me…"

"Sweetheart, you work for DI. That's agency money, regardless of who the check is made out to."

"Darling, you weren't planning on sleeping on the couch tonight, were you?"

He laughed. So did I.

"Stop thinking like an accountant for one minute."

"And think blackmail?"

"I prefer to think of it as negotiations."

"Lee, I will leave this between you and Lila. Besides, I think once your mother sees the amount of that check, it will work in your favor."

"Me, too. But keep the motor running in case we have to make a quick getaway."

We both burst out laughing. Our laughter increased, not diminished, and became so loud, we had to leave the dance floor. Arm in arm, we drifted back to our table, still giggling.

"And about your silk pajamas," Gurn said, while nuzzling my neck. "I ordered you a new pair. Lavender, right? Neiman Marcus, right? Size six."

"You did? Thank you, darling. I—" I stopped talking when I heard Mom's voice singing over the microphone. We sat down and glanced in her direction.

"*I'm wild again, beguiled again,*" she began in her lovely mezzo-soprano voice.

"Oh, no," I whined and leaned into Gurn. "She's singing that song again. I hate that song."

"I thought you liked that song," he said, looking at me in surprise.

"I did. I used to. But now when she comes to the part, 'bewitched, bothered, and bewildered,' I can only think of 'bewitched, bothered, and beheaded.'"

He thought for a moment. "Maybe we should leave for Bali tomorrow."

"Maybe we should. And hopefully, there will be no magic acts and nary a guillotine to be found for thousands and thousands of miles."

~

Books by Heather Haven

The Alvarez Family Murder Mysteries
Murder is a Family Business, Book 1
A Wedding to Die For, Book 2
Death Runs in the Family, Book 3
DEAD...If Only, Book 4
The CEO Came DOA, Book 5
The Culinary Art of Murder, Book 6
Casting Call for a Corpse, Book 7
Love Can be Murder (ebook only), Book 8
The Drop-Dead Temple of Doom, Book 9
Bewitched, Bothered, and Beheaded, Book 10

Love Can Be Murder Novellas
Honeymoons Can Be Murder, Book 1
Marriage Can Be Murder, Book 2

The Persephone Cole Vintage Mysteries
The Dagger Before Me, Book 1
Iced Diamonds, Book 2
The Chocolate Kiss-Off, Book 3
Hotshot Shamus, Book 4

The Snow Lake Romantic Suspense Novels
Christmas Trifle, Book 1

Docu-fiction/Mystery Stand-Alone
Murder under the Big Top

Collection of Short Stories
Corliss and Other Award-Winning Stories

About Heather Haven

After studying drama at the University of Miami in Miami, Florida, Heather went to Manhattan to pursue a career. There she wrote short stories, novels, comedy acts, television treatments, ad copy, commercials, and two one-act plays, produced at several places, such as Playwrights Horizon. Once she even ghostwrote a book on how to run an employment agency. She was unemployed at the time.

One of her first paying jobs was writing a love story for a book published by Bantam called *Moments of Love.* She had a deadline of one week but promptly came down with the flu. Heather wrote "The Sands of Time" with a raging temperature, and delivered some pretty hot stuff because of it. Her stint at New York City's No Soap Radio—where she wrote comedic ad copy—help develop her longtime love affair with comedy.

She has won many awards for the humorous Alvarez Family Murder Mysteries, Persephone Cole Vintage Mysteries, and *Corliss and Other Award-Winning Stories.* However, her proudest achievement is winning the Independent Publisher Book Awards (IPPY) Silver Medal for her stand-alone noir mystery, ***Murder Under the Big Top.***

As the real-life daughter of Ringling Brothers and Barnum and Bailey circus folk, she was inspired by stories told throughout her childhood by her mother, a trapeze artist and performer. The book cover even has a picture of her mother sitting atop an elephant from that time. Her father trained

elephants. Heather brings the daily existence of the
Big Top to life during World War II, embellished by
her own murderous imagination.

Connect with Heather
at the following sites:

Website: www.heatherhavenstories.com
http://heatherhavenstories.com/blog/
https://www.facebook.com/HeatherHavenStories
https://www.twitter.com/Twitter@HeatherHaven

Sign up for Heather's newsletter at:
http://heatherhavenstories.com/subscribe-via-email/

Email: heather@heatherhavenstories.com.

She'd love to hear from you. Thanks so much!

The Wives of Bath Press

The Wife of Bath was a woman of a certain age, with opinions, who was on a journey. Writer and publisher Heather Haven is a modern-day Wife of Bath.

www.heatherhavenstories.com